All the
Pretty Things

All the Pretty Things

EMILY ARSENAULT

DELACORTE PRESS

Text copyright © 2020 by Emily Arsenault
Jacket photograph copyright © 2020 by pbombaert/Getty Images

Visit us on the Web! GetUnderlined.com

Educators and librarians, for a variety of teaching tools, visit us at
RHTeachersLibrarians.com

Library of Congress Cataloging-in-Publication Data
Names: Arsenault, Emily, author.
Title: All the pretty things / Emily Arsenault.
Description: First edition. | New York : Delacorte Press, [2020] | Summary: Ivy's best friend is traumatized by finding the dead body of a young man but as Ivy seeks answers, she learns that her small New Hampshire town hides many secrets.
Identifiers: LCCN 2019007209 | ISBN 978-1-9848-9705-3 (hc) | ISBN 978-1-9848-9706-0 (glb) | ISBN 978-1-9848-9707-7 (ebook)
Subjects: | CYAC: Friendship—Fiction. | Death—Fiction. | Secrets—Fiction. | Amusement parks—Fiction. | Family life—New Hampshire—Fiction. | New Hampshire—Fiction. | Mystery and detective stories.
Classification: LCC PZ7.1.A78 All 2020 | DDC [Fic]—dc23

The text of this book is set in 11-point Sabon MT Pro.
Interior design by Cathy Bobak

Printed in the United States of America
10 9 8 7 6 5 4 3 2 1
First Edition

Gosh, I sound like my father, don't I? But that's what you get from this particular Daddy's girl.

—Ivanka Trump, *The Trump Card: Playing to Win in Work and Life*

ONE

"**H**on. Morgan is missing."

That's how Dad put it when he called. I'd been in the passenger seat, trying to recover from my airplane nerves, wishing my mom would drive a little faster, when my phone buzzed in the cup holder.

Good thing I wasn't driving. Mom and I were both tired after the early-morning flight back to New Hampshire. I had offered to drive home from the airport, but we both knew I was still too rattled to be operating a car.

"Missing . . . like *missing* missing?" I asked. I tend not to be very eloquent when I'm anxious. And Dad has a way of overdramatizing things, so I wanted to clarify.

"Umm . . . yes . . . *missing*," Dad said. "But don't panic, Ivy. It's only since last night. It hasn't even been twenty-four hours. The police are on it. *Everyone's* on it. Including me. But you

1

know, Morgan probably just went off with a friend or a boyfriend and forgot to let her mom know."

That didn't sound like Morgan at all. Morgan is usually pretty careful about not stressing out her mom, since she's raising Morgan and her brother on her own. Morgan is *thoughtful, considerate, compassionate*. Parents and teachers have been using these adjectives about her since we were twelve.

My heart started racing, and I started chewing the drawstring of my peasant top.

"So . . . any texts from her?" Dad asked. "That's why I'm calling. I told her mom I'd ask you. I tried to call earlier, but I guess it didn't go through because you were on the plane."

"Oh." Now I felt even worse. I know that cell phones often work on flights, but I always turn mine off to minimize any chance of inadvertently helping my flight crash.

"So, *hon*. Did you hear the question? Any texts or other contact from Morgan in the last day or so?"

"No," I said softly.

The truth was I hadn't heard from Morgan in three days. And I had been counting.

We'd never gone this long without talking or at least texting. It wasn't like she couldn't text while working at Dad's amusement park, but when she'd stopped replying to my messages on Wednesday, I'd tried calling her. When she didn't pick up for two days, I'd given up, reluctantly figuring we'd reconnect when I got home.

"Okay, too bad. I'll let them all know. And try not to worry. There's a lot of great people working on this. You know I know the deputy chief, right? I've already had a little chat with him about how *important* this is." My dad was talking fast, but he finally stopped for a breath. "I'll let you know if I hear anything else," he added. "How far are you from home?"

"About an hour away," I said, eyeing the speedometer. "Maybe a little more."

"Okay. I'm just pulling into Fabuland now. Talk soon. Bye, Ivy."

"Bye," I mumbled, but he had already ended the call.

I was silent for a moment. Then I drew in a breath, feeling my mom's attention more on me than the road.

"So—" I began.

"I heard everything your father was saying," Mom said, sighing. "Of course Ed *knows the deputy chief.* And he still talks pretty loud on the phone."

She stiffened right after she said it, as if remembering that this was a really terrible time to drop subtle criticisms of one's ex-husband.

"I'm so sorry, Ivy." Her hands clenched the steering wheel. "But let's sit tight and wait for more news. I think with everything that's happened, Morgan probably just needed some time to herself."

Time to herself? That didn't sound right either. Yes, this had surely been the worst week of her life. But up until three days ago, she had been willing to accept comfort from others. From me.

I stared out the passenger-side window, watching the trees whip by as my mom reluctantly passed a rattling pickup truck plastered with bumper stickers from elections that preceded my birth.

To my silence, Mom added, "It's been an exhausting, emotional week for so many people. Let's not jump to any conclusions. She may just have needed some space for a night."

An awful, insane week, more like. And even that was putting it mildly.

"Yeah," I murmured, so Mom would know I had heard her. Then I scrunched down in my seat and started fiddling with my phone, going over my texts from the last ten days.

* * *

It had all started last Friday.

I'd been gone only a few days—to North Carolina with my mom, visiting my grandparents, like we do at the beginning of almost every summer—except my older brother had weaseled out of it this year because of a summer job he had gotten at Syracuse. I'd slept late that morning, waking up to two missed calls and that first terrible text from Morgan:

Ivy are you there? Something bad happened.

Of course I'd called her right back. She wasn't at work. She was home, still crying. I could barely believe it when she told me through sobs. I spent the next couple of days saying, *It's okay, Morgan. It's okay,* into the phone. She let me keep saying it even though we both knew it wasn't really true.

Since I was so far from home, it hadn't felt real until Morgan sent me the link to the first news story that broke. I had it bookmarked on my phone.

4

Danville Mourns Ethan Lavoie

On the night of Thursday, June 29, in Danville, Ethan Lavoie, 19, is believed to have fallen to his death from the train trestle in Brewer's Creek Park.

Ethan, who had Down syndrome, was well known in the close-knit community. He was a recent graduate of Danville High School, where he had been a member of the track team. He worked at Cork's Doughnut Dynasty in the maintenance department for three years, before recently switching jobs to the maintenance department at the Fabuland amusement park, also owned by Edward Cork.

"He was very excited to work at the park," said Steven Jeffries, Lavoie's uncle, at an informal gathering in the Lavoies' High Street yard late Friday evening. "He loved going to Fabuland and he couldn't wait to take his family there now that he had an employee pass. He loved the merry-go-round and especially the food. Pepperoni pizza was his favorite."

It's unclear why Lavoie was on the trestle alone. He was usually accompanied by a friend or family member when he walked to or from work.

"He almost always had a buddy walking him because that was his mom's rule. He knew he wasn't supposed to walk through Brewer's Creek Park by himself, especially at night. I don't know what got into him," said Mr. Jeffries tearfully. "Maybe he just forgot."

Residents—particularly young residents—of the Wilder Hill neighborhood and nearby Rowan Village mobile community, where the Lavoies reside, frequently cut through Brewer's Creek Park when bound for Fabuland because the street route is significantly longer.

Morgan Froggett, 16, took the shortcut while walking to her job at Fabuland Friday morning, when she spotted Ethan lying in the creek bed below. Ms. Froggett attempted to revive him before calling for help. Emergency personnel arrived at the scene within minutes, but Lavoie had already succumbed to his injuries and was declared dead at the scene. Ms. Froggett was interviewed by authorities. As of publication, Ms. Froggett's mother has declined a request for comment on her behalf.

Mr. Cork has set up a GoFundMe to help the Lavoie family with funeral expenses. Mr. Cork donated an initial $1,200 and has pledged to match any additional donations made. The funeral service has not yet been scheduled at the time of printing.

For more information, go to Ethansfundbeam.com or call Chris Nealy at 603-555-0989.

Since that Friday, Dad and Morgan had been giving me daily reports. Dad talked about the police coming and going at Fabuland throughout the week, asking everyone questions. By the end of the week, he seemed frustrated that they were asking the same things, distracting and upsetting his employees. Morgan mostly talked about the funeral, which happened July 5. There were a few hundred guests and the youth choir from Ethan's church sang. Morgan never wanted to talk directly about finding Ethan, though, and I didn't ask her to. She talked a little bit about what she knew—what everybody knew—about his last night at Fabuland. He'd ridden the Laser Coaster with Briony Simpson, Lucas Andries, and Anna Henry. He'd told them that he was calling his mom for a ride home. But then apparently he hadn't. He'd walked home alone, cutting through the woodsy Brewer's Creek area as all the kids without regular access to a car often did. And, while crossing the trestle, he'd fallen to his death. Nobody knew exactly what had happened, or why he didn't call his mom. Usually one of his cousins—Winnie or Tim Malloy—walked or drove him home, but neither of them had been working at Fabuland that night. When the police opened Ethan's locker, they found his backpack in it.

Morgan had reported sadly that everyone was beginning to accept the police's preliminary conclusions. That it was dark, and Ethan had lost his footing and fallen. He might have still been dizzy from riding the coaster, although the kids who'd ridden it with him said they'd seen no sign of that. And his backpack was probably in his locker because he'd had trouble with the lock—he'd had trouble in the past; the old ones get sticky. By Monday, Morgan was able to talk and text about other things—although a little tentatively, a little half-heartedly. She talked about maybe getting a haircut. And I finally got her to laugh, telling her a story about the little snake in my grandparents' pool—my mom wildly Googling *how to get a snake out of a pool* on her phone while my grandpa bumbled around with a net, cursing and trying to scoop it out.

On Wednesday afternoon, while I was at the grocery store with my grandma, trying to help her choose between two seemingly identical rotisserie chickens, my phone buzzed with a text from Morgan.

Want to talk to you about something I saw the day I found Ethan.

Unsettled by the vagueness of "something," and surprised she suddenly wanted to talk about that day specifically, I'd made my way to another aisle to call her. Morgan hadn't picked up but immediately sent me a text saying that she would call me later, after work.

She didn't.

I waited and waited until I couldn't stand it any longer. I texted her at eight p.m. that night, well past when she would have gotten home from the park and had dinner. No response. I called her at nine and texted her again. And again the next morning.

But now this. My best friend was missing.

Since last night?

Things must have been *really* bad. Morgan would never stay out all night without telling her mom where she was going. This had to be worse than my dad was willing to say.

I could feel Mom's gaze on me as I tried to process all this. I turned away, curling into the passenger-side door. She couldn't hide the worry in her eyes. Or the relief that it wasn't *me* who was missing. I know she can't help it. Whenever she hears about something bad happening to another kid, she looks at me that way.

Maybe someone had abducted Morgan. Maybe someone had killed her. Maybe she was trapped somewhere, trying to escape. Maybe she'd told the wrong person about the "something" she had been about to tell me?

My head buzzed with—and then hurt from—the possibilities. After about a half hour of turning them over, I thought I might scream, or explode.

Instead, I rolled down the car window for some air. That was a start.

No sooner had I cracked the window open than my phone rang again. "Dad Cell" flashed across the screen. I fumbled to swipe the screen, my fingers clumsy with nerves.

"Dad?" I croaked into the phone.

"Ivy! Good news. They found her."

I took a breath, feeling some of the tension and fear of the last half hour drain away as I exhaled.

"Who?" I said.

I meant *who was the they that found her,* but Dad yelped back before I could correct myself. "*Morgan,* Ivy. MORGAN. Wake up, sweetheart. Who else? How far are you from Fabuland now?"

"Umm . . ." I looked at the GPS. "About twenty minutes now. Is she okay?"

"Come right to the park," he demanded. "It looks like we could use your help."

TWO

Turns out that when the first workers arrived at Fabuland, a sharp-eyed ride operator had noticed movement near the top of the Ferris wheel. It was Morgan. She was up there by herself. She didn't seem hurt, but when they tried to run the ride to get her down, she leaned far over the safety bar and screamed. They were afraid she'd totally lost it and might jump.

My dad had called the cops and they had suggested using the big blue cherry picker—the one we use to fix the rides—to send someone up to talk to her. A police officer and Morgan's mom tried, but whenever they got close, Morgan would scream and jostle the gondola.

"Ivy's her best friend," my dad was saying to the cops when I arrived. He motioned for me to join the conversation at the ride controls. "She's great. She'll know how to talk to her. Believe me."

It took me a second to realize he was suggesting *I* go up. He repeated these words until the skepticism fell from the officers' faces. Dad is very convincing. Never mind that I'm more scared of heights than anything else I can think of. That's why I never go on most of the rides. But this was different. The terrified look on Morgan's mom's face made it clear—I had to do this.

I got in the cage with the policeman and he secured its swinging door with a heavy metal latch. The cherry picker's engine made a sickly metallic hum as it started to lift our little cage. My stomach did a flip and I grasped the handrail tighter. *You were thirty thousand feet up this morning,* I tried to tell myself. *You survived that, you can survive this.*

Everyone was staring at me and I felt like a princess about to be fed to a dragon. The vibration of the tired machinery rattled my teeth. I gripped the side of the cage and stared at the police officer's dark-blue shoulder so I would not have to watch us leave the ground. My heart thudded as we approached Morgan's gondola.

The cherry picker operator expertly positioned us within arm's length of her—just slightly over her gondola—and then shut off the engine.

"Can your friend come in with you?" the officer called to Morgan.

Morgan stared at us. She didn't move or make a sound. Then— to both my extreme relief and my extreme horror—she nodded.

The officer didn't waste any time unlatching the cherry picker door with a grim *clang.* He held my arm as I stepped into the gondola, then let go once I was safely inside.

I crouched on the floor for a second, hugging my knees to

my chest, waiting for the gondola to stop swinging so hard and for my breath to stop sounding so ragged. For about a minute, I forgot why I was there. I forgot to be relieved that Morgan didn't scream at my presence. I waited for my heart to slow down and for my legs and arms to feel solid again. When I could manage it, I pulled myself up and sat next to Morgan on the metal seat.

"Hey, what's wrong?" I whispered, and glanced at the police officer. He was turned away, toward the open sky—apparently to give us a sense of privacy.

Morgan scanned the treetops and rides and buildings below before letting her languid gaze fall on me.

"You think you want to know," she said hoarsely. "But you don't."

"Morgan . . ." I moved to grip her shoulder but then stopped myself. I didn't know how she'd react. I was afraid she might startle at my touch and send the gondola swinging again.

"Of course I do," I said softly.

That's when I saw her eyes go shiny. Tears rolled down her face so fast I thought for a second it had started to rain. She looked away from me. We sat there silently for a couple of minutes. She didn't sniffle or use her sleeves. She just let the tears slide off her cheeks and drip onto the front of her V-neck T-shirt.

"I'm scared up here," I admitted, folding and refolding my hands because I didn't know what else to do.

"I know you are," she whispered.

"How did you even *get* up here, Morgan?"

She stared at me like I was stupid. The way she looked at me, a stranger would be surprised to know we were ever friends.

12

"Ask Ethan," she said, looking past me, into the air.

Those two words scared me more than our height. And it finally sank in what should have been obvious the moment I saw her up here: *Morgan is not okay.*

She didn't speak after that, but when the cherry picker approached us again, she got on with me. The three of us were safely lowered to the ground. We didn't speak, but everyone gathered beneath the Ferris wheel clapped.

THREE

"Ivy," Dad called through the bathroom door. "I need to get in there and get my Advil. I've got a bad headache."

"Just a second, okay?" I called back as I washed my hands.

"What . . . you doing all kinds of fancy tinkling in there?"

"God, *Dad*."

I hurried up and opened the door so he wouldn't say something even more gross.

"Why the long face?" he asked, looking at me in the mirror while he wrestled open the Advil bottle. As he bent over it grimacing, his bald spot peeked through his slicked-back brown hair. By the end of the day, his hair product starts to break down from the heat.

"Kind of a tough day, that's all," I murmured, and couldn't help thinking Morgan's had been ten times worse.

"I've had worse," Dad said, popping two or three Advil in his mouth and then leaning over to take a swallow of water from the faucet.

"You did a fantastic job," he said, wiping his mouth with his hand and flashing me a quick smile in the mirror.

"I don't know about *that*."

"You talked her down, right?"

"She came down, yes. But she's definitely not . . . herself."

I hesitated. I considered telling him what Morgan said about *asking Ethan*. But I knew it was kind of creepy, and I didn't want to make her sound crazy. Especially if she was going to want to come back to work for Dad soon. Best not to put any ideas in his head about Morgan being unfit or whatever. Still, I'd been thinking about her words all afternoon and into the evening as I'd covered her post at the Pizza to the Rescue counter in the Fabuland Food Zone.

"You know, I was wondering," I said, deciding to come at it sideways. "Did Morgan seem okay to you these last few days? I mean, after the initial shock of finding Ethan wore off?"

Dad looked at me in the mirror again. He sucked in his lips and seemed to be deliberating what to say. "Well, maybe the shock hasn't worn off yet. That's probably the main issue."

"But she seemed okay when I talked to her a few days ago. I mean, not great. But okay. But then . . . *this*."

Dad shrugged and grimaced again, his gaze shifting back to his own reflection.

"This is a complicated situation, Ivy. You have to remember that you can't solve everybody's problems."

"I didn't say that I could. I wasn't talking about everybody. Just Morgan. Morgan is different from *everybody*."

Morgan and I had been friends since sixth grade, although I'd wanted a bestie since kindergarten. I'd had lots of friends in elementary school, but none of them really *stuck*. Until Morgan showed up. I shouldn't have to remind my dad of any of this, but he doesn't really concern himself with certain details of my life—friends, teachers' names, after-school activities. As long as I have good grades, win awards, and show up for my Doughnut Dynasty and Fabuland shifts, the rest is kind of background noise.

"You know she's at the hospital right now, right?" Dad turned and scratched his neck, peeking at his left profile in the mirror. "I ought to find a way to shave in the afternoon. I'm kind of a hairy beast, no?"

"Yeah, I know she's in the hospital," I replied, ignoring his second question entirely. After the Ferris wheel, the EMTs had put Morgan in an ambulance even though she didn't have any visible injuries. They'd said she was going to the hospital for "observation." When I'd texted her mom a couple of hours later, she texted back that Morgan was staying "for a night or two." I was trying not to overthink this piece of news, or let it scare me too much.

"Hospitals allow visitors," I reminded Dad.

"Tomorrow? You're thinking of going tomorrow?"

"Well, I guess. I mean, I'll try to contact her mom and see if I can."

"You might want to give her a few days to herself." Dad

16

brushed down his eyebrows with his forefingers and gave the mirror a subtle smile. "Umm . . . you know they probably have her in the mental part of the hospital, don't you?"

I sighed. "*Yes,* Dad."

I'd kind of figured that from the vagueness of her mom's response, and from the fact that Morgan had seemed fine physically. Still, I was optimistic that once the hospital staff realized she'd *found a body* a week ago, they'd understand that that might knock someone off-kilter for a day or two. And then let her go home.

"Kind of sad to think of her there." Dad scratched noisily at his stubble, now using both hands. "It's probably not a pleasant place."

"Are you trying to make me feel better? Because it's not working."

I stopped watching him and let my gaze meet my own in the mirror. *No crying,* I reminded myself.

Dad shrugged. "Well, you might want to just give her a few days to rest."

"Yeah, you said that."

"And you're going to be busy the next couple of days."

Dad grabbed his electric razor, started it buzzing, and gave his chin and cheeks a few swipes.

"I am?" I asked, surprised.

Dad shut off his razor and plunked it down next to the sink.

"We've got the Princess Parade. Remember, Ivy?" he said.

"Oh. Well, that's pretty well set, I think. All the costumes are hanging up in the staff room of the game house. I've got the eight girls signed up and I've bought all the little giveaways—jewelry and candies and bookmarks." My checklist for the parade had been set before Mom and I left for North Carolina.

"You need a new Cinderella. Cinderella's pretty important."

Crap. He was right. Morgan was out, which meant so was Cinderella.

"You know someone who could fit the Cinderella costume?" Dad persisted.

"We can just switch dresses around if we have to. Even *I* could be Cinderella if no one else wants to do it."

"Nah. The girls love that *Frozen* princess. We need you to be the *Frozen.*"

"Queen Elsa," I reminded him. Not that I was thrilled about the role. I had suggested we do superheroes like Wonder Woman and Black Panther, but Dad had settled on princesses, saying, *Let's take it a step further, Ivy. Let's make it sparkle.* We were probably violating some kind of copyright law, having Anna and Elsa and Belle at our non-Disney theme park. But Dad likes to live on the edge when it comes to this kind of thing.

"Yeah. I need you to be the *Frozen.* Besides, that blue dress looks nice on you."

"Okay, Dad." I turned away from him and headed to my room. "I'll see who I can get for Cinderella."

"Someone with nice long legs," he said, poking his head into my room.

"I'll give it some thought, sure." I rolled my eyes. I was so worried about Morgan that I really didn't want to deal with the princess problem right now. But I was going to have to.

"Thanks, Ivy," Dad said, smiling. And then he left me alone.

I picked up my phone and considered texting Heidi Copley, but instead went to the Fabuland social feed and flipped through the posts from the last few weeks.

Friday would be our second "Princess Day Parade" event and with the last one being partly my idea, I knew I couldn't get out of this one. The first parade was right after Memorial Day, a few weeks before I left for North Carolina. Dad had invested in four new kiddie rides from SecondHandRides.com, which is like an eBay for amusement park owners (*They still have to pass all the inspections,* he'd reminded me). It had annoyed him that the *East County Herald* had chosen not to do a story about the new rides even though he'd offered them free tickets and complimentary pizza pie.

While trying to figure out how to get more parents of small children to want to come to Fabuland, I'd suggested a little kids' event—like a movie night or a superhero character meet and greet—that the newspaper would cover, and then he could mention the new rides as part of the write-up. The parade itself was Dad's idea, but it was mine to have an ice cream social for the kids in the Food Zone afterward. I felt like that had a cutesy-classy kind of a feel to it, to make the more upscale parents feel like they were getting more than a regular old day at Fabuland.

Overall, the event went really well and I knew Dad was pleased. The photos were the best part—Dani Erwin rode a horse as Sleeping Beauty, Morgan and Drea Tomasetti were on a float behind her, throwing dollar-store jewelry and lollipops, while I walked with the other princesses, playing Elsa to Emma

Radlinger's Anna. The little girls were so happy, pointing and waving to us like we were celebrities.

The one sour note, thankfully not shared online, was when Len Daskevich walked by the parade on his way into the Food Zone and saw Drea float by throwing shiny pink beads. In typical dopey fashion, and clearly misunderstanding the transactional terms of the Mardi Gras parades he'd probably seen on television, he yelled, "Hey, Drea! Show me your tits!" Drea had expertly stifled her laughter and Dad's manager, Chris, had grabbed Len by the scruff of the neck and thrown him out of the park.

I knew this princess event on Friday was going to be even bigger since word could only have spread since the first. Switching gears, I checked the details on our Google Doc and saw that Dad had already hired the three horses we had planned. Cinderella, Snow White, and Belle were supposed to ride them. We were also adding a "Tea Party Book Club." Amy Townsend—who would be dressed as Belle—was going to read aloud a couple of stories in the pavilion, and then girls would be paired with princesses to tell them about the last book they'd read. For their effort, each girl would get a certificate for free entrance to the park (for themselves, not their parents) to use another time. This way Dad could say the event was "promoting literacy" when he advertised it or talked to the papers. With how badly he wanted this to work, I needed to find a new Cinderella tonight.

How would you like to ride a horse in a princess costume for ten bucks an hour? I texted Heidi, biting my nails. All the other girls were getting nine dollars, but for a last-minute Cinderella I knew Dad would let me offer more.

What's going on with Morgan? she replied in seconds. I wondered how much she'd heard about this morning.

She's not feeling up for it, considering, I wrote. *So, you in? It's Friday @ 11. We can talk tomorrow if you want.*

I waited for a few seconds. Typing bubbles appeared below my text and then disappeared.

Ever ridden a horse before? I texted. Maybe I needed to sell this a little more.

Once, she wrote back.

Perfect, I typed quickly. *Someone from the farm will be there anyway so all you have to do is sit and wave as they lead.*

K, she wrote back, after a couple of minutes.

Great, I thought. At least I wouldn't have to be texting all night about this. Heidi's reluctant but quick yes was the first thing that had gone right today.

Thx, I texted, and edited the shared Fabuland events spreadsheet before going downstairs to tell Dad and grab a water. He was watching an old *Shark Tank.*

"I've got you a new Cinderella," I said, opening the fridge.

"Great, Ivy," he said, glancing away from the screen for just a second. "That was *quick.* You're awesome."

"You've confirmed the horses, right? And am I right that there'll be handlers for each horse?"

"Pretty sure, yeah." His gaze slid back to the show.

"Okay." I hesitated, the jug of water weighing down my hand.

"I'm working in the morning tomorrow. So I'm thinking I'll see if I can visit Morgan in the late afternoon."

Dad didn't take his eyes off *Shark Tank,* but he smiled a little. "That's sweet of you."

"Maybe I should bring her something."

"Those places don't allow sharp objects. That's one thing I know."

"Right," I said, deciding not to supply a significant reply. I didn't want him to feel he needed to add to that thought.

I watched as Dad took the two long back cushions off the couch and tossed them on the carpet. He does that when he's kind of stressed out. He lies down and dozes off and sometimes doesn't bother to go up to bed. I don't think he slept in his bed for a month when he was the brand-new owner of Fabuland last summer.

As Dad gave the throw pillow a final fluff and lay down, I looked at the gray cushions on the floor. Jason and I used to make forts with them draped with Mom's cheerful tie-dyed quilts. I missed my brother. I wished he had come home for the summer. Dad was trying—sort of—but Jason would've been a better listener, not to mention better to talk to.

"I was thinking, like, flowers," I added, pouring my water and returning the jug to the fridge.

"Ah. Right." Dad paused the show and looked at me. "You need money to help with that?"

"I've got ten or so bucks I can spend at Drake's Grocery. But if you want to chip in, I can get something really nice, like roses."

"Give me my wallet," he said. "It's on the shelf with the keys."

After I'd handed the overstuffed wallet to him, Dad pulled out a ten and a five. He hesitated before putting them in my hand.

"It's nice you can be a good worker and a good friend at the same time. That's one of the great things about you, Ivy. You can do two things at once. You know, not everyone is able to do that."

"Umm . . . ," I murmured.

I knew he was probably about to remind me that Jason sometimes fell short in this category. But I didn't feel like hearing that tonight—even if it was true.

"Thanks," I said, and slipped back to my room.

* * *

With the princess business out of the way for the moment, I could finally focus on Morgan before seeing her tomorrow. I pulled my phone out of my pocket and opened our chat, which at this point was just a one-sided game of twenty questions.

Love you, dearie! Text me when you feel like it.

I knew Morgan probably wasn't checking messages from the hospital, but it made me feel better to write it. Morgan and I used to call each other *dearie* when we were twelve or thirteen. We thought it was funny, I guess, to sound like old ladies. Maybe she'd read this and reply or at least smile.

Then I sat on my bed and fiddled with my iPad, looking through Morgan's posts on social media from the last couple of weeks. I was particularly interested in the day that she stopped replying to me. But just to be thorough, I started with the day I left town for North Carolina.

That day, there was a picture of her on Facebook looking over her shoulder at someone—I assumed it was Emma Radlinger, who had posted it. Morgan's shoulder was mostly bare—except for the little red strap of her bathing suit that showed. It must've been a new suit because I remembered her having only last year's purple two-piece at the very beginning of the summer. In the photo she was smiling coyly, and wisps of her blond hair whirled around her face, caught by a gust of wind. She looked very sunny and relaxed. The opposite of this morning. I scrolled down to distract myself with the comments.

Looking good, Brent Ballard had written. But he writes stuff like that to everyone.

You look a lot happier when you're not slinging meat lovers' deluxe slices, Zach Crenshaw had commented. Now, *that* was interesting. Morgan had mentioned to me a couple of days before I left that she thought Zach was flirting with her. Neither of us knew quite how to feel about it. A couple of years older than us, he was the sort of guy who sometimes wore vintage leather vests with nothing underneath—and you could see that he waxed. The sort of guy who took his cool status so seriously you just wanted to burst out laughing at the sight of him. Morgan and Zach worked together at the Pizza to the Rescue booth regularly. He made the pizzas, while Morgan took orders and served sodas. Sometimes they'd talk about books during the downtime. Apparently they both liked apocalyptic fiction. It was kind of remarkable, though, that Zach was on social media at all. He always acted like he had better things to do.

Sexyyy, Winnie Malloy had added to the thread. Tall, stone-faced, and usually heavily made-up Winnie. Like Morgan, she lived in the neighborhood close to Fabuland with the small ranch houses and the trailer park. She'd graduated from our high school two years ago with my brother, except she stayed local. I'd never talked to Winnie much, but Morgan knew her from the neighborhood, and from riding the same school bus. I was pretty sure Winnie didn't like me. She'd worked at Fabuland for a few summers and was always giving me an angry stare. Or maybe it was just all the eyeliner she wore that made her look that way. Maybe it was that a lot of people don't know how they're supposed to feel about the boss's daughter. I don't blame them. Even *I* don't know how I feel about it most of the time.

I would continue to let it all slide, though. The post was from the day before Ethan, Winnie's cousin, was found dead. It made me sad to think of her happily typing dumb stuff on her phone, unaware of the tragedy that was about to overwhelm her family in a matter of hours.

I glanced at Morgan's picture again. Morgan was an expert at smiling so you could only see a little of the tops of her teeth. She had practiced that smile a lot when we were in middle school. She was self-conscious about the fact that a couple of her front left teeth had grown in wrong. The pointy one was next to her front teeth, rather than two teeth away like it was for most people. *My canine tooth is switched with my lateral incisor,* she used to explain gravely, as if she had some serious condition.

I scrolled through the rest of her Facebook feed, but there wasn't much to see. Morgan wasn't really into Facebook. Two days after she'd found Ethan, some lady named Trista had written on her wall *So sorry to hear about your friend, Morgan. Call if you want to talk.*

I assumed this was Morgan's Aunt Trista—since not many people are named Trista. In any case, Morgan hadn't replied. At least not on Facebook.

I switched over to Twitter. A couple of days before she found Ethan, Morgan had written *It might just be a corn dog kind of night.*

Aw, you don't really mean that, Trevor Baines had replied.

Isn't every night, at F-Land? Emma Radlinger quipped.

F-Land. Not my favorite abbreviation for Dad's relatively new venture.

Frustratingly, Morgan's Twitter feed also had nothing on it after that post. Unlike some of the other people who worked at Fabuland, Morgan had not posted any tributes to Ethan or condolences to his family. Was she still shaken from finding Ethan or was my gut right and there was something more going on? Whatever the *something* was she had been about to tell me—and whether or not she had confided in someone else—there was no sign of it here. I'd have to start asking questions at Fabuland tomorrow. Even if I couldn't get answers to my questions, I wanted to get a better sense of what Morgan had been up to in the last few days. And that was best done in person.

Feeling resolved, I put on my pajamas and crawled into bed. Staring at the white ceiling and hoping to think of anything but

Morgan, I found my thoughts drifting to the day I found out Dad was buying Fabuland.

That was almost two years ago, on the very same day that Dad and I accidentally served a customer a deep-fried rubber glove. I still couldn't tell what the universe had meant by that.

To be fair, Dad had owned and run all the Food Zone vendor trucks at Fabuland for a few years by then without any significant issues. He split his summer between the doughnut shops and Fabuland, and that year I helped him mostly at the park.

David, Dad's Food Zone manager at the time, had just cooked up a batch of onion rings. We were working the biggest of Dad's shiny new vendor trucks, the one with the picture of the smiling french fries on one side. David had excused himself for his lunch break, so only Dad and I were there when a gaunt red-haired lady shuffled back to the window and shoved the contents of her paper plate at us, standing hand on hip as we looked at the plate. Nestled among the onion rings was a light-yellow mass with several stubby, shrunken appendages. It was breaded and fried like the onion rings, but sprang back unnaturally when Dad poked at it with the handle end of a spork. I had to hold my breath so I wouldn't laugh.

"Whoa," he said. "That's something. I wonder why the rubber didn't break down in the hot oil."

I couldn't tell if he was surprised. Maybe he was really good at hiding it.

"You must not have cooked it for long," the lady replied dryly.

I was glad Dad was doing the talking, for the moment, because I wanted to puke just thinking about it.

"*I* didn't cook it," Dad pointed out. "The clown I got working for me in the back did. He's off somewhere on his lunch break or I'd fire him right now."

"Well, I don't want you to *fire* him. I want—"

"I'll get another batch cooked for you. But, you know, it is what it is."

I snatched some breaded onions out of the fridge and plunked them in one of the frying baskets.

"We'll change the oil in the fourth vat in case rubber got in it," I said. "For now I'm going to fry everything, including your new rings, in the middle fryer."

"Don't do that, Ivy," Dad said. "I don't want you to burn yourself."

I knew Dad didn't want me to do the frying whenever anyone else was around to do it. *Your talents are wasted behind the deep fryer,* he said. Usually he liked me to just get the Cokes and smile at the customers while I took their money. But David wasn't here, and Dad wasn't moving fast enough, in my opinion. He might not even know how to cook onion rings.

"I'm fine," I said, and lowered the basket carefully into the hot oil.

Dad watched me for a moment, scratching absently at the chest hair sprouting out of the top of his black button-down shirt. "Okay."

"Dad," I said.

"Yeah?"

I curled one finger toward me so he'd step closer and I could whisper. "Are you going to give her her money back?"

"She doesn't need her money back. She's getting fresh onion rings."

"If someone served *me* a deep-fried rubber glove, would you want them to say to us, *It is what it is*?"

Dad's lips puckered and he bobbed his head back and forth for a moment. Then he stuck his head out the window and said to the lady, "Fresh batch coming up for you. And it's on me. Here's your five bucks back."

He opened the register and gave the lady her money, winking at me as I stood over the fryer. I wiped the sweat off my forehead with the sleeve of my T-shirt. I could feel sweat dripping down my chest too, but I resisted the urge to mop that up with my shirt. The last time Dad had seen me do that, he'd joked, *What do you call the sweat between Dolly Parton's boobs? Mountain Dew.*

That was last thing I wanted him to say in front of a customer. Particularly in an already awkward moment.

Dad's cell phone rang.

"You got this?" he said, brow furrowed. I nodded.

He studied me for a second, then took off—probably to find David and scream at him, or worse.

"I'm sorry," I said to the woman. "We're so sorry about that. Would you like to have some free ice cream, too? How many in your group?"

Her eyes were sad for some reason. "Just me and my son," she said.

I nodded, but before I could say anything else I heard the ding of the fryer and turned around to dump the rings onto a plate.

Bringing the new batch over to the window, I opened the drawer and handed her four free Fabuland cone certificates. I kept them around for such occasions. I was pretty sure ice cream wasn't going to keep this lady from telling people her rubber-glove story. But free ice cream would at least give it a happy ending. The best I could do beyond that was hope she was from out of town.

Maybe the story would be funny with a few days' perspective. That's kind of how food service is, as long as the Department of Health doesn't enter in.

She appeared to be in better spirits when she took the onion rings and certificates, so I was able to relax until Dad returned. His face was red and sweaty, and you never quite knew what was going to come out of his mouth when he looked like that. When he said he had *big* news, my heart thumped hard, because I thought he might be about to say he'd chased David down and slugged him.

"I didn't want to tell you until it was final," he said, when he caught his breath.

He said he was buying Fabuland, the biggest amusement park in our area. This was quite the step up from our doughnuts-and-assorted-fried-goodies operation that had just served a rubber glove. Dad went into explaining how Mr. Moyer had been thinking of selling it for a couple of years, and now it was a done deal. Moyer was washing his hands of the whole thing and moving to Florida with his wife. Dad wouldn't be in charge of only the Food Zone and his doughnut shops but also a whole theme park. I shouldn't have been shocked, because Dad had been toying with the idea since Grandma died and left him a chunk of money. But I'd thought it was only talk, a pipe dream, because really, who buys a theme park?

I wasn't sure if I was excited about this, so I texted Morgan, asking her to meet me at the gates that night. We walked along the edge of the park after the Food Zone closed at seven. The park had two hours left before closing, so the lights were still on and people were still squealing on the swings and at the Pirates' Pendulum.

"I'm not sure that's the kind of thing Grandma had in mind when she left Dad money," I said a little sadly. Grandma and Grandpa had opened Cork's Doughnut Dynasty when Dad was just a kid, and Dad had helped them open the second and third shops when he was in his twenties. Grandpa died shortly after I turned five, and since then Grandma and Dad had disagreed about a lot of things.

"It seems weird that she didn't leave you and Jason anything for college or whatever," Morgan said, a little gingerly. We were both comfortable talking about almost anything. Except money.

I turned red and was grateful that the darkness hid my blush. In fact, Grandma had set up a college fund for me and one for Jason. Mom had squirreled away some money, too. But I hadn't told Morgan any of this. It would feel like bragging, telling her about a college fund. I was pretty sure her mother couldn't afford to save anything for her.

"Well, the doughnut shops have been doing well," I said. "The extra money from my grandma just put him over the top to make the deal with Mr. Moyer less of a risk."

31

"Huh," Morgan said, staring up at the lights glittering along the spokes of the Ferris wheel.

"It's kind of a shame," she said after a while.

"What?"

"You can ride that thing as many times as you want to now. But *you* aren't interested in doing that."

"Maybe I can learn to like that kind of stuff."

We both knew it wouldn't happen, but Morgan humored me.

"Maybe," she said. "You *do* seem more . . . adjustable than some people."

I decided not to take that as an insult or a compliment. It was simply true, and we both knew it. We walked back to the front of the park, where Dad was waiting to drive us home. All the way to Morgan's house, he wanted to talk about whether we would change the name of Fabuland to something else.

"Shouldn't 'fun' be in the name of the park?" he said. "I've always thought that."

"Like, Funland?" I said.

"No. Funland sounds like it's for little kids. Like, maybe, Fun Realm."

Morgan stayed silent the whole drive, braiding and unbraiding the long pieces of blond hair framing her face. But by the time Dad and I got home, she'd texted me.

I'm not sure people feel comfortable in a "realm" was all her message said. She'd been too polite to say it out loud to my dad. She was like that around adults.

* * *

I couldn't sleep. Every time I started to drift off, I got the sensation I was still way up high, in the Ferris wheel, and would jolt awake. After it happened three times, I got up and went out to our back deck to call our cat.

I always feel stupid calling "Emoji! Emoji!" and want to explain to neighbors that she's a rescue cat and came with that name. Thankfully, after about three calls, Emoji flitted up the steps and sat on the back deck, unwilling to make the commitment of going inside.

She's a funny cat—basically outdoor in the summer and indoor in the winter. At the pound, they said they thought she was originally from somewhere in the South and somehow ended up in New Hampshire. She tested positive for heartworm exposure, which is apparently very rare up here for cats, but common in the South. Jason calls Emoji our secret Southern belle, and thinks that's why she hates going out in the cold—she's not used to it, and never will be. I sometimes wonder, though, if she kind of hates us in the summer, and stays out to avoid us.

She opts instead to prowl the neighborhood all night long and only comes inside to eat or drag in a dead bird. She probably senses that I'm a little crazy in summer, always with my foot out the door, heading to Fabuland, scheming with my dad, talking about roller-coaster ribbon cuttings and corn dog prices and all kinds of things that would surely be offensive to cats if they understood them. In the winter, Emoji is a different animal, and I guess I am too. In the winter, she snuggles with me on my down comforter while I study chem or read fantasy novels. She sleeps on my head and tries to lick my hands while she watches me type on my laptop.

I sat on the deck next to Emoji, petting her calico fur and thinking of winter. About how I never used to spend my summers counting the days till Labor Day. Emoji purred for a minute or two, as if she understood. I wanted to pull her to my chest and carry her back to bed with me. She must have intuited my impulse, because she got to her feet, stretched, and then pranced back into the trees behind the lawn.

There was a fairly strong breeze blowing through those trees. I wondered if it had just started, or if I hadn't noticed it while I was petting Emoji. It seemed like a storm might be coming. Usually I liked the noise and the drama of a good thunderstorm. But tonight the hiss of the wind and the rustling of the leaves made me feel anxious. At first I thought I was nervous for Emoji— wishing she'd come inside where it was safe. I hugged my knees, feeling the breeze begin to lift my hair.

Ask Ethan.

I felt the words shudder through me, finally demanding my attention after all the distractions of the evening. I wasn't sure what they meant. Even if they didn't make sense, they reminded me of what Morgan had been through. Finding someone dead. Seeing his face. The dead face of someone she'd known all her life. Someone I'd known all my life, too. We weren't friends with Ethan exactly, but he and Morgan were from the same neighborhood. They'd known each other for a long time.

Want to talk to you about something I saw the day I found Ethan.

What was this *something*? Something specific? Or was I overthinking it? Maybe it was about how horrible it had been, seeing that up close. Maybe I'd just failed to recognize the significance of dealing with it. This dark thing that would forever be in Morgan's head, and that I would forever—probably—fail to relate to in any real way.

"Emoji," I said softly, wishing she'd come back to me.

While I waited and hoped Emoji would reappear, I thought about the last time I'd seen Ethan. It was about a week before I left for North Carolina. As usual, he'd wanted me to let him spin his own cotton candy. And as usual, I'd let him.

"You ever going to get purple cotton candy?" he'd asked as we waited for the first threads of blue candy to appear in the barrel of the machine.

"We've always just done pink and blue," I said. "Probably Chris gets a good deal on the standard colors."

Ethan pushed up his sleeves and gripped his cone. "It's good to try new things."

"Yeah. Maybe I should suggest other colors."

"You're so lucky." He sighed, peering into the machine. "You've got the best job at Fabuland. Look. Here they come!"

"Go for it!" I exclaimed as he started to swirl his cone.

"It's like cobwebs," Ethan said, not for the first time. "You get to be a witch, taming the cobwebs."

"Is that what witches do?" I asked, laughing.

"Why not?" Ethan said, shrugging, focusing his attention on wrapping his cone.

I wished now that I had prolonged that conversation. There was so much possibility in that *why not,* but I hadn't bothered to ask about it. I'd probably been eager to send him on his way wit' his cotton candy. To get back to playing with my phone. And why hadn't it occurred to me to ask if maybe Ethan *could* be on cotton candy duty occasionally?

Now I dreaded going back to the machine tomorrow. I'd probably sit there alone all day with this painful memory amid the blue and pink plastic-wrapped candy puffs.

"Emoji," I called weakly.

She didn't emerge from the trees, or even make a sound. I knew she was out for the night, come what may. I went inside.

FOUR

**BUY TWO HOT DOG'S, GET A POPSICLE
OR COTTON CANDY FREE!**

I sighed as I drove past Dad's big red LED sign before the main entrance. He changes the sign nearly every day—if not with some surprise deal, then some saying about memorable summer days or the value of hard work. He probably came up with the cotton candy promotion early this morning. Probably someone at the Food Zone had alerted him to a pile of hot dogs about to expire, and this was his brilliant plan to get rid of them. Enterprising, sure. But now I needed to chase him down and tell him to fix his apostrophe.

I parked quickly and went in the front gate, but decided correcting Dad on his punctuation could come later. I had about a half hour to ask around about Morgan before I had to start slinging popcorn and cotton candy.

I headed first to the Rotor—the spinning ride where the floor drops out. I used to ride the Rotor all the time. I had all my friends convinced that I loved it. Except Morgan, who knew better. Truthfully, riding the Rotor was a way to look brave without having to go on many of the high rides. The Rotor is just spinning and no heights, and I can handle spinning.

As usual, Ben Yardley—whom everyone calls the Rotor Lord—was there early. He was doing a couple of test runs of the ride, like they do with all the rides in the morning.

"Hey, my friend," Ben said when he saw me. "Here to take a few spins to wake you up? It'll probably work better than coffee."

Ben calls almost everyone "my friend." I'm not sure why, but my best guess is that he smokes pot more days than not, which maybe isn't great for name retention.

"I don't drink coffee," I said.

Ben glanced self-consciously at his Dunkin' Donuts cup. Maybe he wondered if it bothered me that the coffee wasn't from Cork's Doughnut Dynasty. It didn't, but I didn't feel I could volunteer that.

"I was trying to remember recently," he said, raising the cup as if making a toast, "when I started. It must have been sometime in high school. But I don't remember who told me to start drinking it."

As he lifted his arm, a stale kind of smell emanated from his orange Moxie T-shirt. He wore that thing almost every day.

"Maybe nobody told you," I said. "Maybe you tried it on your own."

"Maybe. So, what's up?" Ben asked with a bemused smile.

One of the reasons I chose to go to Ben first was that he was relatively easy to talk to. He generally seemed removed from the Danville gossip mill. He was a year older than Jason, and he hadn't gone to high school here—he went in Dover, where his mother lived. He spent his summers with his dad in Danville, though, which was how he wound up working at Fabuland for so many years.

"Um, did you hear about what happened yesterday morning?" I asked. "With Morgan? On the Ferris wheel?"

"A little bit," he replied. He shook the hair out of his face. "Is she okay now?"

"I'm not sure," I admitted. "I haven't seen her since it happened."

I decided not to mention that Morgan was in the hospital, because then Ben would ask if she was hurt, and I'd probably say that she wasn't, and then it would be fairly obvious that it was her mental state they were worried about. Which I didn't want everyone talking about either, if I could help it.

"If you see her, give her my best, okay?"

There was a look of genuine concern on Ben's sunburned face. He tried again to shake the overgrown blond curls out of his eyes and I remembered fourteen-year-old me who met Ben when he worked in the Food Zone and my dad managed just that and not the whole park—I had a little crush on him then. Maybe I still would now if he took better care of himself.

"Sure," I said. "Also, can I ask . . . how did Morgan seem to you the last couple of days? I don't mean *right* after she found Ethan. I know she wasn't in great shape right after that, for obvious reasons. But I mean . . . after the initial shock. Yesterday, or the day before that?"

I watched as Ben thought about my question. He screwed up his mouth and closed his eyes. This was what I'd always liked about him. That you'd always catch him being surprisingly thoughtful. Like the way he'd watch Rotor riders so carefully, and always stop the ride at the mere hint of distress.

You okay there, my friend? he'd say to younger, winded-looking kids, leading them off the ride with his arm around their shoulders. *Maybe take a little break before trying this one again, huh?*

"Well . . . I saw her crying in the Food Zone the other day," he said slowly.

"Crying while she was working at Pizza to the Rescue?" I asked.

"I think she must've been taking a break because she was at one of the tables." Ben turned off the Rotor and we both watched its inner spinning tube slow down and then come to a stop. "She was with Winnie. It looked like it was getting kind of intense, so . . . Winnie walked her to the bathroom."

"Oh, huh," I said, wondering when Morgan had gotten close to Winnie.

"I had to get back to work though, so I didn't see them after that. I don't think I saw her after my shift ended either, and I have to admit I didn't think about it much. I figured she was still upset about Ethan, you know?"

"Yeah." I swallowed hard, trying not to be so petty as to wonder why Morgan was willing to cry to Winnie Malloy but not answer my texts. "But . . . what day was that? Do you remember?"

"Uh . . . It had to be Saturday, I guess. Because on Sunday I leave early and don't eat at the Food Zone."

I nodded. "Okay. Huh."

That was four days ago, the day she'd stopped texting me. It seemed pretty clear now that something was up that day in particular.

"You know, you might want to just ask Winnie," Ben said. "You're both friends with Morgan, right?"

I didn't know how to respond to that. It had never seemed to me that Morgan and Winnie had much of a connection beyond familiar hellos. But maybe the shared tragedy of Ethan's death had brought them together while I was gone.

"I don't want to bother her right now," I said uneasily. "You know, when her family is going through so much."

I was kind of a liar. Sure, all of this was true. But I also found it difficult to talk to people who seemed to hate me.

"I don't think she'd think of it as *bothering* her."

"Well, it's more that I don't want to say the wrong thing. You know, I wasn't here the week Morgan found Ethan." It felt vaguely shameful to admit. I *should've* been here. For Morgan. For my dad. "I have some questions, but I don't want to upset anyone unnecessarily."

"Well . . . that's nice of you." Ben waved at Emma Radlinger, who was walking by hauling a big clear plastic bag full of cheap stuffed animals for her prize booth. "What kind of questions?"

41

"Umm . . ." I lowered my voice as much as I could—which wasn't much, since someone was testing the creaky Starship 360 ride a few feet from us. "Maybe you could kind of walk me through some of what happened that day? In a general way?"

I knew it probably sounded like a sort of morbid request. But neither my dad's nor Morgan's accounts had felt complete to me. I'd been careful not to press Morgan and risk upsetting her more, and my dad had been so stressed out about running the park short-staffed that I hadn't asked him for details either.

"Well . . . it was a sad day. When I got here that morning, it was kind of chaos." Ben took a sip of coffee, frowned at the cup, and then put it down next to the metal control panel. "They'd already found Ethan at that point. The police were roaming around asking everybody questions. People were crying and talking about it the best they could, and we were really short-staffed, too. . . . Tim and Winnie took off as soon as they found out, of course. Reggie Wiggins was so upset he was in the bathroom puking and crying. Anna Henry was hysterical. Chris sent both of them home, I think. Chris and your dad were just trying to hold it together, deciding whether they should close the park for the morning."

"They didn't, though, right?"

"No. Too many guests had already arrived. Chris had me close down the Rotor and operate the carousel instead of Winnie. They switched around a few other people's duties too, closed a couple of what your dad called 'nonessential rides' for the day."

His account pretty much matched what my dad had told me

about that morning. Chris, my dad's manager, had called a few extra people in to cover all the bases. Dad had even covered my cotton candy post. He'd bragged to me that night about how big and fluffy his puffs were.

"The first couple of days were pretty rough. We tried to keep things upbeat for the guests, but . . . I think the gray mood still came through. It's been back to normal the last few days though. With the exception of yesterday morning."

Yesterday morning meaning Morgan and the Ferris wheel. I didn't really want to get into that specifically even though Ben was giving me a look.

"Were you working till closing the night before?" I asked quickly.

"Yeah. Well, close to it. I wasn't the official closer. Usually it's Winnie on Thursday night. But it wasn't this time—she wasn't around to walk Ethan home."

I didn't know there was a set schedule, but that made sense given that every night a supervisor—usually Chris, but occasionally my dad—closed up with one other person. Usually a ride operator—Ben, Winnie, Lucas, Reggie, or Carter.

"Who was the closer, then?"

"I'm not sure." Ben took a crumpled napkin out of his jeans pocket and dusted around the ride control buttons in a perfunctory way. "I think it was Reggie, but I don't remember for sure."

"Why wasn't it Winnie, if she usually took Thursdays?"

"I don't know." Ben shrugged. "But I'd be kinda . . . careful about asking her about that. Whatever it was, I'm sure both she and Tim feel really terrible about not being with Ethan that night. I know Tim was working his other job at the grocery store, but I don't know what Winnie was doing."

"I wasn't planning to ask her about *that*," I said, a little defensively. Maybe he thought I sometimes lacked a filter, like my dad. Of *course* I wouldn't ask Winnie that kind of question.

Ben adjusted the ride operator's microphone, dusted it, then leaned down and said "Check" into it in a low voice. His voice echoed through the cylindrical interior of the ride.

My phone vibrated and I peeked down at the screen. It was a text from Heidi.

Just realized I can't do the parade, sorry! Forgot I'm driving my grandma to the dr. :(

"Shit," I muttered, and then looked up. "Princess Parade problems."

"Never a dull moment." Ben raised his cup of coffee again. "Not at Fabuland."

"No . . . never," I said, and slipped my phone back in my pocket.

"So." Ben tried to blow his bangs out of his face. "You seem to be acting more like the boss around here every day. You taking over the place when the old man retires?"

"What old man?" I said, before thinking about it. Then I felt like an idiot. I never think of my dad as an old man since he has the enthusiasm of a ten-year-old. "I mean . . . no. I'm not planning on that. Why?"

Ben studied me. In the long pause, I became self-conscious about some of the grooming choices I'd made this morning. I'd thrown on a pink sundress to try to Band-Aid how I'd been feeling since yesterday. And I'd put a little too much product in my hair. It was probably kind of artificially shiny, like Dad's.

"Just wondering," he said. "I'll bet he thinks you'd be good at it."

This line of conversation was making me a little sick. My worst nightmares have me in charge of Fabuland as a middle-aged lady, toothless from too much cotton candy, hacking and scratchy-throated from too many stress cigarettes. I believe this nightmare began precisely when I heard my brother wouldn't be coming home this summer.

"Uh-huh. Well, I'm probably going to end up being a lawyer. Not an amusement park owner."

"Oh yeah?" Ben scowled, apparently taking this answer more seriously than I'd intended it.

"Yeah."

I actually have no idea what I'm going to do with my life after Danville. But people seem to respond positively to *lawyer*. Probably because they think lawyers are a little cold, and think I'm slightly cold as well. I don't agree with either sentiment, but it shuts people up because it apparently sounds like a good fit.

"I'm not sure I can see it, Ivy." Ben squinted at me. "I see you more like a veterinarian . . . or maybe even a park ranger, if you don't mind me saying so?"

"And what about you, Ben?" I said, feeling slightly unsettled at how well he could read me. "What do you see yourself as?"

Ben looked surprised, and then I felt bad. I'd only meant to shift the focus of the conversation onto him instead of me. I'd forgotten, for a second, that he was older than me and I'd never heard him mention college. That there were probably no fancy career plans for the foreseeable future. I wondered, for the first time, what Ben did for the rest of the year, when he wasn't Rotor Lord.

Ben turned on the Rotor.

"A chiropractor." He snorted, taking a slug of coffee. "I'd think that would be obvious."

He smiled and I guessed—hoped—there were no hard feelings.

"See you later, Ivy," he said.

I waved and headed toward the center of the park.

Winnie was kind of the jill-of-all-trades at the park, so I wasn't quite sure where to find her as I walked around. Sometimes she ran the fried dough stand and sometimes she operated the carousel. Occasionally she was the Rotor Lady, when Ben was taking a day off. Clearly my dad must've thought she was pretty competent, because those were all relatively important jobs. When Dad thought someone was a bit of a loser, he put them on janitorial duties or had them run the deadly boring balloon dart booth.

I found Winnie at the carousel. She was running it without riders, checking for mechanical issues, just as Ben was doing with the Rotor. She ignored me for a minute or two, staring at the carousel as it spun. You could practically see her mascaraed lashes flapping in the wind of the passing ponies.

As I approached, I saw that her super-short shorts were cut so that you could see just a sliver-tease of each ass cheek. She had long, enviably tan legs, which made me think of the Cinderella costume that Morgan and Heidi wouldn't be using. Why hadn't

I thought of Winnie before? She was even blonder than Morgan and Heidi. Not that Cinderella needed to be blond, in my opinion, but I had a feeling my dad might disagree.

I stood next to Winnie, smiling faintly at her as I waited for her to turn off the carousel music. The sound of it always rattles me and makes me forget what I'm supposed to be doing or thinking. The low *thump thump thump* beneath the calliope sound seems to reset my heartbeat to its own rhythm.

After the test ride was over, Winnie didn't turn off the music. She just looked up at me and yelled, "Did you want something?"

"A couple things," I yelled back. "This would be easier if you turned off the music."

She didn't try to hide her annoyance at the request, but she did what I asked.

"Yeah?" she said, taking a phone out of her pocket and glancing at it briefly before slipping it back in again.

She was making a show of how disinterested she was in talking to me. I tried not to take it personally. Understandably, she might still be pretty depressed about her cousin.

"I wanted to tell you how sorry I was to hear about Ethan. I was away when it happened, so I haven't had a chance . . ." I trailed off.

"Thank you." She finally made eye contact with me, nodding slightly.

"Umm . . . and I wanted to talk to you a little bit about Morgan."

"Oh. Yeah?" The second word came out unusually high-pitched. Like she was either really surprised or just feigning interest, like you do with a little kid. "Have you guys been . . . talking?"

Had Morgan *told* Winnie she'd stopped texting me? It seemed like maybe she had. My chest started to tighten at the thought.

"Well . . . not in the past few days, no," I admitted reluctantly. "Except for on the Ferris wheel."

"I heard about that. I heard you're like the big hero for getting her down."

I caught the briefest hint of an eye roll as she said this. Probably my dad had been spreading around an exaggerated account of my "heroics."

"Oh, um, anyway, someone told me Morgan was crying on Wednesday in the Food Zone," I said. "While you were with her, talking to her."

Winnie's grip on her hip tightened, her fingernails appearing to dig into the flesh above her hip-hugging shorts. She glanced away from me and looked at the carousel horses as if one of them might help her out with a response.

"What was wrong?" I pressed. Winnie cleared her throat but still wouldn't look at me. "C'mon, Winnie, what was wrong with Morgan?"

"She was upset."

"Yeah," I replied, unsure if that was a deliberate nonanswer. "Okay. I figured that."

"You know . . ." Winnie drew in a breath and leveled her gaze at me. "Since you weren't here, you might not realize what it's been like the past week or so. There's been a lot to cry about."

"I get that," I said. As soon as the words left my mouth, I cringed at how unconvincing they sounded.

"You *do*?" Winnie demanded.

Ouch. I probably deserved that.

"I'm trying to," I mumbled, and found myself the one avoiding eye contact.

"Okay," Winnie said skeptically, folding her arms.

We were both silent for a few seconds. But I decided that just because Winnie was going to be withholding, it didn't mean I had to be.

"I'm not planning on telling a lot of people this," I said quietly, "but I thought you might be able to help me understand. She mentioned Ethan while we were up on the Ferris wheel."

Winnie's jaw tensed.

"What did she say about him?" Winnie asked, staring at me so fiercely that I didn't have time to consider telling her anything but the truth. I reported our brief exchange:

How did you even get up here?

Ask Ethan.

Winnie's expression softened, and she looked more perplexed than angry.

"Does that make sense to you?" I asked.

"No," Winnie said softly. "It's just . . . sad. It's sad she had to go through that. Finding him. But in a way I'm glad it was someone nice like her and not someone else. Someone who might talk about it later like they had celebrity status or something. Like someone who would talk about it on Halloween."

I nodded, feeling the weight of her words, realizing in that moment that I couldn't ask her the last couple of questions on my mind. *Morgan said she saw something the day she found Ethan. Do you know what it was?*

Maybe Winnie knew the answer. Maybe she and Morgan had even talked about it the day Ben had seen them together. Or maybe Winnie would have no clue what I was talking about. And hearing it could be really upsetting, on a number of levels. I didn't want to risk it for now. I'd be seeing Morgan later. Maybe she was feeling better today, and maybe she'd be willing to tell me everything.

Winnie walked over to the red velveteen rope that closed off the carousel entrance. She unhooked it and then turned back to me.

"Was there anything else?" She looked at her phone again. "It's nine oh-one. They've opened the gates by now. I've got to turn the music back on, because Chris and your dad like it to be playing as folks walk in. Like, good-time mood music or whatever. That's why I had it on," she said matter-of-factly.

"Okay, but . . ."

The calliope music drowned out my next thought.

"What?" Winnie yelled.

"I was wondering if you would be willing to be Cinderella in the parade tomorrow."

"I've got fried dough duty!" she screamed back.

"I'll get one of the guys to cover!" I yelled, then stepped closer to her so I could talk a little softer. "Will you do it? I think the costume would fit you."

Winnie shrugged. "Sure. Whatever."

"Are you afraid of horses or anything?"

Winnie laughed. "No. I fucking love horses."

So she wasn't quite as gentle or princessy as Morgan. Or even Heidi. But she'd have to do.

"Never mind," I said. "Nine o'clock we put on princess costumes in the break room behind the pavilion. I'll text you a reminder. Okay?"

"Yep," she said, and then waved at the gray-haired man approaching with two wriggling little boys holding on to his hands.

I felt like there was something Winnie wasn't saying about Morgan, but at least my dad would be happy. All the princesses were accounted for.

FIVE

It wasn't until three o'clock that I finally got off popcorn and cotton candy duty, after which I spent about an hour in the main office checking up on the final Princess Day Parade details. I'd given up trying to text Morgan; when I'd called her mom on my lunch break, she had confirmed that they wouldn't let Morgan have her phone at the hospital, and told me that she was probably going to stay there for a few more days. Her mom also noted that *In the part of the hospital Morgan's in, any visitors under eighteen need to be accompanied by an adult.* Assuming that I wouldn't be allowed to visit by myself at seventeen, I'd called Mom for help. She was willing, and I tried to push away the uncomfortable hint of *the part of the hospital she's in* and just be grateful I was going to get to see Morgan, regardless.

After texting Mom the update, we had agreed that I'd meet her at her place by four-thirty and she'd drive me to the hospital to see Morgan before we picked up dinner.

I still had about ten minutes to kill in my dad's office. And something Ben had mentioned had been bothering me all day. Specifically, that he wasn't sure who had closed the night of Ethan's death—and that normally it would've been Winnie's night to do so.

Chris generally made the employee schedules on his laptop, sent them to each employee, and then forwarded them to my dad. My dad, who's not particularly high-tech, tended to print them out, put them up on the various employee bulletin boards around the park, and then file copies in one of his many over-stuffed folders. He keeps *everything* on paper. He has this persistent paranoia that someday everything on all the computers and phones is just going to disappear.

Still, I found the *Schedules* document on his messy computer desktop, and opened it.

I clicked on the week of June 25–July 1 and scanned down to Thursday, June 29. Under *Closing*, it said *Supervisor: E. Cork. Assisting: W. Malloy.*

There were two unusual things about this. One was that my dad was the closing supervisor. Chris usually did Thursdays. But Chris must not have been available, and had my dad cover. That in itself wasn't all that weird—they traded shifts occasionally. But, like Ben had said, Winnie was scheduled to close that night. And if she had someone fill in for her, it must've been very last-minute, as it didn't make it into the schedule.

I opened my dad's lower desk drawer and found his *Work Schedules* folder. The schedule for the week of June 25 was a few pages back. On the hard copy, *W. Malloy* was crossed out and

Reggie was scribbled in, in blue pen. It looked like my father's handwriting. And he probably didn't know his employees' last names well enough to maintain Chris's more formal way of identifying them.

I flipped to the two previous weeks' schedules to confirm that Winnie *normally* closed Thursday nights. She did. The week before Ethan's death, she'd also been scheduled to work a Tuesday night. But her name was crossed out and Lucas's was penciled in. Winnie was penciled in for Saturday, when Lucas normally closed. They'd obviously traded.

So Winnie had been scheduled to work the night of Ethan's death. But there had been a last-minute change and Reggie had filled in instead. Not a big deal on the surface. Except that if Winnie had been working that night, Ethan wouldn't have walked home alone. I sucked in a breath. No wonder Ben had warned me against asking her about it.

Winnie was supposed to be at Fabuland the night her cousin died. But she wasn't.

My phone vibrated with a text from Mom saying she was getting ready, which was my cue to get going. As I closed the folder and stashed it back in the desk drawer, I couldn't stave off the next thought: *What had kept Winnie away from her shift that night?*

Picking up my bag and heading down the stairs, I pushed the thought down. Asking a painful question like that wouldn't bring Ethan back.

On my way to the front gate of the park, I caught sight of

my dad handing out doughnuts to a group of kids near the game booths. Three girls and one boy, all about middle school age, with a cheerful-looking mom watching them and already chomping happily on a sprinkle doughnut.

I was just going to give Dad a casual wave goodbye—he knew it was one of my nights with Mom—but then I heard what one of the girls was saying to him.

"*Hot dogs* isn't possessive. You know?"

The girl was about thirteen. She was wearing low-rise jeans, a white muffin top peeking out below her too-tight salmon-colored T-shirt.

"And wait"—she smiled slyly at one of her friends—"why are you giving out *doughnuts* for free if you want people to buy hot dogs? Nobody's gonna be hungry for hot dogs if they're full on *doughnuts*."

She kept stressing each pronunciation of *doughnuts* in that high-pitched, exaggerated way younger girls sometimes use to make a word seem ridiculous—even though she was clearly enjoying her chocolate-frosted doughnut immensely as she said it.

"I bet you could manage both," I heard Dad say as the girl brought the last bite of doughnut to her mouth. And then I felt everything go into slow motion. My heartbeat felt heavy and my stomach dropped.

"You seem like you have a good appetite," Dad continued.

I watched Dad's mouth turn downward, into a pout. Red crept up his neck and into his cheeks. There was chocolate frosting smeared on one side of the girl's mouth.

"Dad!" My voice was shaky, so I cleared my throat and tried again. "Hey, *Dad*!"

He turned but seemed to look through me, and then turned back to the girl.

"In fact, you might want to—" I heard him say.

"Dad!" I screamed, and pounced on the platter of doughnuts like a *National Geographic* lioness on a gazelle. "You have any toasted-coconut sprinkle?"

I grabbed a regular chocolate frosted with rainbow sprinkles, took a quick bite, and then talked through the mouthful. "Sorry about the sign. I typed it so fast this morning, I should have checked it."

Dad's mouth straightened, and then formed a gentle smile. "It's okay, sweetheart," he said. "Have a good time with your mom tonight. I'll see you in the morning."

He gave me a kiss on the cheek and then disappeared into another crowd with his stack of doughnuts.

The girl and her little group moved on. I stared up at the swinging Starship 360 and tried to catch my breath. Then I looked down at the doughnut in my hand, one third eaten, frosting melting on my fingers. Funny thing about doughnuts. They're so pretty and enticing when they're sitting together on display, sprinkled and uniform. But they quickly turn gross when you're in the process of eating one.

"Are you okay?" someone behind me said.

I turned around to see Ben, who was finishing the end of a hot dog. He was apparently on his break. I thought of telling him why we were having the hot dog promotion but decided it was too late for that. And I figured he probably had a pretty strong stomach from working here a few years.

"Yeah," I said.

"You look winded."

"I'm fine. I think I've been watching the Starship 360 too long. It makes me sick just looking at it."

Ben stared at the ride with me, waiting to see it do a full loop around. The screams from the riders intensified.

"I know what you mean," he said. "Isn't it amazing, what people do to themselves sometimes?"

I was quiet for a moment, then nodded. His words surprised me. I'd felt that way for a long time, about most of the rides. I feel the same way watching people drink themselves silly at parties. I don't get it, but I'm not sure if that means there's something wrong with me or with them.

"Your dad asked me to switch to that ride last year. Give Rotor duty to Winnie full time."

"Really?"

"Yeah. But I said no, I wanted to stay on Rotor."

To my relief, the Starship 360 completed its final full swing and then started to slow down. Everyone had survived. Nobody was screaming anymore.

"Is this so different from seeing people spin around on the Rotor?" I asked.

"Yeah," he said. "It is. We all like to spin. We do it when we're kids. You spin around and around and get dizzy. It makes sense."

"Uh . . . I don't know about *sense*. I mean, by the same token, some people like to get flipped around, I guess. Is it so different?"

"It draws a different crowd," he said. "I *get* the spinners. I don't understand the flip-floppers, the upside-downers. Best to put someone on that job who understands them."

"Is that what you told my dad?"

"Hell, no." Ben smiled, and I was glad he didn't seem mad at me for my awkward remark that morning. "I just told him that watching that all day would make me puke."

I laughed and I could see the corners of Ben's mouth quirk up as he scrunched the foil into a ball right as my phone vibrated in my pocket. I knew it was my mom, wondering where I was.

"Sorry, gotta go," I called over my shoulder to Ben as I weaved through the wobbly riders exiting the Starship 360.

* * *

After we stopped for flowers and finally found a spot in the hospital parking lot, Mom offered to wait for me.

"I'll be here just in case they *insist* on a chaperone," she said.

She seemed to understand we might need to talk. I walked to the front desk myself, gave the receptionist Morgan's name, and got her room number. The receptionist didn't ask me my age.

"They're going to need to get permission and buzz you in, honey," she explained before pointing me to the elevator and telling me to go up to the second floor, to the McMahon Wing.

I followed her instructions and arrived at a set of big white double doors with a buzzer. I pressed it and then a female voice said, "Open the right-side door, please."

When I did, I reached a desk with a couple of ladies in purple scrubs.

"You're here to see Morgan, right?" one of them asked.

"Yeah."

"Morgan said it's okay. So we're going to have you girls in the meeting room."

"Uh, okay," I said, breathing a sigh of relief.

I glanced back toward the double doors and realized that I'd had to buzz in because they were locked. This all seemed more complicated than it needed to be. Morgan had had a phenomenally shitty couple of weeks and had broken down a little. But she didn't need *this*. I turned forward again, keeping my eyes on the lady's gleaming white sneakers as she led me into a room with a circle of folding chairs.

Morgan was sitting in the chair farthest from the door, turned slightly away from us, looking out the window. She was wearing jean shorts and a long white T-shirt, her hair in a loose ponytail. I was relieved that she wasn't in a hospital gown, but she didn't acknowledge our presence.

"Your friend is here," said the lady. "I'll be at the desk if you need anything. I'm leaving the door open. Okay, Morgan?"

I didn't like how she talked to Morgan—like she was a really old lady who needed every word enunciated to her. It scared me. And the yellow roses in my fist suddenly seemed sad— confirmation that Morgan was now an invalid of some kind.

"Okay," Morgan murmured, still gazing out the window.

I sat close to Morgan, but with one chair between us.

"Hi," I said. The cellophane around the roses crinkled as I sat.

"Hi," she answered, glancing at me for a second and then stiffening as her gaze darted away.

"Your mom and brother been visiting?"

"They went out for dinner. Then my mom's bringing Gavin back home to the babysitter and coming back here for a little while more."

I nodded. "How are you feeling?"

Morgan shrugged. "I want to go home."

"When *do* you go home?" I asked.

"When they believe I wasn't going to jump or anything."

"Do they not believe you?" My words came tumbling out, overeager. "Can I help? Can I tell them that *I* was there and you weren't—"

"They're on the fence, I think," she interrupted. "Once they believe me, I can go home. I don't think anything you say would help. They're waiting for *me* to say the right things."

The topic seemed to annoy her, so I decided not to ask her what "the right things" were.

"So . . . what were you doing up there, Morgan?" I asked.

Morgan released a long sigh, letting her gaze slide over me and across all the empty chairs around us. "I was taking a break."

"I get that," I said, as gently as I could manage. "But—were you up there all night?"

"What better place?" Morgan paused for a moment. "I knew I'd be left alone."

"Until morning?"

Morgan gripped her hands together in her lap. "Well, I guess I didn't realize I'd stay up there that long."

"How'd you get up there?" I asked, and then held my breath, waiting to see if she'd supply the same strange answer as yesterday.

"I climbed."

"Jesus, Morgan." I exhaled. "I'm shaking just thinking about that."

I really was. And I could feel goose bumps forming on my arms.

Morgan took a long breath and glanced around the room before meeting my gaze. Once she did, though, she seemed to be studying my expression.

"Sometimes . . . ," she said, and then shook her head.

"Sometimes what?" I prompted.

"Sometimes I wonder if you're scared of the wrong things."

I wasn't sure what that meant. Morgan has always known I'm afraid of heights—just like I've always known she's kind of afraid of water. For a long time, we helped each other hide these things from the other girls so we wouldn't have to admit to anyone but each other what wimps we could be. It helped us become closer friends. She'd pretend she didn't want to go on the high rides, and I'd pretend to want to hang out in the shallow end.

"Morgan," I said softly.

"Yeah?" Morgan seemed to sink into the chair as she stared at her fingernails. They had a little bit of purple sparkle on them— mostly chipped off.

"Yesterday you mentioned Ethan."

61

Morgan rolled her eyes up toward the ceiling. "Yeah."

I waited for a moment. "Did you want to talk about him?"

"What about him?"

I was silent for a moment. Somehow I'd expected her to take the lead on that subject.

"Some people are making out like it's Winnie's fault about Ethan," Morgan offered. She was looking at me now as she spoke, as if watching for my reaction. "That she was supposed to walk him home. But she wasn't even working at Fabuland that night. That's what people seem to forget. And her brother walked him home just as often—or drove him. It was a rare night that neither of them were there. Ethan said he would call his mom, but he didn't. Why not? Why didn't he go get his backpack out of his locker either? Why was he in such a rush to go home? On foot?"

"Those all sound like good questions," I said quietly. "Are the police blaming Winnie?"

"No." Morgan seemed confused that I had asked. "But since Ethan can't answer those things for us . . . I wonder if there's someone else who can."

I shrugged. "Maybe he just decided to walk. It was a nice night, right?"

"A *hot* night. But nice enough. Yeah." Morgan's expression looked almost feral now, and her voice lowered to a whisper. "I wonder if it's occurred to anyone that he didn't fall."

"What . . . ," I said uneasily. "Like that he was pushed or something?"

"I don't know. Just . . . that he didn't *fall*."

"Who would want to push Ethan? Ethan never hurt anyone."

"I didn't say anyone pushed him. All I asked was if it ever oc-curred to anyone . . ." Morgan couldn't finish her sentence. She was crying.

I wanted to reach out and hug her, but it felt like she was maybe too delicate. It was almost like we were still on the Ferris wheel. One wrong move and she might end up overboard.

"It's okay, Morgan," I murmured. Just like I had on the phone while I was in North Carolina. And just as ineffectively. "Oc-curred to anyone . . . what?"

Morgan sniffled and pulled a mushed tissue out of her shorts pocket. "Never mind."

"No . . . not never mind. I want to know what you were going to say."

But Morgan dried her eyes and said nothing. Her gaze crept toward the ceiling again.

My hands tightened around the stems of the yellow roses.

"Morgan," I whispered—more sharply than I intended.

"Yeah?"

"A few days after Ethan died you texted me that there was something from that morning you wanted to talk about. Some-thing about the day you found Ethan."

Morgan nodded and finally let her eyes meet mine, seeming to focus a little. "Yeah. There was."

"I wanted to ask you about it on the Ferris wheel, but it, um, didn't seem like the right time."

Morgan's face broke into a little smile. "Right. That would've been . . . inappropriate."

I smiled too. Here was a glimpse of the old Morgan. We both

found it funny how people overuse or misuse that word. Like when the local paper characterized the *Fuck off and die* someone had spray-painted on the assistant principal's car as "an inappropriate sentiment."

"So . . . can we talk about that now?" I coaxed.

"Yeah. I actually have it with me." Morgan hopped out of her chair. "In my room."

"What?" I said, stunned by her burst of energy and intrigued by whatever the "it" was that apparently was at the root of all this.

"Hold on a sec," she called as she shot out of the room. "I'll be right back."

After she was gone a minute, I began to wonder if she actually intended to come back. And I wondered what a room in this part of the hospital looked like.

I checked my phone. No texts, of course, since Morgan and my parents were the only people who usually texted me. I put the roses on the floor and stood up. Then Morgan came back in.

"This," she said, and thrust something smooth and round into my hands.

It was a small half-globe paperweight with blue-green glitter on the bottom. Isolated in the middle of its clear plastic domed top was a little brown scorpion.

"Is that real?" I asked.

"I think so. They have these as new prizes at the Water Gun Fun and the balloon dart booths. They're only for this summer. Stuff for older kids to pick from, I guess. Not just toy cars and magic wands and mini stuffed animals. That's what Emma told me."

"Uh-huh," I said. Emma worked a couple of different prize booths, depending on the day.

"The morning I was walking to Fabuland from my house . . . *before* I got to the trestle . . . *before* . . . " She swallowed and took a breath. "Before Ethan. Like a minute or two before I saw Ethan, while I was walking along the path from Braeburn Road to the trestle, I saw this and picked it up. I thought it was kind of cool, so I put it in my pocket. I forgot about it, though . . . when everything happened."

"Okay," I whispered, waiting for more as I handed the paperweight back to Morgan.

"That night I found it in my pocket. Put it on my dresser. Debated if I should get rid of it. Seemed like a bad-luck charm kind of thing, that I found Ethan a minute or two after I'd put this thing in my pocket."

I shuddered and sucked in my breath. I'm not very superstitious, but finding a scorpion trinket seconds before finding someone dead seemed like pretty staggering proof that bad omens existed.

"I almost threw it in the trash, but there was so much going on those few days—talking to the police, and not being able to sleep for a couple of nights and the wake and the funeral and everything—I kind of forgot about it. Until after the funeral. A few of us were hanging out at the pizza place on East Main that night, chatting, mostly just sharing memories about Ethan. And then Emma starts saying how Ethan kept coming to her booth the week before he died, and kept eyeing this one paperweight, one of the new scorpion paperweights. There were a few purple ones and a red one but only one light blue one. He wanted it so desperately that Emma tried to give it to him, but Ethan insisted no, he had to *win* it fair and square."

"And?" I said.

"And he won it. The day before he died. Emma was telling everyone how happy Ethan was, how Ethan hugged her and couldn't wait to show it to his mom, to his cousin Tim. To everyone else it was just a sweet story about Ethan. But . . . for me . . ."

Morgan didn't finish her sentence.

"Wait." I wanted to clarify something. "You found it *before* you found him?"

"Yeah. Ever since I heard it was his, I've been carrying it around with me. I had it with me on the Ferris wheel."

I bit my lip. I didn't like the thought of the bad-luck scorpion having been with us up so high in the sky.

"Do you think Ethan dropped it?" I asked, once I'd recovered from the thought.

Morgan shrugged. "I don't know. I just know it was his. Unless he gave it to someone. Because it was, like, in the middle of the path. Enough people walk that path that it's unlikely it could have been there for long."

I could see why it had unsettled Morgan—aside from the obviously creepy vibe of Ethan's prize. Coming from Fabuland, after you crossed over the trestle, the path in the woods went in two directions. The shorter path went toward Braeburn Road, which

66

was close to Morgan's street. The other, longer path went up a hill, then behind several houses on Sweetwater Road, toward Ethan's neighborhood. It was odd if Ethan had been on *the shorter* path, since it didn't lead directly to or from his neighborhood.

"Did you tell anyone about it?" I asked.

Morgan shook her head. "Not till now."

"Not even Emma?"

"Not even Emma." Morgan's voice was a whisper.

"What about Winnie?" I said.

Morgan looked surprised to hear Winnie's name again.

"No," she muttered, avoiding my gaze.

I could feel her slipping away from me again, so I quickly turned my attention back to the paperweight.

"There are a few ways it could've gotten there," I said, trying to sound casual.

"Yeah. I know."

Ethan's cousins Tim and Winnie also lived up the Braeburn way. Maybe Ethan had given it to Tim. Maybe he'd been visiting them.

"I keep thinking he could have been confused that night," Morgan said quietly. "That's one possibility. He walked up the wrong way, turned around, went back to the trestle for some reason."

"Huh," I said. It was incredibly sad to think of Ethan lost and confused in the woods in the minutes before his fall.

"But I can't help thinking that something isn't right." Morgan shook her head. "That maybe someone isn't being honest about Ethan. About where he was or who saw him that night."

My mind was reeling. It made sense, what Morgan was saying. At least on the surface. But on the other hand, I wondered if she wasn't looking for someone to blame. Surely seeing Ethan like she had made it harder for her to accept that his death was something that simply . . . happened.

I took a breath.

"Morgan, can you remind me who rode the Laser Coaster with Ethan the night he died?"

"Anna Henry, Lucas Andries, and Briony Simpson. Why?"

"I just . . . well . . . if we *were* to ask someone about it . . . I'm wondering who we'd start with."

"I thought of asking more questions after I realized the scorpion was Ethan's, but . . . right after that I got . . ." Morgan's gaze was drifting around the room as she wove her fingers together in her lap. "Distracted," she said softly.

Distracted. I didn't ask for clarification. Distracted by whatever personal demon sent her climbing up a Ferris wheel in the middle of the night? Distracted, maybe, by the memory of Ethan's dead face? Was it bloody? Pained? Were his eyes open? I wondered for the hundredth time in the last few days—even though I tried very hard not to.

Morgan closed her eyes again.

"Morgan?" I whispered. When she didn't reply, I asked, "Why were you crying with Winnie Malloy in the Food Zone on Wednesday? Do you remember? Did she say something to you?"

Morgan's eyes snapped open. Her expression looked like it had on the Ferris wheel.

"There's something I should probably tell you," she said

slowly. "My mom is suggesting I go to Portsmouth in the fall. I'm thinking of saying yes this time. When I get out of here."

I was speechless for a moment. Since the beginning of high school, Morgan's mom had been floating the idea that she go stay with her aunt and uncle in Portsmouth so she could be in a better school district. Morgan had never once taken it seriously.

"But . . . it's senior year. What's the point?" I asked, trying not to raise my voice. "Would you really want to leave now?"

Morgan flipped the paperweight from one hand to the other. "I don't feel . . . comfortable in Danville anymore."

"Because of Ethan?" I asked. "Or . . . ?"

I didn't finish the question.

"Maybe you could leave me alone for a little while," she said, her tone flat. "Don't come and visit me here. Wait till I get home."

"But—" I started to protest. I didn't understand why one minute she wanted to confide in me about the scorpion and the next didn't want to talk to me.

"And can you do me one favor?" Morgan interrupted.

"Yeah . . . anything."

"Don't tell people where I am." She finally let her tired gaze meet mine. "Okay?"

"Of course I won't. Is there a story you want me to tell people?"

"I don't know . . . maybe that I was drunk when I climbed up there? I passed out once I got to the top of the Ferris wheel. That's why I was there in the morning."

I only had to think about it for a few seconds. I wasn't sure I could convince kids of this, but I could probably have about half of the younger Fabuland staff at least *saying* it within the next forty-eight hours. If that was what Morgan wanted. Apparently she felt *drunk out of her mind* was easier to live down than simply *out of her mind*.

"Absolutely," I said, and thrust the yellow roses into her lap.

She looked at them for a moment, and then handed me the sparkle-scorpion paperweight in return.

"Thanks," she said. "And maybe you should take this with you."

"All right," I mumbled.

I felt rattled as I made my way back down to the lobby with Morgan and Ethan's bad-luck charm weighing down my right pocket. But I'd have felt worse if I'd refused. If I'd made her keep it instead.

SIX

As soon as our takeout burritos were unwrapped, Mom peered at me over her new horn-rimmed glasses.

"Do you want to talk?" she asked.

Of course she meant *talk about Morgan*.

I took a moment to decide how little I could say without making my mom think I was deliberately shutting her out.

"Well . . . I think she's still pretty shaken up about Ethan," I said carefully.

"It's hard." Mom nodded knowingly. "When someone we're close to experiences something traumatic and there's not much we can do."

It's hard is my mom's go-to line about everything. She works with little kids—in a charter school during the year and at a day camp in the summer—and she's always affirming their feelings. *I know, sometimes it's hard to share,* she probably says all day

71

long. *It's hard to say goodbye to Mommy. It's hard when we don't get our first choice.*

I always wonder if she ever wants to add, *But you're just going to have to suck it up.* She never had to when Jason and I were little, because Dad was around then to say those kinds of things.

"I wouldn't say that yet. That there's not much I can do." I touched the smooth paperweight in my pocket.

"Well . . . you might want to take a wait-and-see approach, you know? Give her a few days or weeks to work things out a bit. She's wrestling with something. You might want to wait and see if she has a chance to pin it down herself, rather than jumping in. She's already communicated that she's in some kind of pain. Sometimes, in those cases, all we can do is listen."

I decided not to reply—at least not right away. Sometimes all this "affirmation" is infuriating. Instead, I refolded my burrito because black beans were falling out of it. While we ate quietly, I went over in my head all the people I wanted to talk to about Ethan's last night and about his scorpion paperweight: Emma, the three kids who'd ridden the ride with Ethan, and Tim Malloy. But would talking to Tim be any easier than talking to his sister?

"Wanting to help is great, but wanting too much can be a way of making it about ourselves," Mom said. "You know?"

Mom had a lot of therapy after the divorce, and it showed. *Don't make it all about you* is one of her favorite themes. That was how she talked now, at least when something serious came up. Nothing she was saying was wrong exactly, but I occasionally missed the old Mom, who could be a little more laid-back and fun. The Mom who used to be in charge of the kids' birthday parties at Dad's shops. The Mom who could rattle off the color names of at least five different shades of pink sprinkles (*neon pink, Valentine spectrum, taffy swirl, berry blush, sweet sixteen . . .*) and who knew how to operate a ride-on bubble machine.

Now she's an assistant kindergarten teacher at Danville Elementary, and Feelings are way more important than I ever remember them being when I was a kid. Feelings and Respect and giving each other Space. All good things, of course, but sometimes I wonder if she doesn't realize I'm old enough to apply these things with some degree of nuance.

It's hard to believe your parents were ever *married,* Morgan says sometimes. She and I became friends when we were eleven— two years after the divorce—so she never got to see it for herself. *My mom was different then,* I tell her.

"I *know* you want to be a good friend," Mom added.

"Sure," I snapped. "I get it. You don't need to say anything else."

The moment I said it, I regretted it. I wasn't really annoyed with my mother so much as with myself. I *wanted* to be a good friend. I just didn't feel like a very effective one right now. And Morgan's suggestion that she might leave town as soon as she got out of the hospital had put me on edge.

Still, a wounded look came over Mom's face. It's easy to get a look like that from her. And it's hard to so regularly see such a look of defeat on a face that looks so much like yours.

"I mean, what you're saying is helpful. I just don't want to keep talking about it right now."

Mom nodded. We ate in silence until one of us thought up

a safe subject: TV. There was a Netflix series we'd both liked last year, and a new season would start streaming next week. We'd have to binge-watch it some night. Some night when things weren't so busy at Fabuland. Maybe we'd get some of that gourmet dark chocolate ice cream for the occasion.

We talked like that for a few minutes—gently, casually—until the sad look eased from my mother's face.

While we talked, I reached into my pocket and gripped the paperweight once more—to remind myself what I had to do next. By accepting it from Morgan, I felt I'd made her a silent promise. She had questions about the night Ethan died, and I did too. Morgan wasn't in a position to ask them at the moment. I was. And if I wanted to keep her in Danville, I needed to start asking them on her behalf. Even if people didn't like me quite as much as they liked Morgan.

* * *

After dinner, I sat cross-legged on my bed, staring at the scorpion paperweight in my palms, considering who I might start with. The kids who'd ridden the Laser Coaster with Ethan—and seen him last—seemed like the natural place to start. Lucas Andries, Briony Simpson, and Anna Henry. Lucas lived near Braeburn Road, relatively close to Morgan, so he might be most likely to know what the story was with the scorpion. But I knew Briony from chem class. We'd been lab partners for a semester. We weren't exactly friends, but we did chem homework a few times at her house, and I had her number from when we'd texted to meet up. And it felt a little less intimidating to start with her.

I pulled up my chat history on my phone and searched her name. Our last message was from a few months ago, around finals, so I typed out what I hoped was the least awkward text:

Hey, hope your summer's going okay. Kind of random, but wanted to talk to you about something.

Her reply was quick:

What's up?

It felt insensitive to text casually about Ethan, but creepy to keep saying I wanted to "talk about something" until I could set up a way to see her in person.

Are you willing to talk about Ethan?

I guess so

Could we maybe meet?

Like right now?

Yeah

I'm at work but it's dead here so you can come by if you want

Where do you work again?

Stan's Subs on Main

K, see you soon.

Grabbing my sweater and keys, I decided I should get to Briony quickly, before she changed her mind about talking. I dashed through the living room to the front door, promising my mom I'd be back in an hour.

＊ ＊ ＊

Briony was making a customer's sandwich when I got there, stuffing it with peppers and pickles. I waited at one of the sticky white tables until the lady paid and was gone.

"Are you here by yourself?" I asked, approaching the counter.

"No," Briony said. "But the assistant manager doesn't care if I have visitors. As long as I don't bother him while he's in the back doing sudoku on his phone."

"O-okay," I stammered, trying to decide where to begin. "Um, great."

Briony studied me for a moment, a resigned look coming over her big brown eyes.

"You said you wanted to talk about Ethan?" She lowered her voice.

"Yeah," I said quickly. "I mean, I know you were one of the last ones who saw him. How did it all happen that night, that you guys rode the Laser Coaster with him? Was that something you did a lot, or . . ."

"No." Briony grabbed a sponge and started wiping down the counter where she'd just made the sandwich. "We just all happened to be hanging out together in the Food Zone, eating some chicken fingers. I'd gone to Fabuland for the day with my brother, but he had kind of ditched me, so I was hanging out and eating with Anna and Lucas, since they'd both just gotten off their shifts. And Ethan came up to us and asked if we'd ride the Laser Coaster with him. I guess he knew Lucas pretty well from school. We were just like, *sure, if you want*. It was kind of random. But it was like, why not, my day pass meant I could ride all

76

the rides, you know? He seemed really excited about it. He said he'd never ridden it before."

It felt to me like Briony had explained all this *many* times in the past couple of weeks. It came out in a practiced sort of rush.

"And he had fun on the ride? Or did it, like, make him sick at all?"

Briony threw down her sponge and sighed.

"Yeah, the police asked that a lot. Because if he got really sick and dizzy or whatever, that would kind of explain him maybe losing his footing on the trestle. But you know . . . he didn't seem sick at all. He liked it a *lot*. He wanted to ride it again. But . . . no one else wanted to."

I hesitated before asking, "Why not?"

Briony put both her hands out and shrugged. "Personally, I was about ready to throw up and didn't want to risk feeling worse. Anna and Lucas . . . well, I think they kind of had other plans."

"Uh-huh," I said. I didn't know Anna and Lucas well, but I caught Briony's drift that they were hooking up or something. "Got it. And this was right at closing?"

"Yep. Technically, *after* closing actually. Reggie let us go on the ride because Ethan was, like, begging. But after we got off, it was past closing, so we knew Reggie needed to shut it all down. I mean, Reggie was already running the ride for an extra few minutes to let us go on *once*. It didn't seem right to ask for *another* ride after that. Everybody was already leaving and he was probably ready to head out too. Maybe Ethan didn't understand that, I don't know. But we left it that we'd just do it once that night and promised Ethan we'd do it again another day. He was all like, 'I can't do it another day.'"

A dark expression came over Briony's face. "I guess he was right," she murmured.

"That's a strange way of putting things," I said. It gave me a bad feeling. Even worse than when Morgan showed me the scorpion paperweight.

Briony shook her head. "I can't tell you how many times I've thought that myself. And why I didn't just go ahead and ask Reggie to do it again. I mean, if we'd done it one more time, his whole night would've been different and he might not have fallen. Maybe someone would've been walking with him or seen him walking . . . maybe someone would've even given him a ride. Who knows? I just wish I'd said yes, you know?"

I nodded. "Yeah . . . Did anyone walk him out of the park?"

"He said he had to get his stuff, wherever you guys keep the personal stuff in the employee area and call his mom for a ride, so he was going in the opposite direction from us. We said bye and the three of us left the park. Anna and Lucas were heading to Lucas's house. My sense was they were expecting his house to be empty when they got there."

"Ohhh," I said. "So you all said goodbye to Ethan where?"

"Right by the Laser Coaster. I don't know if you heard . . . I gave him my sweatshirt."

"No. When . . . ?"

Briony closed her eyes for a moment. "He was wearing it when he died."

"Oh God. But why . . . ?"

"After we rode the ride, he kept saying he felt really cold." Briony's voice was quavering. She paused and rubbed the outside corners of her eyes. "And I had my big Patriots sweatshirt with me—it used to be my brother's—so I gave it to him and he put it on. He seemed happy with it."

"Was it like a cool night? A rainy night?" I asked. Since I'd been in North Carolina, I didn't know the exact weather that night. But I'd think someone would've mentioned if it was raining, because then the trestle would've been slippery.

"No." Briony shrugged. "It was pretty warm. A nice night, from what I remember. Anyway, I told him he could keep it, because I thought that would distract him a little, like a consolation prize for not riding the coaster again."

"That was nice of you," I said softly.

"Umm . . . I guess." She wiped at the corner of her eye again, this time pushing away a tear. "It doesn't feel nice now."

"I'm so sorry. I didn't mean to make you feel bad, asking this stuff. I was just a little confused about things, having been gone when it all happened. And uh . . . with everything Morgan's been through, I haven't been able to get the whole story from her."

"How *is* Morgan?" Briony asked.

"She's okay," I said noncommittally. "Hey . . . umm, that night . . . and I know this is weird, but do you happen to know if Ethan was carrying around a paperweight with a scorpion in it?"

"Yeah," Briony replied. "Yeah, he was. He showed it to us in the Food Zone that night. Before we all walked over and rode the ride. It was blue, I think."

So Ethan had had it when he rode the ride. Which meant he didn't drop it on his way to Fabuland that morning. He'd had it with him on the trestle that night. And for some reason, he'd made it *past* the trestle. And then turned back *and* fallen off?

"So he had the scorpion thing with him," I clarified, just to be sure. "That night."

Briony nodded, her mouth twisting quizzically—presumably at why, of all things, I'd be asking about this.

"Yeah," she said slowly, drawing out the word.

We were both silent for a moment.

"Thanks for answering my questions," I said. "I'm not as confused now."

Briony nodded again.

"Ivy," she said.

"Yeah?"

"That time you came over and we ended up watching old *Mystery Science Theater 3000* clips on YouTube. That was fun. We should do it again sometime."

I'd forgotten about that. It seemed like a thousand years ago. I couldn't remember how we'd ended up watching videos instead of doing homework, but I remembered stretching out on her basement floor, laughing uncontrollably. It was one of those rare moments when it felt possible to make a new friend despite all my long hours studying and working afternoons at the doughnut shop. Not likely. But possible.

"I'd love to. But this week I'm kind of tied up with Fabuland. Tomorrow there's this princess event I'm in charge of. . . ."

"Oh yeah." Briony grinned. "I heard about that from Drea.

Well, when things are less busy, maybe we could hang out. Maybe with Morgan too, if she likes that kind of thing? And I bet Troy Haines would want in. He loves weird old movies."

"Oh yeah, that'd be cool," I said, and flashed a smile. I meant it. I just didn't think it would happen. At least not until the fall. For now, the summer felt like it would last forever. "Thanks for talking."

It had turned to dusk by the time I got into my car. I tried to focus on the road, but once I turned from the main highway through town onto the rural road that leads to my mom's condo complex, my mind drifted to Ethan. The darkness of the road and the density of the trees reminded me of the path to the trestle. I thought of him wandering it alone in the dark before he fell. What was in his head that night?

I can't do it another day. Why did he say that? Was he about to switch jobs? Was his family about to go away somewhere? Was it somehow related to whatever conflict had kept Winnie away from her job that night? Something happening with the Malloy family that was being kept secret? And why had Ethan been feeling cold on a warm summer night? Was he coming down with something?

I drove a little faster, eager to get back into the light and the familiarity of my mom's place.

And then there was the sparkly blue scorpion paperweight.

Everything Briony had told me suggested that the paperweight had *probably* been Ethan's, and that he had had it in his possession on the day he died. But I wanted to clarify with Emma tomorrow whether it really was such a rare item. Maybe the park had been awash in sparkly blue scorpion paperweights, and the one Morgan found near the trestle was one of many—not necessarily Ethan's.

But if it really *was* rare, it seemed like there were two possibilities to account for the paperweight's appearing on Morgan's path that morning. One possibility was that Ethan had been disoriented, maybe even dizzy, from riding the Laser Coaster and had been wandering around near the trestle and fallen off. Still, the path forked toward Morgan's house quite a bit away from the trestle, so Ethan would really have had to walk far without realizing it.

Another possibility was that he wasn't headed home after work. Maybe he was headed toward his cousins' house but then changed his mind. Or maybe he wasn't alone. Maybe someone knew something more about Ethan's last night.

As I pulled into the parking spot next to my mom's, my mind inched toward the inevitable. The thing Morgan had implied but was hesitant to say out loud.

Maybe someone was lying.

SEVEN

The next morning was the Princess Day Parade, and I kept my eye out for Emma Radlinger while the rest of us were prepping in the big break room behind the arcade. After I spotted her— already dolled up in her Anna garb—I approached Emma and asked for help zipping up my shiny Elsa dress. She nodded and I turned around, scooping my hair to the side so she could get to the zipper. The dress was a little big, so the zipper went up easily. I hoped she didn't notice.

"Thanks," I said, facing her. I straightened her Anna brooch for good measure. "By the way, I wanted to ask you something. About that scorpion paperweight that Ethan won a couple of days before he died?"

"Oh. Yeah?" Emma twisted one of her Anna braids around her thumb. "What about it?"

"Were there lots of scorpion paperweights at other booths?" I pulled on my white Elsa gloves and straightened my blond-white Elsa wig. "Was there really only *one* blue one?"

Emma nodded, looking mournful at the memory. "Ethan said he checked all the booths. There were a bunch of red ones at the balloon booth, and mostly purple and dark green ones at the Wheel of Prizes station. He'd scoped them out. I don't think much thought had gone into which colors were where. There are so many different junky prizes, you know? People only notice the exact mix if there's something they really want."

"Huh," I said, making a mental note to ask Chris about the shipment of prizes. It was almost certainly him who'd ordered them. Chris handled all the administrative minutiae that my dad didn't have the patience for. He might know the total number of light-blue paperweights that came in the early-summer shipment of prizes. Or have a slip that might give the exact numbers.

While Emma and I talked, I'd kept my voice low and an eye on Winnie Malloy. She was on the other side of the room, out of earshot. She was applying lipstick and tidying her hair, glancing at herself occasionally in a tiny mirror she'd produced from her purse. Her hair was twisted up in a chignon that I had to admit was more Cinderella than Morgan had ever looked. I wondered if she'd done it herself. If she had, she was pretty talented with hair.

"Why are you asking?" Emma nudged my elbow to bring my attention back to her.

"Oh . . . Morgan was telling me your story about it yesterday. So I was just curious."

Emma puckered her lips. "You've talked to Morgan? Like, since the thing happened on the Ferris wheel?"

I nodded.

"How's she *doing*?" Emma's eyes widened with exaggerated concern.

"Okay," I said noncommittally, then changed my mind. "Better."

"Was there a guy involved in that whole incident somehow?"

"What makes you say that?" I asked.

"Last week she mentioned she was having trouble with some guy."

"What guy?" I said, startled at this piece of news.

Emma shrugged. "She didn't say. We were working, so it was more of an offhand comment."

"Before or after . . . Ethan?" I said, glancing at Winnie. Now she had her phone pressed to her ear. Her lips were moving, but I couldn't hear what she was saying as she quickly slipped out of the room.

"That's funny. I don't remember. I think it was before. . . . No, wait, actually after. I was telling her a story and it seemed like she wasn't listening. Then she was just like, 'I'm so sorry. I'm distracted. Guy trouble.'"

"Huh," I said. I wondered if this had been a ruse to brush off Emma or something real—another thing Morgan had been keeping from me. You'd think any relatively intelligent guy who was into her would give her a break right after she'd gone through everything with finding Ethan. But maybe whatever guy she had been talking about didn't fall into the "relatively intelligent" category.

"Is she back with Savoy?" Emma asked.

"I don't think so," I said, shaking my head.

Savoy was Morgan's boyfriend until about six months ago. He'd gone to college last fall. They tried to make it work long distance but broke up over Thanksgiving break. Last I'd heard he was spending the summer working at a resort in upstate New York. He hadn't come back to Danville, and Morgan never talked about him anymore. At least not to me.

"Maybe Tim Malloy," Emma mused. "I saw him flirting with her a couple of weeks ago while he was buying pizza."

"He's kinda old," I said.

"Yeah. But I hear he's not so great with numbers. Maybe he hasn't done the math to figure out that he's four years older."

"Umm," I said, lowering my voice as Winnie came back into the room. I grimaced at Emma, trying to convey that we should maybe be quiet about Winnie's brother when she was nearby. "I doubt he'd be prowling for girls right after his cousin died."

Emma waved a hand at this thought, as if to dismiss it.

"So what was *up* with Morgan on the Ferris wheel?" she asked. "I mean, was that just a cry for attention, or what?"

I practiced my fake princess smile to mask my being offended at Emma's unsympathetic phrasing.

"You know what happened, right?" I said. "She was drunk when she did it, and she passed out up there."

"*Really?*"

I nodded gravely. "Yeah."

"Oh my God. Then it's *so* lucky she didn't fall," Emma said, her eyes widening.

"I *know*," I replied, and meant it.

I scanned the room to make sure all the princesses were accounted for. As I did, I saw Winnie pulling a small bottle out of her purse. She began to dab something from the bottle onto her chest, right above the fairly low neckline of her blue princess dress. It took me a moment to realize what she was trying to do. She was applying cover-up to her tattoo. Kind of sweet, in a way, that she was taking the role so seriously. And just as I had that thought, Winnie's gaze met mine, catching me looking.

"Ivy!" a voice boomed from the doorway.

Someone gasped, and as I whirled around, I saw Dani cover her front with her Sleeping Beauty dress, hiding her matching lilac bra and underwear.

"Ivy!" Dad yelled again as he stepped into the room. "There you are. I need you, hon. I need Carl Norton's number."

I marched to the doorway, pulling Dad with me until we were both outside, in the sunshine.

"Jesus, Dad. The girls were *changing* in there."

"I didn't see anything, I promise."

I tried to breathe out my mortification, since I didn't have time for it this morning. "That's kind of not the point."

"Do you have Carl Norton's number? He was supposed to be here with the truck and float by now."

"I thought you had that all set up."

"I *did* have it set up, little miss. But he's not *here*. That's why I need to call him and see what the delay is."

"Where's your phone? Don't you have his number?"

"It's either in my office or my car. I don't have it on me."

"Oh. Great, Dad." My dad likes to "lose" his phone. *If someone really needs me, they'll find a way to get to me,* he's said before. I don't know how he can say this stuff to me and then act all bumbling and innocent when *I* need him to be reachable. Unfortunately, I didn't have Carl's number.

"Okay. You look in your car and I'll look in your office. Okay?"

"Sure, Ivy," Dad replied.

I tried to sprint across the Food Zone to the admin building, but sprinting was nearly impossible in my Elsa dress. I pulled it up to run up the stairs to my dad's office. It's a big room that used to be a hall of mirrors about twenty years ago, before Mr. Moyer bought Fabuland and took the older, cheesier stuff out and made it his big personal office space.

I nearly slammed into Chris at the top of the stairs.

"Is everything okay?" he asked.

I tried to catch my breath. "He wants me to look in his office for his phone."

I realized a second later that I didn't say *my dad*. But Chris didn't look confused at all. There was only one *he* I could possibly be talking about.

"Anything I can help with?" he said.

"He's going to the south lot to look for his phone in his car, if you want to talk to him. He's trying to get in touch with Carl Norton. You have Carl's number, by chance?"

"No . . . but . . ." Chris grimaced. "I'll go to the south lot and try to find your dad, see what I can do. Everything set for the parade?"

"Everything but Carl Norton, I think. . . ."

I pushed open my dad's office door. "But maybe ask him if he needs anything else. Everything's okay on my end. I've got the princesses ready to go. Although I'm not sure if the horse guy is in the north lot yet with the three horses. I don't know if my dad has checked up on that."

"Uhh . . . okay." Chris started down the stairs.

"Oh! Chris!" I called. "I forgot. There *is* one thing."

He turned and looked up at me, his pale eyes weary, his buzz cut a bit flat on one side as if he'd slept on it and forgotten to fix it. He was probably as tired of this princess stuff as I was. There was definitely a possibility that all the stuff Dad had told me he'd "done"—the horses, the float, updating the shared spreadsheet— he'd accomplished by telling Chris to do it.

"How many light-blue sparkle scorpion paperweights were there total, in all the game booths?" I asked.

Chris screwed his face up. "*Excuse* me?"

I sounded crazy, probably. Still, I quickly explained about the paperweights. Not the part about Morgan finding the one that was likely Ethan's, but everything else. About how Ethan had coveted what he thought was the one blue one.

Chris's face pinched up tight with either confusion or curiosity—I couldn't tell which. "I don't know how many there were of each color. I bought them as part of a big bulk order of prizes. The prizes came in a random mix and I selected the scorpions as part of it, but I didn't specify colors. I don't think that was an option."

"Okay," I said. "Just wondering."

"There's one more box of those prizes on the bottom shelf of the second supply closet, if you want to look in there. There's probably a handful of the paperweights . . . for what it's worth."

"Okay, thanks." I wished I had time to go rummaging through the supply closet now. But I didn't. Nor did I think that would supply me with a definitive answer. Even if that box had twenty blue sparkle scorpions, it didn't mean the boxes opened earlier in the summer did as well.

Chris nodded vaguely and continued down the stairs.

I heard the door close. Up in Dad's office, I avoided looking at the three leftover fun house mirrors displayed near his desk. One made you look like you had stilt legs, and one gave you a stretched-out head and neck. The one farthest from his desk made you look really short. Whenever I saw the squished, stubby version of myself in it, I thought of my dad saying, *I've always known that about you. That you wanted to stay small.* I think he said that to me the first time I came to the office to look at the mirrors and say hi to Mr. Moyer when I was a kid. I don't remember exactly why he said it, but it must have been an attempt to make me laugh. About fifty percent of Dad's jokes are flops, but I guess it's nice that he's always trying.

I scanned the big oak desk, then riffled through the papers on it. His phone wasn't there. I opened a drawer. Then I realized I ought to call the phone so I would hear it ring.

I pulled my phone from the little silky Elsa purse knotted

around my wrist and called his cell but didn't hear anything. I wouldn't put it past my dad to turn his phone off, though, since he got such a kick out of being unreachable. I opened another drawer. It was full of little snack packets, chips and Cheez-Its and licorice bites. I rummaged through them, but only for a second, because, of course, on second thought, he wouldn't have put his phone with that stuff. I shuffled through the papers on his desk again. I called his phone a second time.

This time it didn't go straight to voice mail.

"Hey, Ivy," Dad said when he picked up. "Got the phone. I just figured out that I'd left it in the john in the Food Zone. In fact, right as I was about to call Chris, Carl comes tooling into the south lot. The float looks fantastic, superb. He's really outdone himself. You should see it. Looks like a wedding cake. And the sprinkles. *So* many sprinkles. Fabulous."

Dad has always been way into sprinkles.

"Awesome," I said, and mumbled goodbye. After hanging up, I started to straighten the desk papers when something caught my eye. It was a big three-sided plastic picture frame. When I was a kid, there was a picture of me on one side, Jason on another, and my mom on the third. Now it was just Jason and me, with a picture of a pretty stack of Cork's doughnuts on the third. It was dusty. I picked it up to get a closer look at the picture of Jason—he was wearing his cute blue glasses in first grade, way before he got contacts. As I picked up the frame, there was a *thunk*. A small, heavy black-and-gray object had fallen out of the triangular space inside the frame. It looked like a phone—but an old-fashioned phone, not a smartphone. It had a small screen, with the word REC on it. There was a power button, which I pressed. REC disappeared.

I felt my breath catch for a moment. It was a recording device, and someone had tucked it away inside the three-sided frame. Why would my dad have set a recorder up in his office? That didn't seem right. I had a sinking feeling it wasn't *him* who'd set it up. I thought about the surprised expression on Chris's face when we'd run into each other by the stairs. Why would he want to eavesdrop on my dad, though? Either way, I was taking the recorder with me. My Elsa dress didn't have pockets and my little purse couldn't hold two devices without bulging and looking ridiculous, so I shoved the recorder into my bra. I'd figure it out later. For now, I had princesses to line up.

*   *   *

Carl was doing a surprisingly good job with the mic at the parade, announcing each princess as she marched, floated, or rode into the Food Zone.

"Everyone let's welcome . . . BELLE. . . ."

"Put your hands together for . . . ANNA and ELSA."

"And coming in on her noble steed . . . Cinderrrrrr . . . ELLA!"

I snorted and turned to watch Winnie's reaction to this grand introduction.

She smiled and waved. She had the pouch of princess jewelry I'd given her to toss to kids. I saw her take out one of the bigger pieces I'd put in it, a set of purple and blue beads with a giant clear plastic heart pendant—the kind that costs a whole dollar at Dollar Tree, not the cheaper ones that are six for a dollar. She placed it in her palm and looked over the crowd for a second. Then I saw her expression change. I wondered for a moment if she had spotted a sad or sickly-looking little girl whom she planned to toss the necklace to. *Wow,* I thought. Winnie was really taking this shit seriously. And then I saw her arm wind up like a baseball pitcher's. And I watched that huge plastic heart pendant fly out of her hand as the smile left her face. A man cried out in pain. Still waving at the crowd, I looked to my left, and there was Chris holding one hand to his temple. My dad was standing by him, holding one hand to his own back as if it had suddenly started hurting, the other hand on Chris's shoulder.

I couldn't hear him with all the noise, but the words forming on my father's lips looked like *Are you okay?*

I looked back at Winnie and thought I saw shock on her face. She seemed to be trying to recover her smile as she reached into her sparkly handbag again. She tossed a small beaded bracelet to a curly-haired little girl who was jumping up and down.

It took me a moment to take my eyes off Winnie. Something about her expression unsettled me. This was a person trying so hard to smile that it looked like it hurt. A person trying really hard to cover something. I could tell that much. I could even relate. Because I hated playing an ice princess.

But what was Winnie's *something?* Grief about Ethan? Or something more on top of that?

EIGHT

Dad decided we should treat ourselves to dinner out after the success of the parade. While I was hoping for Chinese food because I was craving egg rolls, he drove us right to Danville Pie. I decided not to tell him that I was sick of the summer food trinity of hot dogs, hamburgers, and pizza. I ordered a salad.

"Ivy, it was a great event," he said, after he'd finished most of his medium pepperoni. "We did a fantastic job. In general. I've said it before and I'll say it again, you know how to get shit *done*. We've got that in common."

"Thanks, Dad." That was something Dad used to say more about Jason than me. But I guess that now Jason was gone, he needed to say it to *someone*.

"I think the real highlight was the rainbow flower float. I sure heard a lot of oohs and aahs when that went by. I'm glad I thought of that."

"Yeah, that was pretty impressive," I said, spearing my last cherry tomato.

Dad had asked Carl's wife to fashion a little rainbow arch out of different-colored flowers—kind of Rose Bowl–inspired. Amy Townsend sat under it as Belle, waving. I'd barely gotten a glimpse of it with everything else that had been going on. The arch had been smaller than I expected—Amy had had to scrunch down to fit under it—but pretty.

"You might not have noticed since you were in the parade, but that was what really wowed the parents while all the kids were staring at you princesses." Dad took a gulp from his beer bottle. "But what were you thinking, making the Malloy girl Cinderella?"

"I don't think she meant to hurt Chris." I said it quietly, because I knew I might be lying. There'd been something vicious in Winnie's throw. And I still couldn't forget the look on her face.

"Oh, don't worry about poor Chris. That's not what I'm talking about."

I looked down at the limp remains of my salad. Chris was in his early thirties, and my dad sometimes called him his right-hand man. He'd worked for my dad for several years, starting in the Doughnut Dynasty days, and probably was his highest-paid employee. So it wasn't clear to me why my dad always called him "poor Chris."

"Then what are you talking about?" I asked.

"You *know* about that girl, right?"

I assumed he was referring to the unusual number of guys Winnie had "dated" over the years. I glanced at the booths around us, hoping he'd remember not to bad-mouth one of his employees loudly in public.

"I know you trust her with the carousel and the Rotor," I reminded him. "So why not with Cinderella duty?"

"They used to have a word for girls like her. I'm not gonna say it, but people still think it."

"Not four-year-old girls who want to see a pretty princess. Winnie actually fits the part well, don't you think?"

Maybe I was looking for a compliment on my casting skills. Somehow, after all the work of putting together the parade, I was perhaps looking for more thanks than *Fantastic job. In general.*

Dad stared at me, pulling his lips into a pout. "Their parents think it."

"So what? So she can't be Cinderella?"

"Ivy," he said firmly. "I mean, really. With that boob tattoo all crusty with pancake makeup?"

"Really, that bothers you? A tattoo?"

"Actually, it makes people uncomfortable, seeing that on such a young woman."

"Seeing a tattoo?" This seemed weird, coming from my dad. Danville has its share of tattoos. There's not much to do around here, and getting a tattoo is one fairly harmless way to spice up your life. "It's just a little flower, right? It's not like it says *Born to kill* or whatever."

Dad sipped his beer, then folded his arms. "It says *Zach* under the flower, actually."

"Ohhh." I didn't know what to say to that. *Zach Crenshaw.* Who had maybe been flirting with Morgan when they were working at the Pizza to the Rescue booth. "Huh. Why . . . ?"

"I think they used to date a couple of summers ago." Dad shrugged. "That's what I heard, anyway. It can be hard to keep up with all the Fabuland romances."

I nibbled a piece of baby spinach, trying to hide my surprise. If Winnie was enamored enough with Zach to tattoo his name on her body, and if Morgan and Zach had been recently flirting, this could shed a whole different light on the "Morgan crying with Winnie" incident. Maybe Winnie had been jealous and said something that upset Morgan? It seemed weird in the immediate aftermath of Ethan's death, but it was certainly possible.

"If you have that many boyfriends, it's kinda not smart to put the name of one of them on your boob," Dad continued, apparently oblivious to my preoccupation. "I mean, what are the chances the romance is gonna last?"

That seemed like reasonable advice, but I wished my dad would stop saying *boob*.

"Just don't put her in the parade lineup again, okay?" Dad said.

"Okay," I murmured, resigning myself to the fact that Dad had decided to focus on the one thing about the event that had bothered him. Sometimes he did that, sometimes he didn't. You never knew which way it was going to go.

"Probably by next time Morgan will be back anyway, so it won't be a problem," he added, as if that would cheer me up.

"Maybe," I said. I was beginning to wonder if we'd ever get

the old Morgan back. Or—given her plans to leave—if we'd get *any* version of her back. It was a depressing thought.

"Let's hope for the best, honey."

"Umm . . . Dad?"

Now that the parade was over, I could focus on my silent promise to Morgan. To fill in some of the holes about the night of Ethan's death. Or at least get an explanation about the sparkly scorpion.

"Why was it you, not Chris, closing the Thursday night that Ethan died?" I asked, thinking back to the schedules I had checked and how Dad usually only closed Mondays and the occasional Saturday.

"Chris has been a little tied up lately. He and his wife are having kind of an . . . issue, is the bottom line. So I've been giving him some flexibility. The day before, he came and asked me to switch his night off. I said okay."

Usually my dad spoke of Chris's wife Trisha in an unflattering way, so I was surprised at how neutral he sounded. Usually he complained about Trisha's "sour expression" and wondered aloud why the two of them didn't have any kids yet. I'd never met Trisha, so I didn't have an opinion about her.

"So, I wonder who really *was* the last to see Ethan. Like, did you see him leave that night?" I asked.

"I was in my office most of the night." Dad's expression was sheepish. "Left most of the actual locking-up duties to Reggie, I'm ashamed to admit. I was on my computer, shopping for our next big marquee ride for next summer. Bigger-picture plans, you know?"

Yes. I knew. I knew he wanted me to ask about those plans, but I plowed forward with my questions instead.

"It just seems so *weird* that Ethan would say he was going to call his mom and not do it," I said. "But then leave in such a hurry that he didn't bring his backpack. It just feels like there's something someone's leaving out. Right?"

Dad stared at his beer for a moment, considering the question. He lifted the bottle, almost took a drink out of it, but then put it down and started talking instead.

"Well . . . something not everybody knows, Ivy, and that Chris and I explained to the police, is that Ethan had a lot of trouble opening his locker. He struggled with the combination sometimes. At one point, just about a week before he died, Chris had given him a new locker, because we thought his locker maybe kept getting stuck. But it turns out opening those locks was hard for him. I think instead of asking for help that night, he just decided to leave it be and go home, poor kid."

"Huh," I said. "That's sad to think about."

I thought about Ethan, usually so smiley, maybe a little embarrassed and distracted by failing at opening his locker on his own, and regretting the temporary loss of his backpack. Not really reason to be distracted enough to fall off a trestle, I didn't think. But it made the picture of his last night just that much grimmer.

"It is," Dad said, and shook his head solemnly.

"Did you hear anything about Ethan maybe planning to quit his job soon, or his family being about to move away, or anything like that?"

"No." Dad looked surprised. "Was someone saying that?"

"I thought I heard something like that," I said.

"Huh." Dad contemplated his beer bottle, peeling off part of the label.

I didn't want to talk directly about what Briony had told me. About Ethan saying he couldn't ride the Laser Coaster *on another day*. It gave me a very creepy feeling, and I didn't want to get into that now.

"Umm, do you know why Winnie backed out on her shift that night?" I asked. "Why she couldn't work the night Ethan died?"

Dad shrugged. "Nah. I didn't ask. She's been switching shifts occasionally this summer, but since she always finds a replacement, it's not a big deal. I don't mind people trading shifts if they can cover their own butts. Chris doesn't either."

"Right," I said softly.

Our waitress came and dropped off the check.

"Don't run away, honey," he said to her, digging for his wallet in his back pocket. "I'll pay right now."

The very tan waitress, who was in her twenties and wearing little purple denim shorts, waited patiently as he fished for the right credit card. He tossed it over and it landed right on the plastic check tray.

"Good throw," she said as she walked away.

Dad watched her go.

"I *love* summer," he murmured.

Hoping he wouldn't elaborate, I chose that moment to rummage in my backpack and take out the recorder I'd found in his office.

"Hey. Is this yours?" I asked.

He squinted at it. "What is it?"

"Just a gadget I found . . . umm, when the girls were changing and I . . ." I trailed off, realizing I should be vague, for now, about where exactly I had found it.

"You should ask all the princesses, then. Probably one of theirs."

I nodded, believing he was telling the truth. He didn't seem aware that it had been in his office. "Will do."

If I had told him where I really found it, Dad would probably flip out on someone. Better to poke around on my own first. I didn't want to get Chris in trouble. At least not until I could figure out a little bit more. I needed to hear what was on the recorder and go from there.

"So," Dad said, taking a resolute sip of beer and meeting my gaze. "Kittycat."

"Yeah?" I could tell from his smile that he was about to spring some new Fabuland business on me.

"You did such a good job with this princess stuff. I think you're ready for something bigger. I'm thinking you're really gonna love helping Chris and me with our giant Doughnut Day project too."

"Oh." I smiled like I had at the princess parade—sweetly, but with great effort. "Is that really happening this year?"

"Why wouldn't it?"

I cast around for something that might encourage Dad to reconsider his plan without offending him.

"I kind of thought that was your and Jason's thing," I said, after a moment.

"I can't wait for Jason on this. He might never be coming back."

I'm not sure whether it was the expression on my face that made Dad correct himself. "For a whole summer, I mean."

"And you definitely want to do this big doughnut thing in the summer?"

"Of course, honey. It would be a Fabuland event, primarily. Not as much a Dynasty event. A summer attraction."

I sucked in a breath. Jason and my dad had talked about this for years. The biggest doughnut ever made was a 1.7-ton jelly doughnut made in Utica, New York, in 1993. This was a well-known fact in the Cork household. When we were kids, Dad and Jason would make plans for how they'd top that record someday. Dad would insist their doughnut would be vanilla-cream-filled, with tons of rainbow sprinkles. Jason would talk about the logistics, like what kind of giant vat or swimming pool you'd need for all that oil. What kind of aerial machines or construction equipment you'd use to lift the doughnut, flip it, fill it. They were both kind of inspired, I think, by a book Mom got Jason and me when we were little. It's called *The Giant Jam Sandwich,* and it's about a town plagued by wasps. Everyone pitches in to bake a giant loaf of bread and then trap all the wasps on a slice of it spread with raspberry jam.

When Jason and I were kids, it was clear that it was just a before-bed fantasy, that we'd somehow outdo the Utica doughnut. But since Dad bought Fabuland, he talked about it like it's a real thing. He knows he probably can't top 1.7 tons, and he probably doesn't want to bother. But when he and Jason would discuss it last summer, he would say, "There's something alluring to people about a giant sweet. It brings out a childlike fascination. A Hansel-and-Gretel kinda deal."

So they'd talk about billing it as "the biggest doughnut ever to roll into New Hampshire" or the "world's biggest-ever *sprinkle* doughnut." Dad wanted to unveil the giant doughnut in the middle of the park, where the Food Zone tables are, and give people little sandwich bags of sprinkles and let them throw the sprinkles down from the top of the Laser Coaster or some of the other nearby rides.

"People like to be a part of this kind of thing," he'd say. He felt that the communal spirit of *The Giant Jam Sandwich* bore him out on this.

"When were you thinking this would happen?" I asked, still trying to wrap my head around what this project was going to take.

"Couple of weeks," he said. "Mid- to late July."

"Huh," I said. That sounded both soon and vague enough to be unrealistic. Probably I was supposed to be like Jason and just take up the mantle of talking about it indefinitely. "Well, I'd be honored to help plan it."

"Chris had a brilliant idea. We do about a dozen dough balls, each five feet wide, fry them, and then use frosting to mush them together in a ring that looks like a decorative doughnut, you know? Then we don't have to figure out how to fry one doughnut at once. We can borrow a couple of ten-foot metal vats from the cheese factory up in Landon. I've got a great relationship with those guys. They love me since I use their cheese in the Dynasty danishes, you know?"

"Would that count as a doughnut, though? Dough balls pushed together?"

"It wouldn't be for Guinness World Records. It would just be for the spectacle and the sprinkles."

"Right. Who would spread the frosting?"

"I don't know. I wish I had myself some Oompa Loompas, really."

Dad said this sometimes. I kind of wished he would stop. In fact, sometimes, very occasionally, when he was concentrating intensely on something, he would mutter-hum under his breath, *Oompa loompa, doopity doo,* like in the old Willy Wonka movie. I wondered if that meant he was imagining little orange men working in his head.

"I meant customers or employees?" I said.

"Employees. Customers would only get to do the sprinkles. They can't fuck that up, I don't think."

"Hey, Dad. I'm kind of tired from all the princess stuff. Maybe we can head out now?"

I *was* tired. Not just from the day but from this conversation. And I was eager to be somewhere alone so I could check out what was on the weird little recorder now back in my backpack.

"Sure, Kittycat," Dad said.

NINE

After Dad turned on the TV, I went into my room, closed the door, and switched on the air conditioner to mask the sound of what I was planning to do. It didn't take me long to figure out how to play the recorder. Then I rewound a bit to see what I could find.

It was taking a while, so I stopped in the middle of the rewind, pressed Play, and immediately heard my dad's voice:

"Well, look, Krista, if he wants money from me he should ask me for it himself."

I held my breath for a second, stiffening at the sound of my mother's first name. Then there was a rustling noise.

"Yeah. You know, if he's having trouble paying it, then maybe this wasn't such a good plan. Oh . . . really? Well, those are the breaks. Let that be a lesson, I guess.

"Yeah. I get it, honey. It's been the same thing with Jason for *years* now. He's afraid of hard work."

I winced. They were talking about my brother, of course. But that wasn't the painful part. It was that I knew how much my mom hated it when Dad called her *honey*.

"Yeah. Well, I don't know if I'd call *that* hard work. But you know what, honey, if you're giving him that much, I'll match you. Sure. But you can tell him this is a one-time thing. Once for the summer, and I'm not doing it again in the fall. He's got tuition covered and that ought to be enough. And not next summer either. If he needs more money then, he can come home and work for me. He knows I'll make it worthwhile. He's just needs to embrace the work. That's something he can think about, when he's planning for next summer."

There was silence for a minute. "Uh-huh. Sure, Krista. You know, he's lucky I'm willing to *take* him back. You have no idea how much money he cost me last summer, that kid. Him and his big head.

"But—never mind.

"No . . . never mind.

"Yep. See ya."

Then I heard a sigh and a clunk and a gulp. Then I heard my dad mutter, "Poor little pansy ass." Then he changed his voice and kind of sang the same thing. "Poor lit-tle pansy ass."

I pressed the Stop button, eyeing my bedroom door, wishing I could swing it open and chew my dad out for saying this. But he hadn't said it to Jason's face or to mine. He'd said it while he was by himself. Calling him out—on what was essentially a private thought—would be complicated. And I'd kind of given up trying to get my dad to adjust his vocabulary a couple of years ago.

Dad and Jason used to get along really well. But things hadn't been great between them since Jason left for Syracuse two years ago. And this summer Jason decided not to come back home and work for Dad like he did last year. He got a summer job as an RA and an assistant writing instructor for a high school arts program on campus. Dad had been complaining since May that Jason would make about half the income at that program than at Fabuland. But I could see why Jason wanted to do it. He was majoring in English and music. The campus job was something he could put on his résumé that was more impressive than working rides and frying wads of dough.

Reluctant to hear what else my dad might say when he was thinking out loud, I picked up my phone and texted Jason a simple *Hey* just to see if he'd answer right away. The three dots popped up almost immediately.

Oh hi, what's up?

Princess parade was today. I added a few emojis: shooting star, red dress girl, tired face.

Oh yeah was it okay?

Sure. Dad seemed happy. Did Mom or Dad tell you about Morgan?

Haven't talked to them. What's with Morgan?

Actually, can I call?

Yeah

When Jason answered, I told him about Morgan and the Ferris wheel. He already knew about Ethan because we'd been texting and talking while I was in North Carolina, but I hadn't had time to give him an update in the last few days.

After I was all done, he was silent for a moment. "That's . . . quite a story, Ivy. Whose idea was it for *you* to go up and get her?"

"Dad's," I admitted, even though I wished it had been mine. It would make me feel braver.

I heard Jason snorting.

"Of course it was," he said. "You okay?"

"It's been a few days. I'm fine. It's Morgan I'm still worried about."

I told him about the scorpion paperweight. I felt Morgan had given it to me in confidence, but I didn't think she would mind me telling Jason.

"Huh," my brother said, after thinking it over. "You'll definitely want to talk to Reggie."

Reggie Wiggins, the Laser Coaster operator the night Ethan died. He was on my list, especially since Dad said he had done the locking up at the park. Now that I thought about it, I hadn't seen Reggie since I'd come back home.

"Maybe he saw something," Jason continued. "And Lucas Andries—although I'd be careful how you ask *that* guy questions. I mean, I don't think anyone would want to push Ethan off a bridge or anything. But Lucas is the sort of guy who maybe would be dishonest about what exactly happened. Like, I wouldn't put it past him to refuse someone like Ethan a ride, and then lie about it later because he knows it makes him look like an asshole."

"That wouldn't explain the paperweight on the path, though."

"I know that. I just mean that *kind* of thing could be happening. But you know . . . if you want to talk about Ethan . . . just generally what could have been in his head that night . . . Katy's a good one to go to."

"Oh. *Katy*." Katy was Jason's best friend from high school. She volunteered for an after-school sports program for special needs kids. She had known Ethan pretty well. In fact, she lived in the same neighborhood as his cousins, Winnie and Tim.

"She wasn't around last summer," I pointed out. "Is she in Danville now?"

"She went home this summer, yeah. I think someone said she'd be working at the library." Jason was trying to sound casual, like he wasn't sure, but I knew he always kept tabs on Katy. He was kind of in love with her. Even though technically he had a girlfriend in Connecticut. Still, he'd probably drop her in a second if he thought Katy would give him a chance.

"I called her right after I heard about Ethan," Jason admitted after a moment. "To see how she was holding up."

"And how was she?"

"Not so good, but that was the day after. I've been meaning to check in again."

I stared down at the digital recorder on my bed. I wasn't sure if I should tell Jason about it. I wanted to figure out whose it was first. Plus it would feel like lying, to tell him about the recorder without telling him about *pansy ass*.

"When are you gonna come home and visit?" I asked instead.

"I've got a week off between the July session and the August one. So, the last week in July, maybe. How's Mom?"

"Uh . . . okay, I guess. Tired."

"Right," Jason said. Mom was usually tired.

"Jason? Can I ask you something?"

"Yeah?"

"Why didn't you come home this summer?"

"I got a better job. You know that."

"But . . ."

Something Dad had said on the recording was stuck in my brain, that Jason had cost him a lot of money last summer. I wasn't sure if it was typical Dad ranting or something specific worth knowing about.

"Listen, Ivy. You know how much Dad and I fought last summer. You saw it yourself. I'm kind of over Fabuland. I think you get that."

Yeah. I got it. It wasn't easy work. But we were supposed to be building something together. Dad's parents had opened the first Cork's doughnut shop, and Dad had grown it into a bigger chain. Even if Dad sometimes had an offbeat way of talking about it, or even of going about it—it was all about taking what our grandparents had built and making something even bigger.

"I get it, but it's not really—"

"Hey, can we talk about this a little later? I didn't have dinner and somebody's waiting for me."

"Okay. Text you later, then, bye." I tossed my phone down on my bed.

Fair. That was the word I'd been about to say before Jason interrupted.

I knew I shouldn't throw around the word *fair.* If life was fair, Ethan wouldn't have died. And Morgan would have enough money to go to college. And Mom wouldn't be exhausted by

110

life all the time. And I'd have more friends. I knew I should forget about *fair*. But still, it felt like Jason was cheating somehow, getting to hide at his fancy college while scoffing at all Dad's endeavors that had helped get him there.

I picked up the recorder. I was pretty sure my dad wasn't being cagey when he said the recorder wasn't his. Most likely it was Chris's then, since he was the other person most often in Dad's office. But why would Chris be bugging it?

Chris had worked for my dad for as long as I could remember. Dad said Chris was a teenager when he started working at the original Doughnut Dynasty on Main Street—before I was born, and when my grandfather was still alive and running things. Chris was assistant manager at the first branch shop in Goffsbridge and moved on up from there. After my parents divorced and my mom stopped working for my dad, he gave Chris her old job, putting him in charge of all the sprinkle party managers. It was sort of an important job because it's those parties that made Doughnut Dynasty so popular.

I was in one of the commercials when I was a little kid. I wore fairy wings and a tiara and I said, *Mommeee! Let's have a sprinkle partyyy!*

My mom insisted that I stop being in the commercials after I started kindergarten. I'd been devastated at the time, but now I understand that that was a pretty prescient move on her part. That role would've been difficult to live down.

Given all their history, why would Chris want to secretly record my dad? If in fact that had been his intention. All that *right-hand man* stuff aside, I didn't know how well Dad really knew Chris. He often said Chris was loyal, but that might just be because Chris was quiet and had a military-style haircut. How things *appeared* to Dad was sometimes how they *were*.

If I wanted to know whether this was Chris's recorder, I needed to figure out a way to ask him indirectly. In the meantime, I needed to listen to everything that had been recorded. I pressed Rewind until the recorder clicked. Then I hit Play and waited.

There was a thump and then a rustling and then the faint sound of creaking floorboards. Then a door. And then silence. Whoever had started the recorder didn't have distinctive footsteps and didn't stay long.

The silence went on so long that I got out my iPad and flicked through my Instagram feed, waiting out the recording. Dani Erwin had put up a cute picture of herself as Sleeping Beauty riding one of the horses. A lot of people had liked it, which was encouraging. Especially after Dad's mixed response to the event.

I was about to pause the recorder for a snack when I heard a door opening again. It was my dad's office door, with its creepy hall-of-mirrors creak. I heard a sigh and the sound of someone flopping into the office chair.

There was some rustling, sipping, eventually a burp. I sucked in a breath. I shouldn't be listening to this if Dad likely didn't know he was being recorded. But then again—better me than someone else.

I listened guiltily to my father's sighs and grunts—apparently he was trying to get comfortable in his chair—and wondered who would have the patience to listen to all this. After about fifteen minutes, Dad spoke.

"Yes. May I speak to Janelle Schneider?" A pause. "Yes. You can tell her it's Edward Cork calling."

A sniffle and more squeaking of the chair.

"Helllooooo, Janelle! Yep. I just wanted to make sure you're sending someone to our event this afternoon. There will be some great photo ops, and I want to make sure your Danville reporter speaks to me directly about the literacy angle." Another brief pause. "Yes. You got the press release my manager sent a couple of days ago?" He waited only a beat before launching back into his pitch. "*Excellent*. Oh, and please don't use any old photos you have of the park or its employees, me included, for this story. Only current photos. The park changes a lot from summer to summer, and I don't want anything outdated running. If you can't get the images you want and need to ask us for something, go ahead. Okay?

"Mmm-kay. Thanks, Janette."

I winced. If he wanted newspaper people to do him favors, he at least needed to work on getting their names right.

"Oh, and by the way, I've got something even bigger happening in mid-July. So let's talk about that, too. I can't wait to tell you and your reporter about it."

Dad had a love-hate relationship with the two local newspapers—the town paper and the larger county paper. It irritated him, last year, when the county paper's feature on his new ownership of Fabuland seemed to be more of a goodbye to and remembrance of Mr. Moyer than a forward-looking celebration of all the changes Dad had made. He also didn't like that the county paper ran a somewhat unflattering photo of him pointing up to the top of the Laser Coaster, squinting in the sun, open-mouthed, his teeth sticking out.

I tried not to get too nervous while I listened to the rest of the recording. After his phone conversation with my mother came and went, there was an extended series of sighs and chair squeaks, then complete silence for more than ten minutes. Dad had apparently left the office. Eventually I heard the sound of a door, shuffling, and a muttered *shit* that I recognized as Chris's, not my dad's.

There were a couple of quiet moments, then Chris's voice again:

"Heyyyy." He drew out the word, speaking so softly I had to turn the recorder way up to hear him. "I only have a few minutes. But I'm missing you. I wanted to hear your voice before things got crazy.

"I know, baby. I know. We're going to figure this out. Don't worry. I'm working on it. I know it's hard right now.

"Oh. No. *No*. Don't say that. Listen . . ."

His voice got louder.

"*No*. Come on, now. *Don't say that.*"

Then there was a shuffling.

"So sorry, honey. I gotta go because . . . Hello?"

Then a *thunk thunk*. And then, my own voice. Echoing softly because it was coming from the stairwell. Then there was silence again, and then a rustling that I recognized as me searching my dad's desk, because there was a *clunk,* and then the recording stopped.

I sat there in silence, trying to process what had just happened. I'd never heard Chris use a tender voice like that. It was kind of embarrassing since Chris always had such a businesslike demeanor. He was probably talking to Trisha. Chris had been married for about three years—I remembered Dad dressing up for the wedding.

Was Chris's wife angry at him? Testy because of whatever "issue" my dad had seemed vaguely aware of? Had she hung up on Chris? It was really none of my business, but the upshot was that maybe it *wasn't* Chris who'd put the recorder in the office. Would he record *himself* talking like that? It seemed unlikely.

I put the recorder in my backpack and put on my pajamas.

I had a lot to do tomorrow. I'd start by approaching Chris. And I still wanted to talk to Reggie, plus the two other kids who'd been with Ethan the night he died. I was also curious what Zach Crenshaw might say if I brought up Morgan. Not to mention that I should add Jason's friend Katy to my list of people to talk to. I still wasn't sure what I was trying to find out. But maybe somewhere in all of it there was a path to figuring out what had happened to Ethan.

I lay in the dark and wished Jason and I had talked a little longer. Tucked under the covers, I remembered when we were small and Jason and I had spent all night in one of his expertly constructed living room forts. There was something that had made it a special occasion, but I couldn't pinpoint exactly what. Jason's birthday, maybe, or the celebration of Dad's opening another Doughnut Dynasty branch. Around then he had opened several in quick succession. In any case, my parents, for that one time, let us spend the whole night in the fort, all snug with our pillows and blankets. They even let us decorate the outside of the fort with sprinkles, which stuck to the blue knitted afghan that Jason had used for part of the fort's roof. I didn't remember why our parents had let us be so crazy-messy, but I remember Mom absentmindedly humming and vacuuming up the next morning before Jason and I whipped the afghan around the yard to shake off all the sprinkles.

TEN

Before Fabuland opened in the morning, I spotted Chris in the middle of the central park path, where the Kiddie Town, Food Zone, and Thunder Way roads meet. He was holding one of those superlong measuring tapes that comes on a reel, streaming it from the Starship 360 area to the other side of the road that led to the carousel.

"Hey," I said, jogging up. "What are you up to?"

"Your dad wants me to measure this spot."

"Why?" I asked, looking around.

Chris reached into his pocket and handed me a folded piece of lined paper, then continued measuring. I unfolded the paper and saw a crudely drawn map of Fabuland. *Food Zone, Pavilion, WaterWays, Starship 360,* etc., were labeled in my dad's thick, all-caps style. At three different spots on the map, someone had drawn a circle with a red marker.

"He wants to figure out which spot we should use for the big doughnut gala."

"Gala?" I repeated. I wasn't sure if that was the right word. My dad must have come up with it, because Chris looked slightly uncomfortable when he said it.

"He's got his sights set on July sixteenth."

"That's not really enough time to get a lot of press first. . . ." I trailed off, considering that it would probably fall on our shoulders.

Chris shrugged. "Maybe you ought to tell him that. I already tried."

I glanced at the map again, and then at Chris's slouched shoulders as he straightened and tightened his measuring tape. It occurred to me that maybe he didn't approach my dad's ideas the way Jason and I did: support the doable ones, but try not to feed the crazy ones too much. We all let Dad *talk* about making a giant doughnut spectacle someday. But no one expected him to ever do it. Did Chris not understand this? Was it possible he had forgotten? That he was distracted somehow?

Poor Chris.

Was his wife still angry at him, as she had been on the recording?

Or— I had a sudden suspicion that somehow hadn't occurred to me last night.

Maybe that wasn't his wife he was talking to on the recording. Maybe that wasn't his wife he was calling baby.

Chris took the paper from me and silently marked something on it after looking at the tape measure one more time.

"Wouldn't the Food Zone be the natural place?" I asked.

"Your dad was very clear he wants it to be a whole-park spectacle, not just a food event."

"Uh-huh," I said. "But it would be kind of crowded in this spot, right?"

"He thinks it would be good for pictures, for one. And if there's a big crowd and a need for overflow seating, people could be seated in the Starship 360."

"Right," I said, eyeing the long, boat-shaped ride. It could probably seat about fifty, max. If people squished in.

"Your dad's talking aerial photographs, maybe aerial footage."

"Of course he is," I mumbled.

"What?" Chris said.

"Umm . . . nothing."

Ben was walking by as I said that, sipping a coffee.

"Hey, my friend!" he called. "Caught you looking at the 360 again. You're not seriously thinking of becoming an upside-downer, are you?"

"Umm . . . ," I said, glancing at Chris.

Ben must've realized then that Chris and I were talking.

"Oops . . . sorry!" he said, and turned toward the Rotor.

I stared wistfully at his back for a moment, wishing I'd had a chance to say hi. It took me a moment to recover, and to remember what I'd meant to ask Chris in the first place.

I took the recorder out of my backpack.

"Did you lose this?" I asked.

Chris studied it. "Is that some kind of recorder?"

"Yeah. It's a digital recorder."

"It's not mine, no," Chris said. "Why do you ask?"

His answer was as quick and casual as my dad's had been.

"I found it and can't figure out who the owner is."

"Well, where did you find it?"

"My dad's office," I answered, and then watched his reaction. The skin over the bridge of Chris's nose wrinkled quizzically.

"Then it's probably your dad's."

"It's not. I asked him."

Chris shrugged and started to suck the measuring tape back into its dispenser. "Then ask Tim Malloy, I guess. He's the only other person who goes in there."

Tim Malloy. Winnie's brother. Of course. I wasn't sure why I hadn't thought of him—maybe because he had kind of a dopey and unconniving air. Tim was, however, part of the custodial staff and regularly cleaned Dad's office.

A familiar whirring sound came from behind the Starship 360. The Laser Coaster operator was doing the initial tests for the day.

I could understand why my dad would want to have his big spectacle here, with the Laser Coaster visible in the distance. It had the highest climb and the farthest drop of all the three big coasters in the park. Its tracks were a striking neon green, its cars alternating purple and black. It looked like an exotic snake zipping along the grass when it was moving. It was cool and dramatic and very photogenic. Of course Dad wanted it in the picture.

I checked my phone. There were only a few minutes until nine o'clock, so I said bye to Chris. I was supposed to be ready and smiling at my cotton candy post near the entrance.

Walking back the way I came, I grudgingly took my post,

stowed my purse, and started the cotton candy machine. Dad liked for me to be pulling out the first few batches of pink puffs just as the guests were walking in. I watched as various employees hurried to their stations, my mind wandering back to Chris's words on the recording.

We're going to figure this out.

I know it's hard right now.

And in that instant a few things clicked in my head.

Winnie on the phone right before the Princess Parade—right before I'd gone up to my dad's office and run into Chris and found the recorder. I'd stopped the recorder when I'd found it—and the conversation Chris had had was right before that. Roughly the same time Winnie had been on the phone during princess prep time. So could they have been talking to *each other*? There definitely seemed to be anger or frustration coming from whoever Chris had been talking to. And then, about an hour later, Winnie had hurled a necklace at Chris.

Not to mention the fact that Winnie and Chris were *both* unexpectedly off duty at Fabuland the night of Ethan's death—and both for somewhat vague reasons. *And* that my dad had mentioned that Chris and his wife were having some kind of "issue." In my dad's roundabout way, did that mean they were on the cusp of divorce?

I was so stunned by the possible connections that I was just staring into space when Zach Crenshaw walked by my booth.

"Zach!" I yelled at his back, after I'd had a moment to wake up. I had to scream his name several times because he had earbuds in. "Can I ask you something?"

"Your dad's going to be mad if there's not a row of fresh pizza dough balls rising in my kitchen in twenty minutes," he said, pulling out the earbuds as he stopped reluctantly.

"But nobody orders pizza in the morning," I reasoned.

"It doesn't—" Zach hesitated.

It doesn't matter. I knew that was what he wasn't sure he could say to me. It doesn't matter to Mr. Cork. It's all about how things look.

"Listen, I was just wondering how you think Morgan's been doing the last week or so. If you guys talked a lot after she found Ethan, or how you think she's holding up?"

"Well, I heard she maybe wasn't holding up so well . . . if you know what I mean. And I think you do, since you were the one who got her down."

He raised his eyebrows at me, conveying a reluctant sort of admiration. Maybe. It was hard to tell with such a decidedly cool individual.

"Okay. Yeah. But I mean, before that. I was away for a couple of weeks right before that. And I'd heard you two had gotten closer."

"Closer?" Zach frowned. "Maybe the first few days of summer. But not last week. I've barely seen Morgan for the last couple of weeks since she wasn't working Pizza to the Rescue."

"She wasn't?"

"No." Zach was starting to glance nervously at the Food Zone—apparently still eager to make it to his post at the official start time. "I guess you didn't know since you were away."

"Was she working a different food booth?"

Chris often shuffled people around to accommodate for last-minute no-shows and new hires. But I was surprised Morgan hadn't mentioned it when we were still texting.

"No. She hasn't been in the Food Zone at all."

"What, she hasn't been working these past couple of weeks?"

"No. She's been lifeguarding at the waterslides," Zach said, in the same tone one usually said *well, duh.*

"Morgan?"

Zach sighed. "That's who we're talking about, right?"

"You must be confused. Morgan's not—"

"I saw her in the lifeguard chair," Zach interrupted. "Sorry, Ivy, I've got to go."

"But—"

I was stunned silent for a second as an image flashed in my head. The new red bathing suit Morgan was wearing in the picture she'd posted.

Zach either didn't hear my protest or decided to ignore it. He took off, jogging toward the Food Zone. I stared into the whirling metal of the cotton candy machine. Usually watching it spin didn't make me dizzy. So the feeling in my stomach must've been from the things I didn't have time to say to Zach.

But Morgan's not a lifeguard.

Morgan can barely swim.

ELEVEN

Can I come visit Morgan tonight?

I typed and sent the text before I'd spun a single cotton candy cone, but Morgan's mom didn't reply right away.

It wasn't until I was in the Food Zone eating my bagged lunch—I was still sick of hot dogs and pizza—that my phone dinged with her response.

Morgan is actually coming home tomorrow morning and there is a lot going on at the hospital tonight to prepare for her release. So text me (or Morgan, she'll have her phone back) tomorrow and we'll see how it goes. Thank you for supporting Morgan, Ivy.

Despite all my new questions for Morgan, I felt a weight lift when I read that. Suddenly I had an appetite again. I scarfed down my red pepper sticks and turkey wrap, and was still hungry when they were gone. I didn't want any of the Zone's fried offerings, so I wandered down to the ice cream kiosk between the Food Zone and the WaterWays.

I ordered my favorite, black raspberry. While Drea Tomasetti started scooping, I watched a couple of kids plunking simultaneously into the water from the parallel waterslides.

"You have a pretty good view of the WaterWays, don't you?" I asked Drea. She was on ice cream duty almost every day.

"Yup," she replied, digging deep into the black raspberry. She put her whole body into it, almost disappearing into the cooler before popping back up. "Really entertaining. I get to see all the weird dad bods and the teeny toddler bikinis."

"Someone just told me they saw Morgan working the lifeguard chair a week or two ago, while I was gone," I said, trying for a casual tone. "But I think they must have mistaken someone else for her because she's always been at the Food Zone, right?"

Drea positioned a perfect purple orb of black raspberry onto the top of a sugar cone. "Actually, I saw her there. It was just for a couple of days, though. I guess she was filling in for someone?"

An uneasy feeling came over me, making the ice cream look like something unappetizing. Like a purple bodily organ—a spleen or a kidney.

"Filling in . . . for who?" I asked, trying to keep my voice steady.

Lifeguards were supposed to be certified, of course. A crappy swimmer like Morgan was definitely not supposed to *fill in*.

"Liam Banister," Drea said, handing me a couple of napkins. "He quit at the beginning of the summer because someone got him a job at the lake in Coventry."

I nodded. I knew that. Liam had quit the day before I left for North Carolina. I stared at the ice cream she was patting onto

125

the cone. I wasn't hungry anymore. It was crazy that Morgan would fill in for a lifeguard. Whose idea was that? Chris hired *most* of the Fabuland employees and made the schedules, but Carla Price, the WaterWays manager, hired and supervised the lifeguards. But whoever had asked Morgan to fill in, why on earth had she said *yes*?

Drea held the cone out and watched me for a few moments before taking it back quickly. "Oh! I'm sorry. I totally forgot to ask if you wanted sprinkles."

I wasn't sure how many people knew what a bad swimmer Morgan was, since she hid it well. I also wasn't sure who I could talk to about any of this without getting Morgan in trouble.

"Ivy?" Drea prompted, after a few more seconds of silence.

"Umm . . . no thanks," I said, and held out my hand as she passed me the cone.

Wandering slowly in the direction of the lifeguard chair, I licked the ice cream noncommittally.

A young guy whose name I didn't know was sitting in the chair looking tanned and smiley and confident. I wasn't sure what insight I thought I'd gain by simply gazing up at that chair.

I kept walking, and I'd just tossed the ice cream—barely half eaten—in the trash, when I saw Tim Malloy. He was on a ladder outside the WaterWays shower and bathroom, spackling a hole in the building's outer wall.

"Tim?" I said softly as I approached him, not wanting to surprise a guy on a ladder.

He craned his neck slowly. "Oh. Ivy."

"Can you come down a second, or do you want to talk from up there?"

Tim's mouth went slack, as if he was really thinking about this. I had to admit he was cute. His dark hair was boyish, with a little cowlick sprouting up on top, but he also had casual, masculine stubble. I wondered how calculated the growth was, because unlike Ben, Tim otherwise seemed very clean cut. His jeans were snug, his black T-shirt snugger—just short of looking like he'd bought the wrong size. And just perfect for showing off his biceps.

"You got a message from your dad or something?" he asked.

"No. I wanted to talk to you about . . ." I hesitated. "About a couple of things."

Tim scratched at his stubbly cheek and then descended the ladder. He put his spackling knife and bucket on the grass and wiped his hands on his jeans.

"How's Morgan?" he asked.

"She's okay," I said, hesitating to convey much because I wasn't sure if he deserved to know anything.

"Is she home, or . . . ?"

I didn't know what to make of his gaze, which seemed to shift to one side as he asked the question. Tim's eyes had always had a kind of googly look to them, like the eyes you glue on felt or construction-paper animals in elementary school. Sometimes they made him look goofy. Sometimes they made him look like he was secretly laughing at everything. But either way, he was still a whole lot easier to talk to than his fierce-eyed sister.

"I don't know. Probably. Listen, Tim. I'm so sorry about Ethan. And I'm sorry I wasn't here for the funeral."

"Thanks." Tim nodded, looking away.

"And I'm just wondering . . . would you mind talking about Ethan with me, a little bit? I mean, if you don't feel like it, I understand. But . . ."

Tim repositioned his hands, hooking his thumbs under his armpits. "Like . . . what about him?"

"Well . . . I know this will sound weird. . . . You know the paperweight he won before he died?"

"Yeah. I know about that." Tim's lower lip quivered a little as he formed his next sentence. "He showed it to me. It was pretty cool."

"He showed it to you . . . but he didn't *give* it to you?" I asked.

"No." Tim rubbed the corner of one eye, then the other, getting a tiny streak of spackle on his cheek as he did it. "Actually, I wonder what happened to it."

Something about his slightly spackled face disarmed me a little.

"Morgan found it," I said quietly. "The day she found him."

"She did?" Tim stared at me. "Why didn't she tell anyone?"

"There was a lot going on that day, sounds like." I hesitated. "Would you, um, want it back?"

Tim thought about this, then shrugged. "I don't think it matters now. We have other things to remember him by."

His words made me feel like a terrible person for even asking him these things. Tim seemed to notice my unease.

"Look, should we sit down for a second?" he asked.

"Like, on the grass?" I said.

"Just . . . just so we can really talk. Does your dad expect you to be somewhere right now?"

"Probably," I said, but sat down in the grass anyway. "I'm . . . I'm asking some things because Morgan . . ."

I trailed off. Because Morgan *what*?

"Morgan asked you to?" Tim asked, sitting across from me but leaving a respectful distance between us. "I know you guys are, like, best friends."

Tim yanked a stem of plantain weed out of the ground. I kind of wanted to ask him if he knew why his sister had backed out of her shift the night Ethan died, but thought that might be cruel. Plus he might tell her I had asked.

"Do you know why Ethan was saying that was the *only* time he could ride the roller coaster?" I asked instead.

Tim's face collapsed. His mouth turned down almost despairingly. He stripped the plantain weed of its seeds, scattering them into the grass. It seemed to me he was trying to focus on the weed so I wouldn't notice his eyes turning glassy.

"Umm," he said as I watched his neck and ears turn a painful pink. "No."

"But you've heard that he was saying that?" I said softly.

Tim nodded. There were tears welling up in his eyes. I felt like I'd just swallowed a large stone. I was almost certainly an asshole for asking these questions.

But I had one more thing I really needed to ask him. An easier question, considering.

I opened my backpack and pulled out the tape recorder.

"Do you recognize this?" I asked him, depositing it on the grass between us.

He looked relieved that I'd changed the subject. He shook his head. "No."

"It's not yours?" I said quietly.

"No. Why? What's the deal?"

"I thought maybe it was yours. Someone lost it, and Chris thought I should ask you."

"No. Is it an old-school kind of phone, or what?"

"Uh . . . no. Never mind. Doesn't matter."

Tim started to stand up. "Did you want to ask me anything else? Because Chris wants me to have these holes patched up today. We're painting the outside walls of the changing rooms tonight, so they'll be dry by morning when we reopen."

"Right, no, go ahead," I said, and watched him climb the ladder again. Then he stood there, spackle knife poised against the wall but motionless until I walked away. I wondered, among other things, whether Tim knew there was maybe something between his sister and Chris. But I hadn't felt I could throw that into the already uncomfortable conversation.

I could see why my dad had never made Tim a ride operator. He wasn't good under pressure. Which also made him a terrible liar. When I asked him why Ethan said he couldn't ride the Laser Coaster *on another day*, it seemed pretty clear Tim was struggling to act like he didn't know the answer.

But on the other hand, that meant he probably wasn't lying about the other stuff.

I couldn't wait to see Morgan tomorrow, out of the hospital

and back at home. We'd clear up this whole lifeguard thing, first of all. If she let me, I'd test the waters on the mysterious "guy trouble" front too. I hadn't entirely ruled Tim out yet, although he seemed like a pretty nice guy.

And I wanted to tell her that Reggie and Katy were next on my list—and see if she had anyone else to add. And of course I'd see what she thought about the possible connection between Chris and Winnie, and if it mattered. We'd probably put our heads together like we always had, and figure out who and what we should ask next.

TWELVE

Can I come by this morning? Figured I'd bring some Boston cream and jellies from the Main Street shop. Your mom want anything?

I'd awoken that morning knowing exactly what I'd text Morgan. This was a situation that called for doughnuts. I guess I am my father's daughter. I believe in the cheering power of pastry.

And it appeared Morgan still did too.

Sure! Mom would go for a large coffee, pls and thx! She had late shift and is napping so I'm not gonna ask her about doughnuts now. Not much for carbs lately.

I was so thrilled Morgan had written back and to get an upbeat response that I was dressed in seconds, slid my feet into a pair of flip-flops, and drove straight to the Main Street Dynasty shop like a cruller-loving bat out of hell.

I practically skipped into the shop. I didn't recognize the young guy running the register—probably since I never worked there on weekday mornings. He seemed kind of low energy, nodding sleepily as I listed the doughnuts I wanted.

While he gathered my order, I thought of the days when Dad was still here almost every day. Sometimes, when I was little, he'd wear a chef's hat with his business shirt and tie and entertain the customers. When someone would ask for a Danish, he'd sing "Eat Me, I'm a Danish," which was apparently a song from the '80s parodying a popular song called "Rock Me, Amadeus." At least that's what Dad told us. Often I'd wonder if he made that up. Sometimes he'd flex and kiss his biceps after filling a dozen-doughnut box, as if it had been taxing work. I don't think anyone thought it was especially funny, although a few years ago he used to have one employee, a sweet college student named Penny, who would always giggle politely whenever he did it. Which would, unfortunately, motivate him to do it repeatedly.

"Enjoy," the register guy said as he handed me my order.

I opened my wallet. "What's the total?"

He shook his head. "Come on. I know who you are, Ivy. You came in with your dad last year. And your picture's on his desk in the back."

"But I didn't come in here to get something for free."

He shot me a bored look. "Well then, consider it your lucky day."

I wondered what had happened to Penny, who had left Doughnut Dynasty abruptly. She was way more polite than this guy. In any case, I murmured a thank you and shuffled out of the shop, wishing he hadn't used the word *lucky*. I rarely felt that was the right word for my situation, but people applied it to me all the time.

Delicately placing the white pastry bag on the passenger seat, I slid open my phone to text Morgan. It seemed disingenuous to present my visit as a pastry party and then ambush her with difficult questions. I needed to give her a little bit of a heads-up.

On my way with doughnuts! By the way, someone was telling me you were working the lifeguard chair when I was away? I'm sure it's some kind of misunderstanding but wanted to talk to you about it so I can help. Be there soon with a hug. xo

I drove to Morgan's neighborhood, wondering if her improved mood meant she'd changed her mind about leaving Danville. And considering whether it would be too pushy to bring this up today. As I parked in the driveway of her mom's little Cape house, I noticed that their dog was out on her run in the front yard. Stinkangel was very old, a mix of mutt and bichon frise, with yellowing white fur, a freakishly long tongue, and creepy brown gunk around her eyes.

Her name used to be Lily. But she was constantly rolling around in the yard, scratching her back in slow motion, front and back legs splayed out in a way that apparently reminded Morgan's mom of someone making a snow angel. Over time that morphed into "Stinkangel."

I petted Stinkangel as I passed her, making a mental note to wash my hands before touching any of the doughnuts. True to her name, Stinkangel stank.

I rang the doorbell. Stinkangel panted loudly at my side as I waited. After a minute, I rang the bell again. It was almost a minute more before Morgan's mom opened the door, her hair in a drooping, slept-in ponytail. The tight half smile on her face immediately gave me a bad feeling.

"Hi, Ms. Hodson," I said. Morgan had trained me long ago to use her mother's maiden name.

"Ivy, honey." Morgan's mom drew in a long breath. "Thanks for coming. I'm so sorry, but Morgan's not feeling up for visitors."

"Really?" I said, looking down at the doughnuts Morgan had seemed so happy to hear about earlier.

Morgan's mom stepped out of the house, closing the door behind her. She was wearing a long nightshirt with jeans underneath.

"She just told me she's not feeling well enough, sweetie. I wish I could have you in, but I don't want to push it."

"She and I were just texting," I insisted. "She wanted me to bring these."

Morgan's mom patted my shoulder gently, then nudged me forward, off the front steps and a few paces down the front walk.

"Listen, Ivy," she said in a low voice. "Morgan may be trying to act like everything's fine, even like everything's back to normal. And we all hope that will be the case soon. God, I wish it more than anyone. But these past couple of weeks have been a lot to take in."

"But she really did seem fine, though," I said, knowing I was pushing my luck.

Morgan's mom shook her head. "I don't know what she texted exactly. But she's doing this thing where she acts okay one minute and then the next you see that she's not."

She looked like she was deciding whether to say more. "I'm

so sorry you came out of your way. She just got home last night, hon. Let's give it a few more days."

I glanced around the yard, noting that Stinkangel's ever-dumbfounded expression matched my own feelings right now. I thrust the bag of doughnuts into Morgan's mom's hands.

"Give her these," I said, before adding, "Please. And do you want the coffee too?"

"What coffee?"

I handed her the cup of coffee Morgan had asked for. Some came out of the little hole, splattering on both of our hands. "I'm so sorry," I said. "Here's a napkin. Tell her to text me when she's ready."

"I will, honey," Morgan's mom called after me, but I was already halfway to my car. I couldn't stand to show my clueless, unwanted face in Morgan's yard for one more second.

I jammed the key in the ignition, backed out of the driveway a little too fast, and drove straight to Fabuland as if on auto-pilot.

Of course, I understood what had spooked Morgan. I doubted her mom knew it. I pictured Morgan waking her mom up only a few minutes ago, panicked, asking her to answer the door and tell me to go away. Panicked because of that text I'd written her. About her being on the lifeguard stand.

Apparently I was the last person she wanted to talk to about that. Or about the boy who'd been giving her "trouble." Or about who or what she was afraid of that made her so eager to abandon Danville and spend her senior year elsewhere. Or about anything at all.

Dad had changed the big LED again.

It read:

BIG THINGS AHEAD!
STAY TUNED FOR SUMMER SURPRISES!

I wasn't sure what that meant, but I was glad someone in the family was feeling optimistic. After I parked in the back employee lot, I took my phone out of the cup holder and called my dad.

"Ivy? What's up?" he asked.

"Dad, I'm not feeling well," I said. "Do you think you could get someone else to cover popcorn and cotton candy today?"

"What's wrong?"

"My stomach."

It wasn't entirely untrue. I couldn't stomach another day skulking around Fabuland, trying not to look up at all the people submitting themselves to the Laser Coaster and the Starship 360, fake-smiling and deluding myself that my only real friend wasn't slipping away from me.

"I'll get Chris to wrangle someone from hot dogs," Dad offered. "I think they're overstaffed over there, now that the promotion weenies are gone. That'll be fine for the morning. But check back in and see if you can come in at two or so, okay?"

"Sure," I said, hoping brevity would hide my lack of enthusiasm.

After we'd hung up, I sat motionless for a while, staring at the two older rides stored on the grass behind the employee lot. Dad retired them both at the end of last summer when he made his plan to add more kiddie rides. He'd planned to sell the old rides to other parks but hadn't gotten around to it. One was called the Rocketeer; the other was the Yo-Yo. Despite my fear of heights, I'd been on the Yo-Yo once with Morgan and a bunch of other girls—on a rare occasion that we couldn't reasonably convince them we had other plans. I wasn't really even clear on what the ride did, because I tried not to look at it as we got on. I just knew it was fast and high. Morgan sat next to me. She gripped my hand as the ride operator checked our seat belts.

"Close your eyes," she said. "Close your eyes the whole time. Do you want me to scream the whole time so you know I'm here, or do you want me to stay quiet?"

"Scream," I'd said. And she did. Stupid, exaggerated screaming that was clearly designed to communicate to me that we were okay. Like *Whhhhheeeee! Whooooaaaaa! Yowwwww!*

I sighed at the memory and called up my last text exchange with Morgan. After staring at it for a couple of minutes, I started to type a new text to her.

I will still love you no matter what you decide to tell me, it said. I typed quickly, but my finger refused to send it. I wasn't absolutely sure it was true. Not necessarily because of the thing about the lifeguard chair. That was bad, yes—but I felt like there was something else between us, something that Morgan wasn't saying. Among other things, she seemed to shut down whenever I mentioned Winnie Malloy. Why? And how could I keep pretending to be so confident about our friendship if I didn't know why she was keeping secrets?

I left the message on the screen. But I put my phone down on the passenger seat and then started my car.

* * *

"Is Katy Nealon here?" I asked the lady at the circulation desk. "She works here, right?"

Jason's Katy had never worked at Fabuland. She always said that she loved roller coasters but hated fried food smells and "forced fun." And while I was interested to hear what she had to say about Ethan, I also thought it might be nice to talk to someone who existed entirely outside of the drama of Fabuland.

"She's shelving," the circulation lady said, and pointed behind me. "Last I saw her, she was in nonfiction."

I whispered a quick thank you and walked toward the shelves. Two rows back, I found Katy in the 300s of the nonfiction stacks. She was resting on her elbow, reading, her long, thin limbs bent awkwardly over the cart of books.

"Katy?" I said in a stage whisper. She jumped and slammed her book shut.

"Jesus, you scared me," she hissed. "I'm not supposed to be reading."

"Isn't this a library?"

"Yeah. But we're all supposed to pretend to have more important things to do." She lowered her voice. "There's this creepy old dude who comes in and takes secret pictures of the library ladies slacking off, drinking tea and whatnot. He sends them to the paper and brings them to town hall meetings as numbered evidence to show that the library budget should be cut."

"Are you serious?" I asked. "Does he do it to other people in town? The police, or whatever?"

"No." Katy picked up a book and glanced at its spine. "Just the librarians. I'm pretty sure it's a thinly veiled act of misogyny, really."

"Ugh. Sorry," I said.

"How are you, by the way?" Katy asked, kneeling to shelve the book. She did it so lithely. She used to figure skate early in high school, and still did everything with grace. No wonder Jason was in love with her.

"Okay," I replied.

"Just okay?"

"Yeah," I admitted.

"Heard from your brother lately?"

"A couple of days ago. We didn't talk long."

Katy straightened up and glanced at me. "Did you come to visit or were you just here looking for a book?"

"Visit," I answered. "But I wanted to ask you something, if you have a sec."

"Okay," Katy whispered. She grabbed another book, stepped one shelf over, and began scanning for the book's place. "What?"

"Some things about Ethan Lavoie, mostly."

Katy nodded sadly and returned to her cart. "Okay."

"First of all, I'm really sorry. I know he was your friend."

"Yeah," Katy said softly. She picked up a book but just held it gingerly, not really looking at it.

"I just wonder if you think everything they're saying about the night he died . . . if everything they're saying about it feels accurate to you."

Katy put down the book, absently sliding it back in with the others on the cart.

"How's your friend Morgan?" she asked.

"Okay, not great," I murmured. I paused, hoping I wouldn't have to ask her the question again.

Katy ran her hand along the spines of the books and then looked up at me.

"To be honest, I've wondered some things," she said. "About how Ethan died."

We were both quiet for a moment.

"Like what?" I asked softly.

"Well . . . everyone keeps asking why he was walking by himself." Katy picked up the same book, then put it down again. "Or why he didn't call someone for a ride. And I get it that the Brewer's Creek area is a kind of woodsy, and the bridge isn't like the safest place you can walk. But when I used to hang out with him, he was pretty independent. He walked to places by himself all the time. He walked home from school sometimes, or to the Dynasty when he worked there."

I wasn't sure where she was going with this.

"Back when you were both in high school, you mean?" I asked.

"Yeah," Katy said.

"But the Brewer's Creek area *is* more dangerous," I pointed out, "so that's why his mom didn't want him there by himself."

"I guess," Katy said reluctantly.

She studied me for a second, then wheeled her cart farther into the nonfiction stacks, settling in the 800s, in the back corner. I followed her.

"But that's not what I'm wondering about," she continued, lowering her voice. "There was a time when his mom thought nothing of letting him walk by himself. But about a year and a half ago, maybe two years ago, she started making all these rules. Monitoring him more closely."

"Why?" I asked.

"I kind of wondered that myself." Katy paused for a moment. "I think it was around when he was getting closer to graduating. You'd think she'd have let him become even *more* independent then. But you know, Ethan rebelled a little bit. He told me it was *his* idea to apply for a job at Fabuland this summer instead of at the doughnut shop. He got the job without his mom knowing about it, and then once he had it, she didn't have the heart to tell him no."

I smiled, thinking of Ethan secretly consulting my dad or Chris about a job switch. Probably Chris. I wondered if he had known Ethan was going over his mom's head.

"So anyway, all this talk about why was he alone, why didn't he call for a ride. It all strikes me as kind of . . ." Katy hesitated, sucked on her lip. "Kind of false."

"You think he might not have called his mom for a ride just because he was tired of the rule?"

Katy nodded. "Pretty likely, from my perspective. And he wanted to keep asserting his independence. I don't know why everybody's not saying that. Maybe that would start to feel like victim blaming, to say he walked home on his own because he *wanted* to."

I considered that for a moment. "But why do you think his mom had more rules for him now than before?"

Katy shook her head. "I don't know. His mom's a nice lady. But protective. Maybe she didn't realize she was doing it—trying to hold him closer once he was done with high school. There was this social worker who'd come and check on them sometimes, at least when Ethan was younger. Maybe it was her idea. Or maybe the family had some other trouble and was just closing ranks for some reason, pulling Ethan in with them. I don't know."

"Meanwhile, Winnie and Tim have to feel terribly guilty that they weren't at Fabuland that night to walk or drive him home," I said, fishing, hoping Katy might offer something about the Malloy siblings, since she lived near them.

"Yeah. I don't get that either. Maybe Ethan's mom needs to blame someone. So Winnie and Tim get the blame for not being there."

"Has she said that explicitly, though?" Even though I didn't know what to think of Winnie and Tim, that seemed really rough.

"Well, no . . . but if you read between the lines in what's been quoted to the press, there's all this hand-wringing about a kid walking by himself who was actually perfectly capable of it. It's weird to me, that's all. It's kind of an insult to Ethan's memory."

"But . . . how do you think he fell, then?" I asked.

"I don't know," Katy said softly. "I don't have any brilliant theories on that. I don't think anyone does."

"Do you think it's possible he was headed to his cousins' house after work instead of his own?"

Katy cocked her head skeptically at the question. "It's *possible*. He spent a lot of time at their house, yeah. And vice versa. I don't think it matters whose house he was headed for, really. Either way, he didn't make it there."

Katy's voice broke as she said this. She closed her eyes for a few seconds—willing back tears, it looked like. When she opened them again, she scanned the spines of the books on the top shelf and sighed.

"Jesus, this town just gets sadder and sadder." Katy shook her head. "Your brother's smart to take a break this year."

I wasn't sure I wanted to talk about Jason and how lucky he was not to be here.

"So, why did you decide to come back here this summer?" I asked instead. "Weren't you somewhere really cool last summer? Like Portland, Maine?"

"Yeah, that's where I was. But that option wasn't available this year."

"Why not?"

"I was working there with my girlfriend. At her parents' restaurant."

"Girlfriend?" I repeated.

"Ex-girlfriend," Katy said. "We broke up in March. So that would make it kinda awkward, you know, for me to stay at *her* parents' house and work in *their* restaurant."

"But . . . wait. You had a girlfriend?"

"Oh, *God*. Jason didn't tell you?"

I took a moment to digest this. Katy liked women. Now that I thought about it, the fact wasn't actually that surprising. What was weird was Jason's failure to mention it.

"Well, how long has he known?" I asked.

"About two years. Maybe a little more. It figures. I hope you don't mind me saying this. Your brother is so sweet, but he kind of has a tendency to ignore information that's not convenient for him."

I was silent for a moment.

"I'm sorry, Ivy. Should I not have said that?"

I wasn't sure how to reply. I was used to hearing Jason criticized in the past year or so. Mostly by our dad.

"You know I love Jason," Katy added quickly. "I mean, as one of my oldest friends. You know I don't mean it in a vicious way."

"Of course not," I murmured.

I thought about my phone, still sitting on the passenger seat of my car, with the words *I will still love you no matter what you decide to tell me* still unsent. There was a *reason* I hadn't sent it. There were things Morgan couldn't tell me. Things I wasn't sure I could bear to hear. I had known this, instinctually, the moment I met her eyes on the Ferris wheel. I knew it now too. So it wasn't vicious at all, what Katy had said. It was simply *true*. And not just of Jason.

"Are you okay?" Katy asked.

"Yeah," I lied. "But I should go. I'm supposed to be working."

THIRTEEN

It was only a five-minute walk from the scenic turnoff on Brewer Road to the trestle where Ethan had fallen and died.

When we were a little younger, Morgan would hold my hand when we walked over the trestle. Eventually, I started to feel it was wide enough that I didn't need to be afraid. I could focus on the tracks beneath my feet and the trees ahead of me and not really think about it.

Now I took the well-worn path into the trees. After a minute's walk, I could still hear faint carousel music and roller-coaster screams from Fabuland. But it felt very distant and irrelevant here—like the low hum of a neighbor's television through an open window in summer. For a minute or two, I could block it out; enjoy the relative quiet, the seemingly endless leafy green. Until the trestle came into view.

It terrified me to think of Ethan approaching the trestle by himself in the dark.

My heartbeat quickened as I came closer to it. I could hear my own strides—the determined *thpt thpt thpt* of my skirt against my knees. I kept my spine straight and my head up, to make my posture match the sound. If someone was watching from the other side of the bridge, they'd never know my legs were shaking.

When I got halfway across, I slowly lowered myself to a sitting position, dangling one leg over the edge, then the other. I knew Morgan liked to sit here like this with other friends—legs swinging, hair blowing in the breeze, sipping leftover lemonade from Fabuland. She never made me stop and sit, because she knew I hated it.

Looking across to the other side, I saw a little makeshift memorial for Ethan. There was a sign I couldn't quite read from where I was, a few stuffed animals, and some flowers in a narrow black plastic vase. From where I was sitting, the flowers looked like fresh lilies and gerbera daisies. Someone had either put them here in the last couple of days or was replacing them with new ones.

I pulled my attention away from the flowers and forced myself to look at the creek bed. I wasn't good at calculating distances, but it was a long way down. At least three stories, if you were going to compare it to a building. Some of the rocks below looked viciously sharp. Whatever had happened to Ethan, I hoped it was quick. I hoped he'd died as soon as he hit the rocks and not suffered, lying there by himself.

I took out my phone. The message I'd typed an hour ago was still there.

I will still love you no matter what you decide to tell me.

I stared at the message and then looked down again at the creek bed. I couldn't decide which sight made me feel more ill, or more scared. It occurred to me that I had come here not so much to figure anything out about Ethan but to determine if I was really going to send the text.

Glancing away from my phone, I could see the faintest blur of my reflection in the shallow water of the creek.

Then I held my breath and hit *Send*.

I stared at my phone for a minute. And then another. The leaves around me rustled. A random thought came to me, stirred by my interaction at Cork's earlier in the morning. Penny, the girl at Doughnut Dynasty who'd laughed at Dad's jokes. *Shiny Penny,* my dad used to call her. She *did* have shiny, eager brown eyes—and would always ask me about school and friends and boys. I'd liked her, but it was weird how she just left without saying goodbye.

A bird chirped. I waited, and willed Morgan to write back.

I thought about our last night together before I'd left for North Carolina.

We'd been eating pizza at her place and decided to health it up with a side salad. While she was washing the lettuce, she'd said, "Any chance your dad would consider naming a ride the Salad Spinner?"

This was a running joke we'd had since last summer, when my dad was toying with the idea of renaming some of the older rides to make them sound more exciting.

Privately, Morgan and I would try to think up the dumbest and most unappealing ride names possible, attempting to one-up each other.

"How about the Brain Fart?" I shot back.

"You've said that one before," Morgan reminded me. "But I have a new one. The Face Lift."

I washed a tomato and started cutting it, thinking hard.

"The Intervention," I replied.

"The Kiddie Fiddler." Morgan grinned wickedly and took a red pepper out of the fridge.

"The Time Manager," I said quietly, still going for boringly awful instead of viscerally awful.

"The Expectorant," Morgan countered, after a few minutes of silence.

"Gross," I said. "You win."

Now I closed my eyes to keep myself from boring a hole through my phone. Another minute or two passed, and it was still silent.

I gazed at the rocks and wondered if anyone had ever thought the one thing about Ethan that they might have thought *first* if he hadn't had Down syndrome.

Had anyone considered that he could have *jumped*?

It felt very simple now—why Morgan might have said *Ask Ethan* while at the top of the Ferris wheel. Maybe she'd been thinking of jumping, and she'd wondered if he'd jumped as well.

She'd asked me to consider the question of "if he didn't fall." But then she'd said she wasn't necessarily talking about him being *pushed*. The stuff everyone was wondering about—the backpack he'd left and the fact that he hadn't called his mother—none of those were inconsistent with jumping. Someone who was going to jump wouldn't care about leaving their backpack. Someone who was going to jump wouldn't ask for a ride home. Someone who was going to jump might ride a roller coaster they'd been afraid of before, and say, *I can't do it on another day.*

And it was narrow-minded of all of us, thinking that Ethan couldn't experience the kind of pain that made someone think about doing something like that. Because of course he could. Even if we didn't understand *why*. Ethan could have had secrets just like the rest of us.

My phone vibrated. I gripped it hard, like Morgan's reply might save my life.

Hello Ivy?

The text wasn't from Morgan. It was from my dad. I stared at it for a moment. Then he wrote again.

Ivy honey.

And right after that:

Are you feeling well enough to come back?

I put the phone down next to me. I watched my blurred reflection in the shallow water, swaying slightly at the edge of the trestle.

Anyone could feel that way sometimes. Even if it was just for a moment here and there. The way Morgan had probably felt up on the Ferris wheel. People felt that way even when no one would ever guess. Smiley, innocent guys like Ethan. Beautiful girls in Cinderella costumes. People who otherwise looked and acted like they were busy or happy engaging in generally sunnier, sparklier things.

It was about as believable as Ethan spontaneously falling.

It was about as believable of Ethan as it was of me.

I looked down at my wobbly, distant reflection again.

I've always known that about you. That you wanted to stay small.

I heard those words in my father's voice. But I didn't quite know if the tone was affectionate or critical. I couldn't remember if the thing had really been said near the wonky mirrors in his office, or somewhere else. Or why I would think of those words now.

Write back, Morgan. I prayed this in my head until I was saying it out loud.

"Write back, Morgan."

She didn't.

And I felt as small as ever.

It scared me to be up there on my own. I grabbed my phone, pulled myself to standing, and walked the rest of the length of the trestle, to the other side. Approaching Ethan's memorial, I saw that the sign said *We love you, Ethan.* And then underneath that, in different, lighter handwriting, *Heaven has a new angel.* Up close, I could see that all the stuffed animals were turtles. Some were brownish and very realistic-looking. Some were bright green with goofy smiles and googly eyes. One had a rainbow-colored shell. I stared at the turtles, and then looked back at the rock bed where Ethan had fallen, and then back at the turtles, and burst into tears.

I stood there crying for the better part of five minutes. I wasn't sure why I was crying. Maybe it was for Ethan, even though I hadn't known him, really. Maybe it was for his family. Maybe it was because now that I wasn't on the bridge anymore, a couple of the thoughts I'd had up there had scared me. Just momentarily, but still.

And I wondered if Ethan really liked turtles all that much. Or if his family just *thought* he did. My dad didn't stop buying me unicorn plushies until I was about fourteen because I didn't have the heart to tell him I'd stopped collecting them when I was ten. I wondered if there were things even Ethan's mother and cousins didn't know about him. Or if it was true what Katy had said— that he maybe hadn't wanted anyone walking him home. That he didn't want to be babied like that.

As I sniffled and pulled up the shoulders of my dress to dry my face, I remembered Ethan hadn't ridden the Laser Coaster ever before. He'd told Briony and the other kids that.

Of course. Possibly he hadn't ridden it before that night because *he wasn't allowed to*. Because his family had been protective of him lately. But why? Maybe it didn't matter why. Maybe he was being *sneaky* that night. And that answered some of the questions about his choices. It was a rare night that neither of his cousins were around. And he chose that night to ride the roller coaster. He *couldn't do it another night* because one of them was almost always there, making sure he followed his mom's rules. And on a night he'd broken his mom's rules, it made sense that he might not call her for a ride—out of guilt or rebellion or some combination of the two.

On the other hand, that still didn't explain his backpack. Or the sparkly scorpion. I glanced up the alternate path in the woods—the one that led to Braeburn Road, and Morgan and Winnie's neighborhood—and wondered exactly how far up that path Morgan had found the paperweight.

My phone vibrated with another text from my dad.

Ivy. Come in or at least call now. Chris and I need to talk to you about something.

I couldn't tell over a text, of course, if the matter was really as urgent as my dad was making it sound. My heart jumped a little. Maybe he and Chris had talked and were going to ask me about the tape recorder. Or maybe not, I tried to reassure myself. Sometimes my dad just liked to make people hop to it.

Coming now, I typed back before walking over the bridge and through the trees to my car.

FOURTEEN

I found Dad in his office.

"Hey, Ivy," he said, leaning back in his chair. "You recovered from your tummy ache? You need anything? Pepto-Bismol? Smelling salts?"

Chris was sitting on the old couch opposite my dad's desk, staring down at the clipboard in his hands. I noticed that he was wearing the same shirt as yesterday—a dark-green polo shirt with a tiny smear of mustard near the collar buttons.

"I'm fine," I said, trying to sound upbeat and innocent. "What was it you wanted to talk about?"

"Two things," Dad replied, unbuttoning the top button of his dress shirt and loosening his tie. "First of all, we thought you ought to know how much progress we're making on this giant doughnut thing."

I glanced again at Chris, whose gaze had shifted to the window. From the couch you could see the lifeguard chair that towered over the WaterWays slide area.

"What kind of progress?" I asked, relieved that this wasn't going to be as serious as his text had made it sound.

"Well, the cheese guys in Landon are on board with renting out those big vats. We've got someone delivering them tonight. I can't wait. I've got a recipe for a dough that I think will really hold up even if it's done in big batches and formed into giant balls. I mean, it doesn't need to taste great or even have the consistency that people are used to for doughnuts. Chris agrees with me on that. Right, Chris?"

Chris nodded. His eyes looked glassy to me. I wondered how long he and my dad had been having this conversation.

"And Chris and I had another good idea: stringing the dough balls together with a thick bendable wire. You won't see it, but it'll keep the balls tight together. We might allow people to view the frying of the doughnut balls the night before, to kind of build things up. But I'm not sure about that—we'll see. Then we'll construct it in the wee hours, so people don't see the wire . . . see the sausage being made, so to speak. And then the doughnut will be all ready for frosting and sprinkling when we open the next day. So, Ivy . . . I hope you've already cleared your calendar for July sixteenth. And the day before, of course, for preparations. No tummy aches allowed."

"I will." I hesitated. "But that's so . . . *soon.*"

"That's usually a high-traffic week to begin with. We don't really need to draw a lot of *extra* people in. I mean, sure, *some* extra. We definitely want a crowd. But it's mostly for the fun of it. Maybe a teaser for something even *bigger* later in the summer."

Something *bigger* than the giant doughnut, come August? What could *that* be? Were we going to find a way to rain sprinkles over Danville? Shoot a doughnut-filled rocket ship to the International Space Station? My head was spinning.

"Chris, do we do a ribbon-cutting of some kind, you think?" Dad continued.

"Umm . . . what would the ribbon go around, exactly?" Chris asked.

"I don't know. The doughnut?"

"I wouldn't mess with the simple beauty of the doughnut itself." Chris yawned. "Frosting all over the ribbon?"

"Okay. Never mind." Dad tapped his pen on his desk. "No ribbon. And I was thinking of officially calling it Doughnut Daze. Isn't that cute?"

"Is this event going to be more than one day?" I asked, slightly alarmed.

"Well . . . no," Dad said.

"I was asking him the same thing," Chris volunteered.

"You decided on the site?" I asked.

"Yup. In the crossroads area between the Starship 360 and the Laser Coaster."

"That won't be too tight a fit, if you're planning to draw a big crowd?"

"Some people can watch from the Starship 360. And we've got those extra bleachers for the doughnut-eating contests in August. We can stage those on the opposite side. Having people at different heights will really build things up, make it feel very exciting."

"But then . . . people can't ride those rides that day?" I asked.

"Ivy." Dad tapped his pen on his desk again—more noisily this time, like he was beating a drum. "We figured you and Chris would share the publicity duties. I think the local papers are getting sick of hearing from me. If they're dealing with a fresh new face, I figure they might pay more attention. And since Jason's not here, the Fabuland Facebook feed's been kinda neglected. I'd like you two to give it a little more attention. I'm thinking Chris will handle most of the traditional media contacts, and you'll do all the social media. At least to start. Does that sound good to you both?"

I glanced at Chris, who nodded perfunctorily. Clearly they had already worked all this out.

"Good deal," Dad said, without waiting for a nod or a word from me. "We can nail down some of the details later, but you probably need to be back on cotton candy right now. I had Carol bag some before she went on pizza duty, but we need someone doing the live-action cotton candy. People lag in the midafternoon. They need the pick-me-up, the stimulation."

"Yeah," I said, relieved for the opportunity to get out of the office. "I'm headed over there next."

"Wait," Chris said. "Ed, you forgot why you called Ivy in. Remember?"

"What?" Dad looked puzzled for a second.

I held my breath, waiting for one of them to demand the tape recorder.

"The waterslides?" Chris prompted.

"Oh! Right," Dad said, and then twisted his mouth into a serious expression. "Ivy, we've had a report of a safety concern and we thought you could shed some light on it."

"Okay?" I squeaked. This sounded worse than something about the tape recorder.

"You might not have been aware of this when you were gone, but one of our lifeguards left unexpectedly and we were in a pinch. Carla put Morgan in the chair. She assured me she was going to check credentials before she put anyone in the post. Now Chris and I are concerned that the proper steps weren't taken."

"Why is this coming up now?" I asked, my pulse quickening fast.

"Maura Taft came to me with her concerns this morning," Chris said, glancing at his phone and then slipping it into his back pocket. "She'd heard someone who didn't have the proper training was put in that post."

Maura Taft was Drea Tomasetti's best friend. *Damn.*

"Umm . . . what was your question?" I murmured.

The wheels were starting to turn in my head, but maybe not fast enough. Maura Taft worked one of the prize booths, but at school she was on the swim team. I wasn't sure if she had lifeguard credentials, but she was probably at least working on them.

Dad leaned back in his chair and jangled the change in his pocket for a moment. "Does Morgan have lifeguard training? We didn't want to bother her, under the circumstances. But we thought you would know."

"Umm," I said.

Drea had probably told Maura what I was asking yesterday. And some bells must have gone off for Maura. Maybe she knew that Morgan wasn't a great swimmer. Or maybe it just annoyed her that someone had asked Morgan and not her.

"Speak up, hon," Dad said.

"Can we maybe talk about this privately?" I murmured.

Chris perked up at the question, and nearly leapt off the couch.

"Sure," he said.

He was gone in seconds. After I heard him reach the bottom of the stairs, I turned to my father.

"I don't want to get Morgan in trouble," I said, talking fast now. "Because I think she was having a tough time right before the Ferris wheel thing, and I'm sure there's been some kind of misunderstanding."

"Noted," Dad said. "No one's getting *Morgan* in trouble. I'll promise you that."

"Umm . . . is Carla here today? Can I talk to her?" I knew what the answer would be. I was just trying to buy a few more seconds to figure out how to respond.

"No." Dad folded his arms. "You can't. I'm the boss. Not you. Please answer the question."

When I looked into his dark eyes, I felt myself become disarmed a little, like I had looking at Ethan's turtles. Like I no longer had to hold on so tight to everything. Because it was just Dad and me now, and his promise had given me permission to let go.

"I mean . . . Dad . . . didn't you ever notice . . ."

I was about to ask my dad if he'd ever noticed that Morgan was kind of aquaphobic. But then it occurred to me that he probably hadn't. First of all, she did her best to cover it up. Second of all, he didn't really know Morgan all that well. It took two or three years of me having her over before he stopped mixing her up with my other blond friends from middle school. I'd always gotten the feeling, then, that he'd found my friends interchangeable—extensions of me whom he'd buy ice cream for and tell jokes to, but whose exact facial features, preferences, strengths, and weaknesses were of little consequence. He probably never knew Morgan wasn't a good swimmer or that diving terrified her. He was only vaguely aware that his own daughter was afraid of heights.

"Dad. I need you to promise me again. Because Morgan isn't doing well right now, and I think she may have been pressured into a bad decision or something."

"Yes. I promise. I *already* promised. Now spit it out, Ivy."

I wondered for a moment about Chris—if he shared some of the blame with Carla. Had *he* scheduled Morgan in that lifeguarding spot without asking about credentials? I decided that wasn't my concern at the moment. There were a number of things I'd been wondering about Chris, and I was having trouble figuring out how to address any of them.

"Ivy!" my dad barked.

"Morgan isn't a good swimmer," I blurted out.

Dad's arms tightened, moving higher up his chest, like they had a life of their own. Like he was part python, squeezing another part of himself up and out.

160

"She . . . umm . . . barely ever goes in the deep end. She's actually never been a fan of water."

Dad's mouth slackened and he looked from the window to me and back again.

"Dad," I said softly. "You didn't know that?"

Dad stared at me. But he only looked me in the eye for a moment, then seemed to let his gaze graze over the rest of my face—my mouth, the color in my cheeks, the wrinkle in my forehead—like he was quickly assessing the sincerity of what I was saying.

"Where the fuck is she?" he demanded.

"Who?" I felt my breath leave me for a moment. "Morgan?"

"No. *Carla*." He swung his office door open, calling, "Chris, is Carla here right now?"

He flew down the stairs and I followed him.

"Uh . . . what?" said Chris, who was waiting at the bottom of the stairs. "She's usually monitoring the wave pool, right?"

Dad nodded and walked in the direction of WaterWays. The wave pool was farther than the waterslides, but I could already hear the *wheeee!* and *whoaaa!* of kids riding the waves.

"Dad," I said, walking alongside him.

"Yeah?"

"We probably should get the whole story first, before you do anything about it. Don't you think?"

Chris was following us, not saying a word.

"I'll handle this, Ivy," Dad said.

"Just . . . talk to her in *private*, will you?" I pleaded.

"What is this, honey?" Dad walked faster so I was a couple of paces behind him. "Business Management 101 from my sixteen-year-old daughter?"

"Seventeen," I reminded him.

"Still kind of comical, honey. *Carla!*" Dad yelled when he caught sight of her sitting on one of the two lifeguard chairs. The waves were on low tide. A few adults turned to look. Most of the kids kept playing in the waves. Kids are used to yelling, and learn to ignore it, I've found.

I stopped in my tracks to watch some of the midafternoon moms watching my dad make his way around the pool to Carla. He looked out of place here approaching the tanned, muscular lifeguard in his sweat-stained blue business shirt.

Carla was a hyperathletic woman in her twenties. She always had a very serious expression, and rarely spoke except to tell someone to quit running around the pool. It had surprised me when my dad hired her because he always preferred people who smiled a lot over other qualifying job skills. But his last Water-Ways manager had quit abruptly at the beginning of last August and Carla had been a quick hire.

"I need to talk to you, Carla," he was saying. *Plip plop plip* went his feet along the shallow puddles next to the pool. His speed and determined tone made my pulse quicken.

"Dad," I called, but found my voice inadequate. It came out breathy and girlish. No one heard me over the kids playing in the pool. I tried to straighten my spine like I had at the trestle, but the attempt just made me feel numb. I was frozen, watching Carla.

She quickly climbed off the chair, expert and catlike. She

looked at my dad expectantly, calmly. Until he got close enough for her to really see his face. Then her tidy little frown disappeared, and her mouth opened slightly.

"Excuse me," Chris said from behind me. He was trying to catch up with my dad, and I was blocking the narrow way next to the pool. I squeezed aside for him, hoping he would intervene.

"We can talk in the gazebo," he called to my dad.

There was a gazebo just beyond the cyclone fence of the wave pool, for people to snack in since they weren't supposed to bring food into the wave pool area. The gazebo was usually empty—as it was right now.

"There really ought to be two lifeguards here at all times," Carla said quietly. "When the waves are going."

"Then turn the waves *off*," Dad said through his teeth.

Carla blew her whistle and yelled in her usual drill sergeant tone, "Waves'll be off for a few minutes!"

A couple of kids in the pool seemed to droop with disappointment. Carla nodded to the younger male lifeguard across the pool and then followed Dad and Chris.

I followed the three of them, even though I hadn't been given an invitation. Dad was too riled up to notice and the other two certainly weren't going to protest.

We'd barely reached the gazebo when Dad started laying into Carla.

"Did you check Morgan Froggett's lifeguard certification?" he demanded. "Did you make sure she got that information to you?"

"What?" Carla said, crinkling her nose at the question. "She's not on lifeguard duty. That was just an emergency—"

163

"Simple question," Dad interrupted. "Did you make sure she was actually a *lifeguard*?"

"Well . . . I guess I thought . . . You said you wanted her to start quick, and you said—"

"Yes. Quick. But she still needed to be a real fucking lifeguard!"

"Dad," I growled. I turned to the pool and saw that there was at least one black tankini-clad mom looking at us.

Carla's face was stunned. She stared at Dad, then glanced over at Chris.

"I think there must be some kind of misunderstanding here," she said slowly.

"Did you or did you not put Morgan Froggett on lifeguard duty at the waterslides?" Chris asked.

He sounded exhausted.

"Yeah, but—"

"I don't want to hear any *buts,* Carla," Dad interrupted. "*You* ask for the certification. *You* make sure you get that paperwork before you put someone in that chair. *You* check the references. And isn't there a basic skills test you're supposed to do, even when you have all that stuff?"

"Not when you—"

"Not good, Carla. It doesn't look good at all."

"But you told me—"

"Yours is one of the most important jobs in the park. Because if *safety* at Fabuland goes out the window, *Fabuland* goes out the window. You know what I'm saying? Do you know how many Fabuland jobs this town relies on? How hard it would be if we went down the tubes for a summer because some dumbshit didn't ask for certification from a new lifeguard?"

Dad stopped to take a breath. I glanced at Carla, whose posture seemed to crumble at *dumbshit*.

I think Carla was trying to say something, I wanted Chris to say. Because I couldn't manage to say it myself.

"And you know why I gave the job to *you*?" Dad continued. "Because I thought you were a smart cookie. But you know what, Carla? No smart cookie would do this. Only a dumbass would do this."

I watched Carla standing there. I felt bad that on top of everything else she had to endure this while wearing only a bathing suit.

"I mean, am I wrong?" Dad demanded. "*Tell* me I'm wrong, Carla."

Carla opened her mouth, but Dad didn't let her say anything.

"Now, I know that Morgan was partly in the wrong. Who the hell knows what that kid was thinking? Maybe it was a dare. Maybe she wanted to impress someone. Maybe it was a money issue. I don't know. But you're the grown-up in this situation, and *you* were supposed to be the one to check that shit. That's your *job*."

"Ed," Chris said softly, and then cleared his throat. "*Ed*. I think you've made your point."

"It's a point that needed to be made. It's about kids' *safety*. A lot of people don't know that about me, that that's the thing I care the most about."

"Of course," Chris said.

Dad sighed. "Carla, I think you need to pack your things and go."

Carla looked confused for a second, and then looked at me. She seemed to be studying me—looking me up and down. Was there something she wanted to say to me?

I think Carla was trying to say something shot through my head again. But the air was so thick with my dad's anger, I could barely breathe, much less speak.

I felt very small and pathetically girlish. I might as well have been saying, *Mommeee! Let's have a sprinkle partyyy!* I wondered what Carla thought of me. And why, in this particular moment, it was *me* she was choosing to look at.

I always knew that about you. That you wanted to stay small.

Mercifully, Carla stopped looking at me. She turned and headed for the dressing room, presumably to gather her things. Chris disappeared quickly, his phone up to his ear as he went.

"Ivy, why are you here?" Dad demanded. "Get back to work, honey."

I nodded. I was stunned silent and motionless, my head and limbs still prickling with the sting of what Carla probably thought of me. She probably thought I'd *told on her.* Among other terrible things.

Dad wanted Oompa Loompas, and he wanted me to be his Charlie, like Jason had been. I tried so hard, but somehow I always ended up as Veruca Salt.

FIFTEEN

Spinning cotton candy is actually therapeutic.

That's why I asked my dad for the job at the beginning of last summer, when he first became the boss of everything.

The buzz of the machine helps me drown out the noise of the rest of the park. And I love that moment when you start to see the first few wisps begin to fly up the metal cylinder of the machine. It really is like magic, how they appear out of nowhere. And I love corralling the gossamer threads onto a little paper cone, twisting them into a cloud.

Kids love to watch the spinning. *Stay behind the bubble, kids,* I say as I put on my latex gloves. I think it all looks like something quite expert to them. It's a cheap thrill for everyone involved.

I spun, looped, and bagged a couple of blue batches to have on hand, letting the noise of the machine calm my nerves from Dad's shouting at Carla earlier. Then I waited, perched on my stool, for customers. After a few minutes, a wave of parkgoers came off the Ferris wheel, a handful of them wanting fresh-spun candy. But after they'd gone, I was alone with my grim thoughts again.

I'd screwed up royally. I'd *thought* I'd been talking very casually to Drea, but she'd turned around and told Maura, and then big trouble ensued. For Carla, for my dad, probably now for Morgan. Because even if my dad was willing to overlook Morgan's role in the whole thing, people would certainly be talking about it. At the hospital, Morgan had said she wasn't comfortable in Danville anymore. Whatever that meant, I'd just made it worse.

"Shit," I muttered. And of course, two little girls—about kindergarten age—chose that very moment to walk right by, probably within hearing distance. Then I saw Anna Henry following close behind them. Her perfect black bobbed hair always stood out in a crowd. People at school used to call her *Helmet*. I resisted the urge to yell that.

"Anna!" I called instead. "Your friends want some cotton candy? It's on me."

The girls came running to my stand, Anna chasing after them.

"I guess that'd be okay," Anna said. "You giving it out for free today, or what?"

"No . . . just . . . free for you guys. I'd been hoping to run into you or Lucas."

"Ava and Portia!" Anna exclaimed rather suddenly, almost as if she hadn't heard me. "Do you recognize Queen Elsa here?"

The two girls stared at me. One of them—the one with curly blond pigtails—put a thoughtful finger up her nose.

"You were at the parade?" I asked. "I guess I didn't see you."

"Yeah," Anna said. "This is my summer babysitting job. Ava and Portia aren't sisters, but their parents both pay me for the two of them so the girls can hang out and the parents can get a cheaper sitter. They send us here, like, once a week."

"Sounds like a good deal," I said, nodding at the machine. "Pink or blue, girls?"

The girls whispered to each other for a moment, and then the finger-up-the-nose one chirped, "Pink."

I poured the pink floss sugar into the machine. Anna rummaged around in her large tote bag and extracted a wallet and round hairbrush.

"One for you?" I asked Anna.

"Oh! No thanks." Anna grimaced. "I don't eat that stuff."

Probably she didn't want anything that sticky anywhere near her hair.

"How are you holding up?" I asked, hesitating before starting the machine.

Anna shrugged, tidying her hair and twisting a couple of strands to curl playfully along her chin line, then tossed the brush back into her bag.

"Well . . . how do you mean?" she asked.

"It's been a hard time for everyone, I know. It's been hard on you . . . hard on Morgan. Listen, after the girls get their cotton candy, do you have a sec to talk?"

"I guess," Anna said slowly.

After I spun each girl a giant cone, Anna told them to sit on a nearby bench.

"So . . ." Anna glanced back at the girls for a moment. "What is it? Briony mentioned you were trying to piece some things together from when you weren't here."

Of course Briony had. But I caught myself before letting an exasperated sigh escape me. There was no such thing as a private conversation in this town, apparently.

"Yes." I played with an empty paper cone, tapping it along the edge of the machine. "Do you mind? I mean, I know it's still a hard subject."

"I don't mind." Anna glanced back at the kids. "As long as the girls don't hear. They don't know about Ethan. They don't need to."

I put down the paper cone. I needed to try not to look fiddly and nervous. Maybe that was how I'd seemed to Drea yesterday.

"I think I got the basic picture from Briony, about how it was when you last saw Ethan," I said. "But I just wanted to make sure I understood something else about him. Did he tell you *why* he'd never ridden the Laser Coaster before?"

"No." Anna shrugged. "Maybe he was too scared."

"But then why was he magically brave enough *that* day?"

"Well . . . who knows? Why are we ever brave enough to try something new? I guess it was just the right day."

I didn't reply. It hadn't been the *right day* for anything for Ethan at all. But it would be cruel to point that out.

"You know . . ." Anna hesitated, looking thoughtful. "I'm not absolutely sure it *was* the first time he'd ridden the Laser Coaster. I think he might have just been saying that to get us to go on it with him."

170

A wild yodel came from the top of the Ferris wheel. We both glanced over as the gondola of the noisy rider moved down closer to us. It was a young dad in a baseball cap, apparently trying to entertain the little boy sitting next to him who was very much on the low end of the legal height permitted on that ride, from my estimation.

"What makes you say that?" I said, turning back to Anna.

"Well . . . right after we got off, he was saying something kinda weird. He kept saying, *I feel like I've actually done that before. It feels like this is something I've done before. Isn't that weird? It feels so weird.*"

"Wooo-*hoooo*!" The dad screamed again as his gondola swept near us and then upward.

"He *said* that?" I asked.

"*Yes.*" Anna looked slightly impatient.

Behind her back, one of the girls had yanked most of her cotton candy from its cone and was positioning it over her chin to resemble a beard. I decided not to say anything, because I wanted to continue the conversation.

Had it really been the first time Ethan had ridden the ride, then? Or was that just the story everyone told now? Because it dramatized and saddened the narrative of the night he died? I could feel my theory about him *not being allowed to ride the Laser Coaster* slipping away.

"Did he say it in a joking way?" I asked.

"I don't know, exactly," Anna admitted. "Maybe he was remembering that he'd gone on some other roller coaster somewhere else or something."

"And was he *okay* on the roller coaster?" I asked. "Not seeming sick? Not too terrified? Like, not begging to get off or whatever?"

"Absolutely," Anna said quickly. The word made me feel a little funny. Except for my dad, I hardly ever heard anyone use that word outside of television. "He was fine. I mean, he was screaming and stuff, like all of us were. But he was having a great time."

The other girl pulled half her cotton candy off its stick and put it on her head, bobbing it up and down like a big bouffant.

"But after you guys said no to riding the Laser Coaster a second time, you didn't see him actually go to the front gate and leave?" I asked. I cocked my head as if that might somehow soften the question. I knew I was getting into more sensitive territory here.

"No." Anna shook her head sadly. "I think we'd have offered him a ride in that case. It's just . . . the way it all happened, we didn't see him. I think he may have gone to the bathroom right after we said goodbye. Lucas says he's *sure* Ethan went into the bathroom after we said goodbye to him. He told the police that. My guess is that Ethan spent some time at his locker after that. I mean, I know he didn't take his backpack from his locker. But maybe he was struggling to get the locker open for a while before he actually left."

I nodded, taking this in. I had a feeling that Anna, like Briony, had gone over all this many, many times. But it was interesting that Lucas said he saw Ethan go into the bathroom as they parted ways after the Laser Coaster. I hadn't heard that before.

"We should've gone on the ride with him again," Anna added,

looking at the ground. "It would've meant a lot to him, probably."

"I'm sorry," I said. "I don't want to make anyone feel bad. I'm just trying to understand what happened."

"Yeah, I know," Anna mumbled. "You talked to Reggie at all?"

"Reggie? No, not yet. I haven't seen him, actually."

"He's not working today," Anna said. "I've been wondering how he's doing. I was going to check in on him too, but someone else is running the Laser Coaster today."

Now that she mentioned it, I realized I hadn't seen Reggie since returning from North Carolina. Reggie was hard to miss. Short with slightly spiky hair and a silly little mustache, he was always playing way-too-loud Celtic punk music on his phone to accompany his every move. He'd been a friend of Jason's last summer, and maybe before that too.

Anna finally turned around and looked at the girls on the bench. Both were sporting fluffy hair *and* beards.

"Cute," she said, putting one hand on her hip. "But Ivy gave you those to *eat*, my lovelies."

I handed her a plastic bag and a few napkins.

"They can put whatever they're not going to eat now in this," I said. "Just try to leave some air in the bag before you tie it. It'll last longer."

Anna thanked me again and walked toward the carousel with the girls. After she wasn't visible anymore, I turned the cotton candy machine back on and kept busy for the next twenty minutes bagging a few pink batches. As I worked, I couldn't shake one thing Anna had just told me about Ethan.

That thing he'd said after going on the Laser Coaster.

I feel like I've actually done that before. It feels like this is something I've done before.

And the term he *hadn't* used for that sensation—at least not according to Anna's account—kept whirling around in my head to the rhythm of the spinning cotton candy machine, feeling more significant with each turn.

Déjà vu. Déjà vu. Déjà vu.

SIXTEEN

On my way home from work, I thought about a conversation my parents always used to have. I hadn't thought about it in years, but Anna's words had called up the memory.

When we were kids, Jason used to try to get away with riding his bike without his helmet. And then our mom would lecture him, usually over dinner, about why he needed to wear it. She would tell this long story about how when she was a kid nobody wore helmets and how once she wiped out on her bike and hit her head. She was unconscious for a couple of minutes and then she and her sister walked home and didn't even tell their parents. That evening my mom got a really weird feeling, like everything that she and her family were doing—the shows they were watching, the things they were saying, even the way she picked out her nightgown and put it on—had all happened before. And then by bedtime she had started puking. She confessed the fall to her parents, who rushed her to the hospital to have a CT scan. Turns out she had a concussion, and she didn't recover for several weeks. She had headaches and couldn't really do her math homework for a while—her brain was too foggy.

And I got off easy, our mom would conclude. *I don't want you to go through that—that or much, much worse.*

Our dad would always match our mom's concussion story with his own.

In high school, when I was catcher, a kid from the other team made a clumsy swing and knocked me clear out. But I was back up and hit a home run next inning. I insisted on batting even though I felt like crap. Doctor told me later what a bad idea that was. But I went for it, and our team won by that point.

And then our mom would inevitably say something like:

Well, we don't want Jason to miss the point, *Ed. I've heard this story about a hundred times and I still don't understand why the hell your coach let you do that.*

I'm fairly certain Jason finally started wearing his helmet so that we could all stop having to experience this conversation. As I parked in Dad's driveway, I observed a brief moment of gratitude that my parents were no longer married.

My dad was in the living room when I stepped inside. The TV was on, but he wasn't watching it. He'd positioned several shovels around the room, leaning them on the couch and the armchairs. Two were snow shovels, one looked like a heavy garden shovel, and one looked more like a giant spatula than a shovel.

"What're you doing, Dad?"

"Mostly just killing time till my vats arrive. I can't wait. I'm taking a dinner break and then I might go in later to check things out, make sure the vats fit where we plan to do the frying. I want to get started on a practice-run doughnut right away. But I'm glad you're here; I was wanting to ask you what you thought of them. You've got a flair for this sort of thing."

"For . . . shovels?" I said slowly.

"Don't think of them as shovels," Dad said, picking up one of the snow shovels and waving it gracefully back and forth, two-handed. "Think of them as frosting spatulas. I'm not sure this one would work that well for the gentle contours of a giant doughnut."

"Okay," I murmured, wondering if the Carla incident occupied even a tiny fraction of his brain anymore. I wondered how someone could ever get used to firing people, let alone doing so publicly.

"Whichever type I think is best, I'll be buying a few so we can have several people frosting at once. Not for efficiency's sake so much, but I think it'll give it a fun, frenetic kind of look."

I glanced over the shovels. *Fun and frenetic*. Translation: make all his employees sprint around like busy Oompa Loompas.

"What you do is you get ones with a strong, shiny round metal scoop like this one," I said, lifting the heavy garden shovel with its shiny scoop. It looked brand-new, and I wondered if he'd bought it on his way home from work. "Then paint the wooden handles really bright."

"That's great. What color, you think?"

I shook my head. "Not just one solid color. Diagonal stripes, like a candy cane. Maybe red and white is too Christmassy, but it is kind of candy-festive. Okay, I've got it. They shouldn't all be exactly the same. But they all have candy stripes. They all have white as one color and something else as the other. So you have candy-stripe pastel green, pink, purple, whatever. They all match in that way, and it also ties in with the rainbow color, candy fun of the sprinkles."

"Perfect," Dad said, clapping his hands as if I'd just performed a backflip. "That's what I love about you, Ivy. This stuff just comes out of you like a faucet. Are you hungry?"

"Umm, what were you thinking for food?"

"There are a few frozen meals in the freezer. You mind heating a couple of those up? In the oven, not the microwave. They get too gummy in the microwave."

"Sure," I said, and headed for the kitchen. I turned on the oven and opened the freezer, where I spied some enchiladas. After I shoved them in the oven, I decided to hang out in the kitchen for a while. I didn't want Dad to feel too eager to turn on the "faucet" again. I took out my phone and texted Jason.

Do you have Reggie Wiggins's number?

Before I'd left Fabuland, I'd taken a quick look at the week's shift schedule. Reggie wasn't slated to work all week, and hadn't worked the previous week either.

No immediate response from Jason. As I waited, I heard my dad leave the living room and go up the stairs. I took a deep breath and opened a different chat.

Did you get my last text? I wrote to Morgan. My phone vibrated almost immediately.

Yes.

I practically hugged the phone.

Can I come over and see you? I fired back.

Not right now.

What about in an hour?

Not tonight, I mean.

Do you think I don't mean it? What I said in my text from before?

No response.

I do, I wrote, after five minutes had passed. *Because you're like my sister.*

Neither of us really knows what it's like to have a sister, Morgan replied.

Well, *that* was cold, I thought. I wondered if I was even supposed to reply.

What's going on, Morgan? I typed back. *Are you still thinking of leaving Danville?*

And then—no response.

I'm not sure how many minutes I gazed at my phone before a noise came from upstairs, making me jump from the chair. Something had come crashing down in my dad's bedroom. I left my phone on the counter and went to the foot of the stairs.

"You okay?" I called up.

I wondered if he'd brought one of the shovels upstairs and knocked something over while dreamily frosting a giant fantasy doughnut. If that was the case, it definitely felt like a moment I didn't want to walk in on.

"Yes, hon," he called back. "No worries."

I grabbed my laptop from the living room and settled at the kitchen table with it. There was something I'd been wanting to look up since my discussion with Anna.

I googled *concussion, déjà vu,* and *cold feeling.*

The first thing that came up was titled "Facts About Concussion and Brain Injury." The first symptoms listed were headache, nausea, and dizziness. But further down the list was "a feeling of déjà vu."

I clicked out of the site and found a couple of health forums in which people were discussing their possible concussion symptoms, with "a weird aura of déjà vu" and "a feeling like I've been here before" among them. I didn't see anything about a cold feeling being a symptom, though.

I wondered if it was possible that Ethan had somehow hit his head while riding the Laser Coaster. It seemed unlikely because passengers were always strapped in pretty tight in the double shoulder straps. The backs of the seats had a little padding. But could he have been jolted the wrong way somehow? Or knocked heads with someone?

I googled *roller coasters* and *concussion.* I found a couple of articles from about a decade ago addressing the issue of whether the increasing speed of some of the fastest new roller coasters could lead to the risk of brain injury. I saw very little at first glance about cases of such a thing happening—except when people were breaking the rules, getting out of their seat belts, climbing on their seats, things like that. There were a lot of people *wondering* if they could get a concussion on a standard roller-coaster ride, but there was very little definitive information from medical experts on how likely it really was.

Still, it felt like a reasonable working theory to me, even if I wasn't exactly sure *how* Ethan might have banged his head. Among the other symptoms were *blurred vision, balance problems, difficulty thinking clearly, difficulty concentrating,* and *difficulty remembering information.*

Those were all things that could have led to Ethan not only losing his footing on the bridge but also possibly wandering up and down the wrong path, unsure of his direction or destination in the dark. Which could easily account for the dropped paperweight on the wrong path. Not to mention forgetting to call his mom or leaving his backpack at the park.

I returned to my original Google results and sat back in the chair, feeling sad again at this image of Ethan wandering alone in the woods. I didn't know Ethan well, but I remembered his enthusiasm, his wanting to be a part of things. I'd let him spin his own cotton candy many times. He asked me when my birthday was once, and then every other time he saw me, he'd tell me how many days till my birthday. Someone told me once that he did that to everyone—that he had a phenomenal memory for birthdays.

"Is the food ready?"

I jumped. My dad was standing right behind me, shovel in hand. Then he squinted at my computer, where the search *roller coasters concussion* was clearly visible.

"What're you looking *that* up for?"

"I don't know," I mumbled. It was too late to slam the laptop shut.

"You don't go on the roller coasters," Dad pointed out, grinning. "So you don't have anything to worry about."

"It seems like no one really thinks roller coasters on their own cause concussions anyway," I offered.

"Right," Dad said, opening the fridge and grabbing a canned seltzer.

"Dad?"

"Hmm?" He opened the can and took a long gulp.

"Would there be any reason someone with Down syndrome couldn't go on a roller coaster, that you know of?" I asked.

"No." Dad frowned and wiped his mouth with the back of his hand.

"Has someone asked you that before?" I said, noticing how immediate his response was.

Dad shook his head. "Not directly, no. But I know that last year a park in New Jersey had a problem because a ride operator refused to let a girl with Down syndrome get on a ride with her dad. They got a lot of bad press for discrimination. I remember reading about it. Chris forwards me amusement park stories sometimes, just as a heads-up."

"I'm sure the operator didn't mean to be discriminatory, right? They probably thought of Down syndrome as a medical condition and were being cautious?"

Dad shrugged. "Yeah, I guess it's a fine line. You can see how that family would see it more as discrimination, you know? I think the medical conditions that are really the biggest concern are heart conditions, because they're so common and a ride operator can't spot them. Chris and I have told all our ride operators if you see a borderline old person you're worried about, make sure you make a general announcement and direct *everyone's* attention to the sign with the restrictions. I mean, what more can you do? You don't want to offend the elderly thrill seeker, right? More power to them. I'll probably be one myself someday soon. And someone might look to be in shabby shape but have a good healthy heart. My ride operators have been told that if they're really, *really* worried about someone, they should inquire politely. Try not to offend, but make safety the priority. Makes sense, right?"

"Yup," I said softly, closing my computer.

You never could tell when and about what my dad would decide to become detail-oriented. It happened sometimes. But it was completely random.

My phone buzzed and I picked it up. Jason had sent me Reggie's number.

"Anyway, the food's not ready yet," I said, not looking up. But my dad was already wandering into the living room anyway.

I thought about shooting Reggie a text but opted to ask Jason a different question.

Actually, do you know where he lives?

The dots appeared, before his response came.

I do, but what's up?

Can you talk?

I wanted to track down Reggie. But I also wanted to talk about Chris and Winnie, and I couldn't think of who else to trust with that topic besides my brother. Same with the tape recorder. My phone vibrated again.

Yeah, one sec.

I peeked into the living room. Dad was standing in the middle of the room, sketching something on a legal pad, muttering to himself. I heard *confectioners' sugar* among the otherwise inaudible words. I stepped close enough to see that the drawing was indeed doughnut-shaped.

"I'm going out for a little bit," I said.

"What about dinner?" Dad pressed down to draw a dark arrow on the pad, then scribbled something next to it.

"I'm not actually hungry. Maybe I'll fix a sandwich later. You can eat both the enchiladas if you want. Okay?"

"Have you made any Facebook posts about the Doughnut Daze yet?"

"I will tonight," I promised. "The timer's all set for the enchiladas."

"Okay, hon. See ya. And, Ivy?"

"Yeah?"

"You'd do well to remember that I saved your friend's ass today." Dad didn't look up from the legal pad as he spoke. "Our reputation for safety was on the line and I had to fire *someone*. But it couldn't be Morgan, because everyone knows Morgan's already suffered enough lately, and what kind of an ogre *am* I, right? Not to mention you would've hated me for it. So maybe be careful who you talk to about what, yeah?"

"Umm . . . what do you mean?" I said. Even though I was pretty sure I knew exactly what he meant.

Dad was finally looking at me, his face reddening a little. "You might not realize that *your* mouth is a *big* mouth. Like mine. I mean, yeah, you look in the mirror and you see that pretty little pink mouth of yours. But when you're at Fabuland, everything you say is amplified, whether you want it to be or not. People listen. People listen *hard*. Because you're my daughter."

"Uh-huh," I said, my voice weakening to a whisper.

"Like, you can *wonder* if roller coasters are bad for people's brains. You can research that all you want, in your own house, on your laptop that I bought you for Christmas. But it would be awfully foolish . . . no, let me rephrase that . . . really stupid, actually, for you to let people hear you talking about something like that."

Dad finally stopped speaking, but before I could respond, he leaned over and kissed me on the head.

"Don't stay out too late," he said.

SEVENTEEN

I was still shaking when I called my brother from a grocery store parking lot.

"Hey," he said when he picked up. "What's up?"

"I'm killing time in the Drake's Grocery lot. I . . . wanted to talk to you."

"About Reggie, you mean? What's up with that? He, uh, doesn't seem like your type."

"My *type?*" I repeated absently. It seemed weird that Jason could think he knew something about what my type was. I was foggy on that myself. Maybe someday I'd have time to figure it out. "No, it's not like *that*. I've just got some things I want to ask him. And he hasn't been to work in a while."

"What, are you Dad's truancy officer now?"

"I just want to *talk* to him," I insisted.

Trying not to lose my patience with Jason, I took a breath and watched people strolling in and out of the grocery store. An elderly lady with a slow walk and a big smile pushing an enormous sack of generic dog food. A little girl in a fairy costume skipping and yanking her dad's arm as she raced through the automatic sliding doors.

"Okay . . . about what?" Jason asked.

"There are some things I want to clarify. On Morgan's behalf, sort of. About Ethan."

"Hmm . . . ," Jason said doubtfully. "I hope you'll keep in mind that Reggie's my friend."

"What do you mean?"

"Be *nice* to him, that's all. You know how it can be hard to make and keep friends when they work for Dad, right? He's one of mine, and I want to keep it that way."

"Got it," I said, even though I didn't sense that Jason and Reggie were ever all that close. "So are you going to send me his address or not?"

"Yeah, sure. I guess. I'll send it when we hang up. Just FYI, he doesn't live in Danville anymore. He lives in Leverton, in an apartment with a couple of buddies. So, are you just going to show up at his place? A visit from the boss's daughter might kind of startle him, don't you think? Is that what you want?"

Of course I didn't. But I couldn't always help it if people reacted that way to me. They had to deal with it—just like I had to.

"I've been meaning to ask him about the last night with Ethan," I explained. "But maybe he's quit since it happened. I haven't seen him since, and he hasn't been on the schedule."

"Did you ask Dad? Or Chris? Dad sometimes doesn't know the employee roster, but *Chris* always does."

I kept gazing at the grocery store doors. After a moment, someone hurried into the store whom I recognized. Tim Malloy, wearing a deli uniform. I always forgot that there were a number of Fabuland employees who worked other jobs, and Tim was one of them. By all accounts, he had been working at the deli counter of Drake's the night Ethan died.

"It didn't dawn on me how long it's been since I saw Reggie till this afternoon," I murmured. "I didn't think to ask Dad before I left the house."

That was an understatement. I didn't recall having any coherent thoughts as I left the house and drove to Drake's. Only a feeling. A feeling that I needed to get away and talk to my brother.

"Ivy," Jason said after a thoughtful pause, "whenever someone has the good fortune to escape Fabuland, we should have the good grace to stop ourselves from drawing them back in."

Jason's tone made me wonder if he ever wrote about Fabuland. It was probably great fodder for his college writer persona—his dad's shitty amusement park that he was too smart to work at. Fair game because he'd endured several long summers as Dad's lackey. But I wondered if *I* was fodder now too.

"Are we talking about Reggie still, or you?" I asked.

"Touché. Hey, how is everything else lately? How's it going, being Dad's . . . right-hand person?"

"Is that what I am?" I pulled down the rearview mirror and glanced at my reflection. I wondered if my voice sounded as dull as I felt. The question made me think of my dad referring to me as a *faucet*. It wasn't the weirdest thing he'd said this summer by a long shot. But it would probably take me a couple of days to forget it.

"He always has one, and I'm assuming *you're* it this summer."

"Not Chris?" I mumbled.

"Chris doesn't count. Chris is just an employee. His *real* right-hand man . . . or woman . . . always has to be someone who has some other attachment to him besides money."

I wrinkled my nose at the mirror. Jason was right. When we were little, it was Mom. After that, it was his girlfriend Kayla. Jason and I never got to know Kayla all that well because she and Dad always hung out on our nights with Mom. But Kayla had the most beautifully shaped black eyebrows I'd ever seen, and always read thriller novels in the first booth of the Main Street Dynasty store, which she "managed" for a year or so.

Once Kayla and Dad broke up, Jason was old enough to be Dad's main guy. Now that Jason was gone, it was me by default.

"Speaking of Chris . . . ," I said, pushing the rearview mirror back into place. It had occurred to me that Jason was the only one I could ask about this, without fear of it boomeranging back to me in some mortifying way. "Do you think it's possible that Chris and Winnie have some kind of . . . connection?"

Jason was silent for a little while.

"Hello?" I said.

"Why are you asking that?" he asked.

"I've just picked up on some . . . things," I admitted.

I summarized those things for him eagerly—the simultaneous phone calls, the fact they'd both canceled somewhat mysteriously on the night of Ethan's death. When I was finished, Jason was silent for a full minute.

"Hello?" I said again.

"I dunno, Ivy." He paused for a few more seconds. "That's not enough for me. And considering who you are, and who *she* is, I would maybe leave this alone."

"What's *that* supposed to mean?" I demanded.

"It's not supposed to mean anything cryptic. It's just . . . my advice. Let's leave it at that."

I tried not roll my eyes. Great brotherly advice from Mr. Avoidance Behavior.

"People gossip about Winnie too much," Jason added. "And I never thought of you as a gossip."

"I'm not gossiping," I said unconvincingly.

We were both quiet for a moment.

"So, is Dad behaving himself?" Jason asked.

"That's a complicated question," I said. "What do you consider behaving?"

"Well . . . any . . . outbursts lately?"

I considered the incident with Carla. I decided I didn't want to talk about that right now. Jason would probably ask me what I had said or did and I would have to say, *Nothing*. And I didn't have the right words to convey how miserable it felt to stand there quietly while she got fired in a bathing suit.

"You know . . . I think it's pretty different being his daughter," I heard myself say, "than it is being his son."

I wasn't quite sure how or why I'd let those words escape my mouth. It almost felt like I'd stepped out of myself for a moment as I said them.

I thought I heard Jason suck in his breath.

"Are you saying one is harder than the other?" he asked.

"I don't know. Maybe." And now I was stepping back into myself—hedging, as usual. Hiding, even.

"Which one's harder?" Jason reworded his question, lowering his voice.

"It's not a competition," I murmured. "I just wanted to point out that it's different."

"Okay," Jason said uncertainly.

"Can you send me Reggie's address, please?"

More silence on the other end. I wondered if I was supposed to be embarrassed by what we'd just almost kinda sorta half-discussed.

"All right, Ivy," Jason said. "And by the way, if you want to know what it's like to be his son, take a closer look at the Yo-Yo."

"What?" I said.

"The Yo-Yo. The ride."

"The one you guys stored away this year?"

"Yeah. You look at that thing and *then* let's talk. I need to hang up to get Reggie's address out of my contacts. Bye, Ivy."

He ended the call.

A few seconds later, a Leverton address and a phone number popped up on my phone.

Tell him I said hi, Jason had written beneath it, which disappeared as my navigation kicked in and I shifted my car into drive.

EIGHTEEN

Leverton was about twenty-five minutes away. Reggie and his friends lived in Upton Village, which was basically a semicircle of squat brick apartment buildings that looked a little like dorms. Each apartment had a flimsy eggshell-colored door with a number on it. Reggie was in building B, apartment 3, according to Jason's text.

After I parked, I grabbed my phone from the cup holder and saw that a new text from Jason had come in while I was driving.

You surprised me when you said that thing about being Dad's daughter. It's not a surprising sentiment, I was just surprised you said it and I didn't know what to say back. I know it's probably hard for you being up there by yourself.

Since I'd been expecting something more about the Yo-Yo ride, I was a little startled by his sympathy and texted back immediately so he'd know I'd seen it.

Thanks

At Reggie's, more later . . .

I got out of my car and went up to apartment 3B. It had an odd, tippy little square of concrete in front of the door—standing in, I guessed, for steps. All the other apartments had actual steps. I leaned forward and rang the bell. A noise like a pot clattering sounded before Reggie opened the door. He looked skinnier than when I'd seen him a few weeks ago, and he had shaved off his little mustache. His eyes popped slightly when he registered who I was.

"Hi," I said as cheerfully as I could.

"Jason's sister," he said, slightly disbelieving.

"Yeah."

"Mr. Cork's daughter, then."

"Uh-huh." *Keep it good-natured, Ivy.* "That too."

"What does your dad want?" Reggie asked, leaning against the door.

"What do you mean?" I said, trying to keep my friendly smile in place.

Reggie tapped his fingernails against the door. They were long and pointy, and gave me the creeps for a moment—until I remembered something someone had once said about Reggie playing classical guitar.

"Did he send you?" Reggie stuffed his hands in his pockets. He'd caught me looking at his nails. "He knows I've been taking some time off, so . . ."

"Umm . . . no. My brother gave me your address because I wanted to talk to you."

"Your *brother*?" His hands went deeper into his pockets. I had the feeling he wished he could jam his whole self into those pockets to get away from me.

"Yeah. I wasn't sure who else to ask. Do you have a minute or two?"

"I guess." Reggie hesitated, then opened the door wider. "You want to come in? One of my roommates is here, but he's in his room. I think he's sleeping. Or watching Netflix or whatever."

"Sure. I'll come in. It's kind of hot out here."

But when I stepped inside, I realized the apartment was actually hotter, although I knew I couldn't say so. There was a big red couch in the living room, which was right inside the front door. Reggie sat on the couch and I followed his lead. In front of us was a plain black coffee table littered with plates, a chip bag, and a couple of beer cans. There was an almost gag-inducing smell of cinnamony air freshener, as if someone had had a little too much fun spraying the aerosol can.

Reggie saw me looking at the chip bag, which I was considering using as a barf bag if the smell got to me.

"Umm," he said. "Can I get you something to eat? Or to drink?"

I shook my head. "No thanks. I just . . . Let me go ahead and tell you why I'm here. I've been talking to some people about Ethan. And I wanted to talk to you, too."

I didn't know what to do with my arms, so I folded them across my chest.

"Okay . . ." Reggie picked up the chip bag and glanced into it. "Like, what about Ethan?"

"Just, well . . ." I unfolded my arms, wondering if having them crossed made me look like I was cold, or haughty boss's daughter–ish. "If you don't mind talking about the night he died . . . how did he seem in those last few minutes you saw him? Like, right after the ride?"

Reggie hesitated, then scratched his elbow. "He seemed okay."

"I heard Lucas Andries saw him go into the bathroom right after everyone said goodbye outside the Laser Coaster."

"Hold on a sec." Reggie went into the kitchenette, opened the fridge, and took out a beer. He gazed absentmindedly into the fridge before asking, "You want one?"

"No thanks," I replied, trying not to sound uneasy.

"Okay, I just didn't want to be rude. So . . . ," he said as he sprawled on the couch again, opening the beer. "So . . . what was it again? You want to know if I saw Ethan come out of the bathroom?"

"Uh . . . yeah." It sounded weird now that he'd rephrased my question. "I haven't talked to Lucas yet, but I feel like that's the last moment anyone can account for. I kind of wonder if Ethan was getting sick in there or something."

Reggie stared at his beer thoughtfully before taking a sip. "I didn't see him come out. I was closing up the coaster, and then I was helping your dad with the normal shutdown—checking for stragglers, walking through the Food Zone, taking a look at the clipboards to make sure all the cooks did their shutoffs and safety checks, then checking the other locks besides the main gate's. Your dad was in his office, mostly."

"Checking for stragglers?" I hesitated. "Does that include bathrooms?"

"Yeah. Well, when there's time. I don't remember if I did

it that night. It's not usually that important, because what're the chances someone's hanging out in a dark bathroom after closing?"

I nodded. "It was supposed to be Winnie closing that night, wasn't it? But she canceled at the last minute? So you had to do it instead?"

Reggie took a long gulp of beer. "Yup."

"I wonder why," I said in what I hoped was a casual tone.

"She's been doing that a lot lately."

"Canceling at the last minute?"

"Well . . . canceling. Not always at the last minute. Two weeks in a row, Chris couldn't do one of his regular night shifts, and Winnie would cancel right after him. They've *both* been kind of flaking out on their shifts this summer."

Bingo, I thought. I'd been hoping someone would verify this, despite Jason's doubts about the topic. "So that night wasn't the first time?" I pressed.

Reggie looked bored as he took another sip. "No."

"Did Winnie say *why* she couldn't do that shift?"

Reggie shrugged. "Nope."

"Are you guys friends?" I asked.

I figured I should establish this before probing too much.

"Winnie's cool," Reggie said noncommittally.

That didn't give me much to go on, but it didn't seem safe to float my Chris-and-Winnie-sitting-in-a-tree idea, in any case. Maybe it was the reason for Winnie's absence that night. But even if it was, that wouldn't have been the *cause* of Ethan's death.

"I was thinking," I said slowly. "Is it at all possible that

Ethan got a concussion or something while he was on the Laser Coaster?"

Reggie was quiet for a minute before putting his beer down on the coffee table.

"A concussion?"

"Some of the kids who rode with him are saying things that make me think *maybe* he could've somehow hurt his head on the ride."

"Like what things?" Reggie asked softly.

"Subtle things," I said reluctantly, realizing that it might have been a big mistake to talk about my "theory" this early—and with this particular person.

"Like *what*?" Reggie demanded, leaning closer to me. He was taking this personally. Of *course* he was. He was in charge of the Laser Coaster that night. If Ethan had hurt himself on the ride, it could mean Reggie had done something wrong.

"He was feeling cold all of sudden, and he was talking about having déjà vu." Now that I said it, it seemed kind of vague. "A déjà vu feeling is sometimes a sign of concussion. I read that online."

Reggie shook his head. "If he mentioned that to the other kids, I didn't know about it. He wasn't dizzy or throwing up or anything. I know sometimes a concussion takes a while to creep up on you, but . . . I . . . don't know what to say. I've run that ride hundreds of times and no one's ever gotten hurt or hit their head. There's no way Ethan could have hit his head unless he unbuckled his seat belt."

"Is it *possible* that he did?" I asked quietly.

"No," Reggie said quickly. "I double-checked it before he rode—I remember checking his specifically."

There was a pained, almost twisted expression on his face that made me decide I needed to back away from the discussion.

"And he still had it on when he . . ." Reggie seemed to be struggling to keep from crying. "When he got to the end of the ride."

"Well, it's only a theory," I offered. "I guess I have a *few* theories. I guess we *all* do, you know? I mean, just this morning I was wondering why no one ever really seemed to ask if Ethan might have jumped off the bridge."

I could feel myself reddening at this admission. I'd blurted it out to change the subject. But Reggie didn't look shocked. He started nibbling on one of his long fingernails.

"Maybe because people don't usually think of kids with Down syndrome as being suicidal," he murmured.

"Is that fair or accurate, though, is what I was wondering."

I drew in a breath, immediately regretting how I'd arranged those words. I probably sounded cold. Regardless, Reggie really seemed to be considering his answer. He gnawed his nail harder. To my surprise, he bit the pointy tip off and spat it across the room. Then he frowned at the relatively bald index finger from which it had come.

"Probably not," he mumbled. "But . . . I don't think that was the case with Ethan."

"What makes you say that?" I said. It felt weird to be discussing this with someone I barely knew. But the fact that Reggie was a friend of my brother's made it seem vaguely okay. And I was glad that the horrified expression had slowly eased from his face.

"I don't know how much you talked to Ethan." Reggie closed the hand with the bitten nail and rested it in his lap. "But he had kind of a philosophical way of looking at things."

My phone buzzed and I pulled it halfway out of my purse to check who it was. Jason's name lit up the screen and I quickly read the text.

I didn't know if you were trying to tell me that Dad is starting to treat you like he used to treat Mom.

For a second, I felt the room flip-flop. The dingy beige carpet was on the ceiling and the cobweb-cornered white paint was on the floor. When it righted itself, I stood up, sliding the phone into the front bib pocket of my dress.

"Is there a bathroom I can use?" I asked.

"Sure. There," Reggie said, pointing.

"Thanks," I replied, running for it and closing the door behind me.

I stood at the sink and stared into the vanity mirror. It was a small medicine cabinet–type mirror. The kind someone in a movie opens and closes right before they gulp down a bottle of pills and almost die on their sad bathroom floor. I opened and closed it. Not so much because I was curious what was inside—though I noted there were only plastic razors and a bottle of Delsym—but to distract myself from my own reflection. My eyes kept coming back to my pink lipstick. The shade was Candy Peach. I'd started wearing it two years ago.

Back then, my dad and I worked together a lot at his french fry and hot dog cart at Fabuland. At the time, I didn't understand his sudden interest in the little food carts, which only brought in a fraction of the revenue that the Cork's Doughnut Dynasty shops did. Of course, I understand now that he was checking out Fabuland, deciding whether he wanted to buy it. I'd often wear jean shorts and a sparkly Cork's T-shirt while I served up the snacks and sodas. Dad would always tell me that the T-shirt looked cute on me. One day he said it while we were all eating breakfast together. Dad said it with kind of a wink and a shimmy, and Jason put down his spoon and stared at Dad. For the next minute or two, I tried to concentrate on my rice flakes and pretend not to notice Jason staring at our dad staring at me. I couldn't manage it. I put my bowl in the sink and stalked away, unsure which of them I was angry at.

It was around then that I stopped wearing shorts and T-shirts and started shopping for flowery summer dresses. I decided that I didn't need to advertise doughnuts with my boobs. And that a tasteful dress—like my dad's suits and ties—was a better advertisement for us all. In my fifteen-year-old head, it felt like a sophisticated sentiment. I added the lipstick sometime soon after that.

Now I stared into the mirror and thought of my dad's words. *You look in the mirror and you see that pretty little pink mouth. . . .*

The lipstick shade was all wrong and maybe always had been. But why had no one ever told me that? Why hadn't Morgan, at least?

I grabbed some toilet paper and wiped off the lipstick. Then I shut off the light and stood in the dark for a moment, deciding what to do next. I took out my phone and texted Dad:

Decided to stay with Mom tonight, fyi. See you at Fabuland in the morning.

He wrote back almost immediately: *K.*

I listened to my own breath for a few seconds before stepping out of the bathroom.

"Actually, can I have one of those beers?" I called to Reggie.

He started to stand. "Uh . . . what? Yeah, sure. I guess."

"Don't get up," I said quickly, walking across the kitchen to the fridge. "I can get it myself."

The fridge was full of beer. I snapped one open and drank as fast as I could. I'd only ever had beer at a couple of parties I'd gone to with Morgan, but I knew I didn't want to make this one last like I had with the others.

"What's going on?" Reggie was in the kitchen now, eyes wide like he'd never seen a girl in a sundress drink beer before.

"Nothing." I slammed the fridge shut. "Can we maybe sit outside?"

"Sure," Reggie said.

I led the way out the front door and sat on the tippy concrete square. Reggie stood a couple of feet away. Keeping his distance from me, just as Tim had. I took a cleansing breath, and then another gulp of beer.

"Slow down," Reggie said, hooking his thumbs in his front pockets. "Are you okay?"

"Of course," I said.

"How's your brother, by the way?"

I didn't feel like talking about Jason right now. I was angry at him without being certain why. Maybe for that moment two years ago at the breakfast table. Or maybe for texting me questions that made me want to down a beer.

"He's fine. Hey . . . what did you mean when you said Ethan was philosophical?"

Reggie cringed slightly. "I wasn't, like, making a joke about him."

"I know you weren't," I rushed to say. "I could tell. I just want to know what you meant."

Reggie stared at his sandals. Feeling awkward, I looked in the same direction. His feet were really dirty.

"Did you ever notice that aquarium hat he always wore?" Reggie asked after a moment.

"I remember he always wore the same navy-blue hat," I said. "Is that the one you're talking about?"

In fact, I had a picture of Ethan in my head, wearing that hat while he tried out the cotton candy machine.

"Yeah. Did you ever ask him about it?"

"No," I admitted.

"Well, if you had, he would have told you that it was from this one time he went to visit his great-aunt in Florida, when he was younger. She brought him to this aquarium, where she bought him that hat at the gift shop. He would tell you about all the cool jellyfish he saw, and the sea lion show. And then, if you were willing to listen long enough, he'd tell you that that aunt had since died, and that he would probably never go back to Florida because he didn't know anyone else who lived there. To Florida or that aquarium. 'I'll probably never be back there, but I have my memories of it,' he would say."

"He'd say that every time?" I asked, my heart sinking at the sincerity of it, wondering if he saw a lot of turtles on that trip.

"Yeah. I wondered at first if his mom had fed him that line or something. But you could tell by the way he took the hat off and looked at it that he meant it. And that's, you know, something a lot of us have trouble with. Appreciating something even when it's gone forever."

I considered asking Reggie if he really thought Ethan had accepted that he was never going back to Florida or whether he was trying to convince himself that he accepted it. But when I looked up and saw Reggie's face, I decided against it. He looked like he might cry if he tried to say anything else.

"I'm sorry," I said softly. I hadn't realized Ethan and Reggie were friends. Now it sounded like they were.

Reggie stayed by the door, leaning on it, and eventually closing his eyes. I finished my beer. I was feeling kind of floaty, and I didn't want the feeling to end. It would probably be easier to respond to Jason if I could keep feeling this way.

"Can I have another beer?" I asked.

Reggie opened his eyes but seemed to struggle to find a response.

"I'm sorry," I said, standing up and starting to walk away. "Never mind. Forget I asked you that. I'll leave you alone now. I'm sorry to have bothered you. My brother, uh . . . says hi."

He waved and thankfully went back into the apartment. I was

glad he didn't stay outside and watch me drive away. I needed a few minutes to chug some water, to make sure the fuzzy feeling had dissolved before I started the car.

When I finally took off, straining not to push the gas pedal too hard, it occurred to me that there was something similar about Reggie's face just now and Morgan's on the Ferris wheel. A kind of indecision, somewhere between devastation and disbelief.

I wished I could forget it. But that wasn't an option.

NINETEEN

My mother was asleep on the couch, collapsed under an afghan with CNN still on, when I got to her apartment. I turned down the air conditioner and the volume on the TV, then took off her glasses and set them on the tea table behind her. Without the glasses, she looked like her old self. Like the person who wore contacts and makeup and a whitening-strip smile.

Not wanting to go to bed just yet, I sat at my mother's feet, almost tripping over her laptop on the floor next to the couch. Sometimes she went on Facebook while she watched TV and posted inspirational quotes set against pictures of sunsets or kids blowing dandelions. I often wondered if she'd picked up the habit from her kindergarten-teacher buddies, who were presumably fairly positive people. Maybe more positive than she was, in her heart of hearts, these days.

I opened the laptop, minimized the web browser with her Facebook feed, and navigated to the files with our old family photos. Scrolling through, I found one of my favorite pictures of my dad and me. In it, I was riding on his shoulders right before a parade was about to start. I was wearing an American flag T-shirt and a pink tutu, eating popcorn out of a striped paper box, making Dad's hair all greasy with the artificial butter. I remembered that day really well. We had been visiting my mom's parents. I was about five. Before the parade we were picnicking in a park, and my parents were trying to get me to eat a ham sandwich my grandma had made. I hated ham and didn't want to eat it. So did Jason, but after Dad told him to *man up* he'd somehow managed to force his sandwich down. I, on the other hand, had no interest in *manning up*. I'd just finished filming a "sprinkle party" commercial a week or two earlier and was pretty enamored with my sparkly, princessy self. Dad had lectured me about eating what I'd been given. When he was a kid, he told me, he ate everything that was put in front of him and didn't complain. He threatened to not let me watch the parade if I didn't eat the sandwich. I stared at that sandwich for five minutes, then ten, while my dad eyed me, muttering under his breath. I took a small bite and his face softened. I put the sandwich down and stared at it some more. And then something magical happened. A German shepherd who for the past few minutes had been playing fetch with its owner careened over, casually snatched my sandwich up in its jaws, and ran away with it, chomping wildly.

Dad had stood up and yelled at the dog's owner for having her dog off its leash. But once she was out of earshot, my dad started laughing hysterically, telling me that I was the luckiest girl in the world.

You're like Cinderella and Snow White in the old cartoon movies, he said. *The animals all want to come to your rescue.* He bought me popcorn at the parade and lifted me onto his shoulders.

Mom's not in that picture, but there's a different one of her that day, where we're all standing together, posing by the car after the parade. She was wearing a lilac linen sundress that tied behind her neck. Her hair was all swept up to the back of her head in a bun, and she looked sophisticated and out of place framed by my cheap tutu, Jason's chocolate ice cream–stained shirt, and Dad's silly sunglasses slipping off his sweaty red face. She was squinting from the sun, but smiling wide all the same, showing off her perfect teeth and expertly applied coral lipstick. I looked over at Mom's sleeping form, watching her breathe. She didn't wear lipstick anymore.

I scrolled down to a picture from about a year later.

It was my seventh birthday, and we were all smiling. The cake was the biggest, sprinkliest thing you'd ever seen in your life— smooth fondant frosting, polka-dot ribbon, purple and pink sprinkles. Three tiers, as if I was getting married. Dad was grinning from beneath a fresh haircut and Mom was looking gorgeous in her indigo wrap dress—even though one arm was in a cast from when she slipped and fell on the ice that year. Jason was distracted by the size of the cake—staring at it instead of the camera. I studied his face for a moment, considering the question he and I had raised about being Dad's daughter versus his son. Jason had spent a lot of time trying to be Dad's right-hand man. But I didn't remember him ever getting a big birthday cake like mine.

"Mom?" I whispered. I wanted to show her the picture, to see what she remembered about that day. And to see what she might say about that year in general.

"Ivy?" My mom opened her eyes and pushed her feet against me, stretching. "What time is it?"

"About ten," I said. "You going to bed?"

"I think I'll stay here for a while." She closed her eyes again. "I'm going to try to stay up for the monologue."

"Mom, you're asleep," I reminded her.

"Yeah," she murmured, curling herself up tighter.

I glanced at the picture, then closed the laptop.

"Okay. Good night, then."

"Good night."

I got up from the couch and went to my room, looking at my phone once I shut my door.

An hour ago, Jason had texted, *Ivy? You there?*

I decided to text back an answer to his earlier question—about our dad treating me like he had our mom:

He doesn't yell at me the way he used to at her.

You're special to him right now, Jason replied. *That's why you don't get that shit.*

Mom used to be special to him, I wrote.

Until she wasn't, Jason wrote back.

I felt a hollow, almost sore feeling in my stomach as I considered how to reply.

Do you remember that night we slept in the cushion fort? I asked.

It took a few minutes for him to write back the word *Yes*.

Should we talk? I texted.

I prefer to type, he wrote back.

Probably a smart choice. We didn't ever talk about that stuff. It would maybe be too weird to start saying anything out loud. We'd just end up shutting down and hanging up.

Why didn't we come out of the fort all night?

Jason: *We built forts like that more than one time, so I'm not sure which night you're remembering.*

Me: *The night when you put that folk music on Mom's iPod and had me listen to it on repeat.*

Jason: *I did that on more than one night. Because I was worried about you hearing too many bad words. But there was only one night when we stayed in there until morning.*

Me: *Why did we do that?*

Jason: *We were afraid to come out because Mom left the house and didn't come back all night. That's why we slept there.*

I felt uneasy reading those words. Funny, you could live with a memory your whole life and not think much of it. But then once you forced yourself to step out of the age you were when you experienced it, you started to see it differently. To my seven-year-old brain it wasn't weird to spend a night in a cushion fort. It was kind of cool. But if a seven-year-old kid told me now—told seventeen-year-old me—that she'd done the same thing, I would think, *Wait, that doesn't sound right.*

Me: *We couldn't go to bed because Mom wasn't home?*

Jason: *I guess that was how I looked at it. They were yelling at each other, and she took off like she was scared of something. And if it was scary enough for her to leave and not come back, shouldn't we just stay put? That's how I looked at it at the time.*

Me: *But they let us bring a picnic into the fort, and decorate it with glitter and sprinkles.*

Jason: *No.*

Me: *Why do you say no?*

Jason: *You're funny.*

Me: *How am I funny?*

As soon as I typed it, I half knew the answer. I was "funny" because I was still kind of remembering it like I was seven.

Jason: *That wasn't decorations. They were throwing shit at each other. There was a big bag of party supplies in the living room. And a shipment of sprinkles. Somehow they ended up opening them and flinging them at each other.*

Me: *That's not how I remember it.*

It really wasn't. Of course I remembered our parents fighting other times. I just didn't remember that night being one of them. And yet I didn't find Jason's version terribly surprising. Numbing, maybe. But not surprising.

Jason: *Maybe because you were barely seven and had earbuds in. I was ten and didn't.*

Me: *What was that music that you would always play for me?*

Jason: *Mom's Shawn Colvin. The song called "Polaroids" that you always wanted me to repeat. Why are you asking about all this now?*

Good question. When I'd looked at the couch cushions on Dad's floor the night after the Ferris wheel incident, I'd felt an overwhelming desire to crawl beneath them and hide. I typed back, *I've just been thinking about it lately.*

Which was why I'd almost asked my mom about it. But it hadn't seemed possible when it came down to getting the actual words out. I gripped my phone hard as Jason's reply came in.

I try not to think about that stuff. I'm the biggest fucking snowflake cliché there is. Because you could say I find sprinkles triggering.

Do you ever write about that? I typed back quickly.

Jason: *Are you kidding?*

Me: *No.*

Jason: *No, I don't write about that. I write about memory sometimes, but only in a fictional way, usually. I try not to write autobiographical stuff. I think people would find me unsympathetic.*

Me: *And weren't you going to say more about the Yo-Yo?*

Jason: *Are you at home right now?*

Me: *Mom's.*

Jason: *Tomorrow. Go look at it in the daylight.*

Me: *I was just looking at it the other day and didn't notice anything.*

Jason: *Before I said anything about it?*

Me: *Yeah.*

Jason: *You weren't really looking, then. Look again.*

I sighed. It seemed like lately everyone had an assignment for me.

I put on my pajamas and turned out the light before typing back *Good night.*

211

TWENTY

My alarm didn't go off because I had forgotten to set it. And my mother hadn't woken me before she left for work. When I rolled over and grabbed my phone, I saw that it was 9:20. And then I saw that Jason had texted me more than an hour ago.

WTF?

DID YOU GO TO REGGIE'S LAST NIGHT AND TALK TO HIM?

I leapt out of bed, my heart pounding. Clearly, something bad had happened for Jason to be screaming at me like this.

Yes, why? I typed back, and forced myself to send with a shaking finger.

The phone began to buzz.

"Jason?" I said, picking up.

"Reggie overdosed last night." Jason was nearly yelling. "He's in the hospital."

"*What?* Is he okay? I mean, I just saw him."

212

"He's going to be okay. But his roommate thinks he did it on purpose."

It took me a moment to remember to breathe.

"What kind of drugs?" I asked.

I wasn't sure why it mattered. I just needed to ask *something*.

"That's the thing. It wasn't all, like, recreational drugs. He had old prescription painkillers lying around from when he had a broken bone a while back, and some Tylenol and booze. Reggie's an intelligent guy. He would've known that wasn't a smart combination."

"When?"

There wasn't a hell of a lot of *when* between when I'd visited him and this morning. I sat on the bed to steady myself.

"Last night. I don't know what time. Katy texted me that his roommate was posting updates, and I looked on Facebook and Twitter and there are threads about him. People sending their thoughts and prayers and whatever until it looked like he was going to be okay. Some people were starting to theorize about what the cause of it all was, but luckily somebody shut that down pretty quick."

"Oh," I said slowly, trying to swallow the rush of dread that I felt coming up my throat. "People were saying it was kind of about Ethan? I'm guessing?"

"Some. Yeah. But the thing is, Ivy . . . the story his roommate is telling is that some girl in a weird flowered dress came over, they talked for a little while outside, and then Reggie got really drunk after she left, and then he did this, up in his room. Good thing his roommate checked on him."

Weird flowered dress. I didn't really hear the words that followed those three.

"Is he still in the hospital?" I asked, my voice quavering as I thought of the locked doors of the ward Morgan had been in. Likely Reggie was behind them now. How many people was Fabuland going to send to that ward before we were done?

"Yeah. I'm not sure when he'll get out. I think the roommate was telling this around because he thought it was some kind of breakup that Reggie wasn't handling well."

We were both silent for a minute. I glanced around my room. The summer sunlight was slanting in, making a cheerful rhombus on my light-purple carpet.

"I assume he's got it slightly wrong . . . unless you haven't been honest with me about Reggie," Jason said.

"Uh-huh," I squeaked. I hated the girlish innocence of my room. Mom had set it up this way when she and Dad first got divorced, but she couldn't afford to change it now.

"I assume you made it to Reggie's place after I gave you his address?" Jason asked, his voice low.

"Uh-huh," I repeated, creeping to the kitchen. "He's wrong."

"Jesus," Jason muttered. "What did you guys *talk* about?"

"Ethan . . ." I opened the fridge and stared into it even though it felt like I might never eat again. "The night he died."

"What the fuck, Ivy?"

I sat on the cold kitchen floor and started to cry. Then I sniffled into the phone for a few minutes. Whenever I tried to recover my voice, I found I had nothing to say.

"I'm sorry," Jason said, sighing. "I shouldn't have said it like that."

"Please come home," I managed to say. "Without Morgan, I don't really have—"

"I can't. Not for the next couple of days, anyway."

"But what about for the big doughnut unveiling? Dad said he emailed you the date."

"He did, but—"

"Please come home for that, at least."

Jason hesitated. "I'll see what I can do."

"Yeah," I breathed. "Please."

"In the meantime . . . try to stay out of trouble, okay?"

"Okay," I whimpered. Even though I had no idea how to honor that advice. I'd never been someone who got into "trouble" before. I wasn't quite sure how it had happened so suddenly and so disastrously.

After we hung up, I dragged myself up and yanked on some old shorts and a T-shirt. Maybe if I dressed more like everyone else today, the *weird flowered dress* girl might be less identifiable to everyone who had read that social media rumor.

While I brushed my teeth, my reflection caught my eye for a moment.

You look in the mirror and you see that pretty little pink mouth of yours. But when you're at Fabuland, everything you say is amplified, whether you want it to be or not. People listen. People listen hard. Because you're my daughter.

I spat out the toothpaste and didn't bother to rinse. And I

215

didn't bother with a shower either—just grabbed my phone and purse and headed to Fabuland.

When I got there, I parked at the far side of the employee lot near the two rides my father had retired last summer. I got out of my car and walked around the Yo-Yo a couple of times, looking upward at its plum-purple beams, its white riding cars with red and yellow seats. There was nothing particularly noticeable about the ride except that it looked sort of sad and lonely here, away from the park, its lights off, pushed up against the trees. Did Jason maybe see the ride as a metaphor for himself, off on his own away from the frenzy of Fabuland, out of our father's favor? I snorted at the thought. Maybe that was how an English major looked at things.

I wondered why of all the rides in the park, these two were the ones that got eliminated when the four new kiddie rides took precedent. I wondered if Jason was part of the selection process. I didn't really want to talk to him again this morning, though. After the news about Reggie, I felt kind of small, and our discussion about this ride seemed insignificant.

Everything seemed insignificant, really. Was I supposed to go back to spinning cotton candy when I'd just maybe driven someone to try to kill himself? And why in the world had I brought up the notion of *Ethan jumping* to Reggie? Had I put an idea in his head that he'd carried through with when he was drunk enough later in the evening?

I stared up at both rides for a little while, trying to solve my brother's riddle, then remembering Morgan and me riding the Yo-Yo and wondering if I should bother texting her again.

I decided not to. I wished I was someone else. And I wished I could go home and burn all my floral summer dresses, for what that was worth. I was starting to picture it—me lighting a match, the flames rising from my newest baby-blue dress with the white eyelet trim—when my phone jumped with a text from my dad.

Good morning! I want to talk to you—got a different job for you today.

It was always something with Dad. The demands never stopped. But I would welcome almost any distraction from Reggie at this point. I slipped the phone into my pocket and hurried into the park.

A couple of minutes later, I found my dad on the lawn behind the east side pavilion. He was standing behind a large blow-up kiddie pool that had a big sheet draped over it propped up with a bunch of unlit tiki torches.

"Ivy!" he yelled when he saw me coming. "Take a look."

He was holding a large coffee in one hand and used the other to lift the sheet and reveal a giant mass of creamy-white dough almost as tall as me.

"It rose *so* well. *Look* at that thing."

I did. We both did. When I turned to him, he was still staring. The right side of his hair had collapsed over his face, oily and uncharacteristically limp.

"Have you been here *all night,* Dad?"

I wondered if he'd even heard about Reggie yet. But I didn't want to ruin his bright and ambitious mood.

"Yep. Oh, Ivy. Isn't this a thing of beauty?"

"Well . . . it's big," I said slowly.

"Yeah. Kinda looks like a big tit, actually. But not in a bad way."

"Mm-hmm," I said.

I took a long, slow breath. I taught myself to do this years ago. Let the comment pass, and don't feed it with a scowl, a protest, or even an eye roll. I had bigger things to worry about right now anyway.

"Can't wait to see it golden brown," Dad said. "All slathered with frosting."

"Do we have enough sprinkles?" I murmured.

"Don't you worry about *that*, honey. Shipment's coming today. Twenty pounds of sprinkles."

I made a note to myself to make a social media post about the arrival of so many sprinkles.

"Did you do this all yourself? Mix up the dough and shape the ball?" I asked.

"Chris helped at the start. But he's got something he needs to deal with. He left in the wee hours and might not be back until after the doughnut event."

"*What?*" I said in disbelief.

Dad was still gazing at the giant ball of dough. "Yep. Chris was a trouper all night with this thing, but he's got some personal issues, so I'm cutting him loose for a few days. He humored me last night, though, since the vats came in. We were here all night, mixing the dough, giving it time to rise. I *did* take a nap on the couch in my office for a while, so don't worry about me.

I'm all ready for another fabulous day at Fabuland. Although I probably stink. Do I stink, Ivy?"

He paused for a second to take a sip of coffee but didn't wait for an answer.

"So I was thinking about who I trust to take over the publicity for this event since Chris won't be available. And I'm thinking the only person who will do a good enough job for me is *you*."

"Oh. Okay. You mean the print media too? Newspapers and stuff? Not just Facebook and Instagram?"

Dad pushed the floppy side of his hair back behind his ear. "You got it, hon. All of it. It'll be good for college applications. You can say you were a publicity and marketing intern."

He waved at the giant ball of dough and continued.

"You can start in my office. Chris has a spreadsheet of his media contacts and the dates each of us has contacted them—to his knowledge, anyway. Sometimes I make spontaneous calls he doesn't know about, when inspiration hits. He's got most of the numbers and email addresses you'll need. Janelle at the *Herald* and Daniel at the *Gazette* are top of the list. I've got the number of the features desk chair at Channel Twelve News on speed dial in the contacts in my phone, if we decide to go that route."

"But . . . where do you want me to start?"

"Just look at the spreadsheet. Chris will have noted who he reached out to when and what kind of response he got. Use your judgment about which are the live ones, which ones you want to follow up on right now."

"Okay . . . but how should I explain myself? My job at the park? Aren't most of these people used to talking to a business contact who's . . . uh . . . an adult?"

Dad lifted the sheet again and touched the dough ball gently with his fingertips. "You're adult enough, Ivy. I trust you."

"But . . ."

He pulled the sheet back down with such force that it fell off the tiki torch on one side.

"Shit," he muttered, then turned to me. "No one's going to ask you how *old* you are. You carry yourself like a woman. You have for years."

I was silent. Dad took a gulp of coffee, then fiddled with the sheet, trying to throw the loose end back onto the tiki torch.

"Why don't you go to my office now and start your work? Julia Shaw is selling bagged cotton candy at the ice cream kiosk, and we'll put you back on the machine in the afternoon."

"It shouldn't take me long to update the media stuff." I hesitated, reluctant to go up to his office and spend the morning alone. "You need any help here?"

"No. John Wisniski is helping, and Carl Norton. And Winnie."

Winnie. No last name required. For some reason that irritated me. Why did Winnie get to do the fun stuff, while I was stuck in his office, calling media contacts who were probably tired of overenthusiastic Fabuland personnel calling about a giant pastry?

"Who's on carousel?" I asked.

"I've got it all covered, honey. We're going to try out the big frying vat right back here. Tim's going to cordon off this section so nobody can wander back here and hurt themselves, but people will be able to see the big dough ball being fried from a distance."

"Does everyone have safety gear? Isn't hot oil going to go splashing everywhere when you guys try to lower this thing into a giant vat of oil?"

"I've already thought of all that, okay? Of course we're not going to just toss it in there. What do you take me for?" Dad grinned. "We've got a whole plan, with the cherry picker and a net and a pulley and beekeeper suits."

I stood there for a moment, trying to determine if he was joking about the beekeeper suits. Or all of it.

"I'm going to snap a picture of your preparations," I said, pulling my phone out. "To post on social today."

"Great idea, Ivy."

Dad pulled the sheet off the tiki torch again and posed with a warm grin, his arms folded, one foot up on a small cooler that was sitting in the grass. The exuberance in his expression made me feel guilty that I couldn't muster anything close.

"Good one," I said, replacing my phone in my pocket.

"Go on ahead to the office now." Dad grabbed me by the elbow and pointed me in the direction of the administration building. "My laptop's open on my desk with Chris's spreadsheet."

* * *

First I took care of the social posts of Dad by his dough ball. I swiveled around in his office chair for a while, trying to decide on the perfect caption to convey my father's voice and enthusiasm.

Practice doughnut!! Can't wait to share the real thing with you all on Saturday, July 21!

I gazed at the words for a moment, deleted them, and then typed, *Kinda looks like a big tit, actually. But not in a bad way.*

I stared at those words the same way one stares over the side of a bridge or the railing of a long stairwell—with this weird, counterintuitive feeling that if you look too long, you might just get a rogue impulse to jump. I hit the Delete button quickly, before my index finger could get a chance at a similar impulse with the Return key.

We were up all night testing the perfect dough recipe, and it's coming out fabulous. Join us on Saturday, July 21, for our Super Doughnut unveiling!

I hit Return this time.

Then I checked Chris's spreadsheet. Based on his notes, it looked like he'd planned to follow up with Janelle at the *Herald.*

A secretary answered the number I called, saying, "*East County Herald,* how can I direct your call?"

"Is Janelle Schneider available, please?"

"What is this regarding?"

"An event at Fabuland," I said.

"And who shall I say is speaking?"

"My name is Ivy Cork." I swallowed self-consciously. "I'm filling in for our manager, who's been in contact with Janelle recently."

"I see. One moment, please."

While I waited, I studied the contact list a bit farther down.

Chris had Channel 12 News listed near the bottom, with an email address but no notes.

"Ma'am? Janelle is actually on the phone right now. She'll call you back. She knows the day and time of the special event, if that's what this call is about. And she will be sending someone. Were there additional details you wished to discuss?"

"Yes," I said. "I'll chat with her about those particulars when I get her return call. I'll give you my number. Our manager is unavailable right now, so I'll be the contact for the event."

After I'd given the secretary my number and thanked her, I got up from the desk.

I found it emotionally taxing, pretending I cared this deeply about a doughnut, willfully ignoring the obvious fact that these people were only humoring me. I needed a couple of minutes to breathe and replenish my intestinal fortitude before making another call.

I wandered over to the file cabinets and opened the one labeled *Rides*. I found a sea of colored plastic folders with alphabetized tabs: *All-Star. Boing-Boing. Cazam!* It didn't take me long to find *Yo-Yo* in the back.

The top piece of paper in the file had *New Hampshire Department of Safety* across the top. Below that it said *Tramway and Amusement Ride Division*.

The document was from the summer before last. So the ride had last been inspected under Mr. Moyer's ownership. Dad had taken the Yo-Yo out of the park sometime around the end of last summer, when he'd first started expanding the little kids' section.

I brought the Yo-Yo file to my dad's desk and looked at the minimal paperwork, which included a manufacturer description of the ride.

Manufacturer: Zumpro
Weight: 48 tons
Power: 125A 400V
Capacity: 24 riders
Mount Type: Portable or park
"The Yo-Yo" is built on a single trailer. A rotating hub with four gondolas that swing to a maximum height of 70 feet. It features over-the-shoulder safety restraints.

There wasn't really much information—it was a simple brochure, more of an advertisement than a technical document. It had a couple of color photos. A typed paper behind it showed that Mr. Moyer had purchased the ride four years before he'd sold Fabuland to Dad.

In the brochure photographs, the ride had neon yellow beams and red and yellow seats. I did a double take. This morning, I'd noticed that the ride was purple. Did the Yo-Yo come in different color options? I examined the brochure and didn't see anything about color choices.

I tried to remember what color it had been the one time I'd ridden it with Morgan and a few other friends. Of course, the memory was simply of terror—Morgan's good-natured screaming, my praying for an end from behind closed lids. It was a memory generally devoid of color and other visual details.

I picked up my phone.

Did the Yo-Yo used to be a different color? I typed, and sent the message to Jason.

As I returned the file to the cabinet, I heard the *vroom* sound of a text message coming in. It wasn't my phone, which was set to vibrate, but my dad's, which was just sitting on his desk. Of course he'd wanted to be unavailable while tending to his dough balls.

I glanced at the message that had come in.

Let me know if you need another set of those big tongs, someone had written.

Below that was another, earlier message that had come in the night before at 11:24. I knew I shouldn't be looking at my dad's texts, but two words in particular—the first words of that text—caught my eye. *Your daughter.*

I pressed the home screen again so it lit up for longer, then leaned closer to the phone and read the whole message.

Your daughter came to my place tonight and was asking me questions. I didn't know what to say. Did you know she was coming?

Your daughter. Me. I didn't recognize the number. I'd talked to three people last night—my mom, Jason, and Reggie. It wasn't my mom's number, and it was unlikely she'd write him a message referring to me as "your daughter." And of course it wasn't from Jason.

I picked up the phone and looked at the number, comparing it to the number for Reggie that Jason had given me. It was a match.

I could hear my heart in my ears now. I took a breath.

A text buzzed on my phone.

Yup, Jason had written.

I paced the floor of the office. I sat down on the couch for a second, then stood up again. As I did so, I caught a glimpse of myself in the shortening fun-house mirror. There I was, all squished and squat.

I always knew you wanted to stay small.

I stared at my shortened self and considered those words. I wasn't sure my father had ever said them. I just *thought* them when I looked in this mirror.

Wearing plain summer clothes now, I looked not only shorter but also younger. Or . . . actually . . . older. I wasn't sure. I was confused. My heart was beating too hard for me to decide.

And in any case, I had some questions for my father, and I intended to ask them. I pocketed my phone and ran down the office stairs.

TWENTY-ONE

Someone had delivered three beekeeper suits. Dad was trying on yellow beekeeper gloves. Almost everyone else on the lawn behind the pavilion was smiling and laughing. Except Winnie, who was connecting all the cables running from the pavilion to the vat on the lawn. She looked bored.

"Dad, I need to talk to you," I said in a low voice. I knew it was going to be difficult to pull him away from this miniature circus of his own making.

"Can't now, sweetheart." Dad was looking at his gloved hands. "We're just about to heat up the oil."

Winnie put one hand on her hip, watching me from several yards away. Her posture accentuated the ample curve of her chest—which somehow scared me more than her determined stare.

"It's pretty serious," I said quietly.

Dad looked up. "Something with one of the media contacts?"

"Umm, no. Can you just . . . come to the office for a sec?"

"Let's talk in the pavilion and we'll see if I need to come to the office."

I nodded, and once we were under the shade of the pavilion, I showed Dad his phone.

"What's this about?" I asked.

Dad glanced at the phone, then tried to grab it from me with his gloved hands. He missed several times, then yanked the gloves off. "What were you doing reading my text messages?"

"Dad—that's not really the point. Why would Reggie have written you last night?"

He stuck the gloves under his arm and snatched his phone away. "I don't know. Beats me. I haven't been on my phone all night."

"Why would he tell you I came to see him? Do you know what *happened* last night? Why would—"

"Ivy, the bottom line is that you shouldn't have been snooping."

That didn't seem like the bottom line to me at all. It didn't seem like my dad knew what had happened to Reggie, but I didn't want to talk about it within earshot of Winnie and the others.

"I wasn't," I said. "You're the one who made me your press secretary. The phone made a noise and I looked at it. And you yourself said your Channel 12 News contact was in there."

"You *were* snooping." Dad's face was red. "And I *trust* you not to do things like that. You're one of the few people I trust that way. I hope you're not about to make me regret it."

"I need you to tell me what this is about," I insisted, ignoring the smarter voice in my head saying, *Shut up, Ivy. Shut up right* now.

"I'm not having this conversation. If you can't figure out how to respect my privacy, then we're going to have a problem. And I don't need any more problems right now. Can't you see that I have a lot going on?"

I opened my mouth. I had words, but none of them came out. Instead, I sucked in a breath and held it.

"We'll talk later," Dad said through his teeth. "Not in front of these folks. Go back to the office."

I folded my arms. I gazed beyond him. I saw Winnie was staring at us, openmouthed. I wondered if she'd heard about Reggie and the *girl in the weird flowered dress.* Neither of the two other guys was watching us, at least. One was wearing a full beekeeper suit and talking in a loud alien voice while the other laughed.

"Go *back* to the office!" Dad said, his voice becoming a yell.

I considered standing my ground. But I was afraid he would yell louder and louder until I left.

So I turned and walked away, feeling Winnie's gaze on me but trying not to look rattled.

◆ ◆ ◆

I sprawled on the office couch and texted Jason.

Dad just blew up at me. This doughnut thing is getting to him.

Jason didn't write back. I kept typing anyway.

I think Dad thinks Winnie is more competent than both of us, I typed, and set the phone on my stomach while I closed my eyes.

A couple of minutes later, my phone buzzed.

Winnie Malloy?

Do we know any other Winnies? I was typing furiously now, encouraged by his unexpected response. *Yes, Winnie the queen of the carousel. Mistress of the fried dough.*

Jason came right back with: *Dad just doesn't want you to get any grease burns. And he knows how much you like the cotton candy machine. Do you really care about any of this? Next year you'll be headed to college. And if you're smart, you'll find a summer job somewhere else, like me.*

I couldn't help rolling my eyes before typing, *Don't you ever feel bad that you turn your nose up at Fabuland, when it's paying for your fancy college?*

Jason's reply was immediate: *I'm not turning my nose up.*

Yes you are, I shot back.

After a minute or two, Jason's response appeared.

Fine, maybe a little. But what I want to know is why Winnie just came up again. Did you hear something about her? Did she say something to you?

Something like what? I typed.

No reply. A sharp *tweeeeet* sounded from outside. I sat up and glanced out the window. A lifeguard named Jayna was on duty at the waterslides. She was standing and waving her arms at someone. Then she sat down and spat the whistle casually out of her mouth.

I decided to call Jason. And he actually picked up.

"Hey," he said. "I only have a few minutes. Did it have something to do with Winnie, when you said that thing about being his daughter?"

Well, *that* was an interesting theory. Did Jason think I felt like an inadequate daughter in Winnie's cool and competent presence? Did he feel the same way when he was with Dad and Chris? I decided not to ask. Instead, I watched Jayna for a moment. She took a drink from a water bottle, then folded her hands behind her head.

"Not really," I said.

"Oh. Okay." Jason sounded tired. "Then why are we talking again?"

"Let's talk about the Yo-Yo," I offered. "So, it used to be a different color?"

"Yeah." Jason paused for a moment. "We painted the two rides at the end of last summer. Tim Malloy and Ben the Rotor Lord painted the Scream. I painted the Yo-Yo."

"Even the parts way up high?"

"Even those."

"All by yourself?"

"Yeah. I mean, Tim helped me get the cherry picker in the right position. But I was the only person doing the actual painting."

"Huh," I said, grateful I'd never been given such a task.

Score one for Jason. Score one for the son having it harder than the daughter. Even if Jason wasn't afraid of heights like me.

"Who decided those would be the rides that would go?"

"Dad and Chris."

"Why paint them?" I asked.

231

"Dad said, *We want to make them look snazzy.* He said it was customary to tidy up the ride before selling it."

"Ivy?"

I jumped. Dad was in the doorway.

"I wanted to talk to you, honey," he said. "Now that we've had a little while to cool off."

"I've gotta go, sorry," I muttered into the phone, ending the call. I sat up straighter, crossing my feet.

"Ivy. I want to clarify something." Dad sat at his desk, leaning back in the swivel chair just slightly.

"Yeah?"

"I wish you hadn't snooped like that." He made a clucking noise and shook his head. "It's really disrespectful, like I was saying. And I like to think you're a respectful person."

"Uh-huh."

I liked to think so too.

"But I'm going to give you an explanation." Dad opened a desk drawer and took out a package of peanuts. "I'm not sure you *deserve* one, but since you're my right-hand woman, you're going to get one."

Dad opened the bag and threw a handful of peanuts in his mouth.

"Okay," I said, trying not to let my mind linger too much on the word *woman.*

"Reggie has been struggling," Dad said. "I don't know if you heard about what happened last night, but he was struggling before that. I can't say that I'm surprised, although I *am* deeply sorry."

232

"Struggling . . . how?" I asked. I hoped it wasn't a stupid question.

"He was . . . you know . . . upset." Another handful of peanuts. "He's been struggling since Ethan died. Like, grieving. Depressed. He hasn't been up for working. But I feel for the kid, you know? So I told him to take as much time as he needed. With pay."

I stared at my dad. He licked salt off a couple of his fingertips.

"With *pay*?" I repeated.

"Yes, hon." Dad peered into the snack pack and picked out what I had to assume was a particularly choice-looking peanut. "There are things you don't know about being a boss, Ivy. When you manage people, sometimes you make a judgment call, things like that. Quietly. Without making a thing of it. Like I'm doing for Chris. I'm giving him a few weeks to himself with pay. Then we'll see where we are."

I sat up straighter. "What's going on with Chris, Dad?"

Dad tipped his head back and poured several peanuts into it. "His wife. She's got cancer."

"*What?* Why didn't you tell me? What kind of cancer? Is she going to be okay?"

"I hope so. We all hope so." Dad chewed the peanuts heartily. "Uh, it's colon cancer, I think. Or . . . no. Cervical? One of those. It began with C, anyway. Either way, at least they caught it pretty early. But she's in the hospital right now."

"But . . ." I studied Dad's shiny red peanut package, finding its presence during this conversation particularly distracting. "Why didn't you tell me earlier?"

"Because you're not the boss, Ivy. Remember? *I* am."

I thought about all this. It wasn't surprising, really. Dad gave money to lots of different people for different reasons. There was Ethan's family and his funeral expenses, of course. And a year ago, he had helped a local family fund reconstruction of part of their house to accommodate a wheelchair ramp, an extra bathroom, and living space for their son—once a Doughnut Dynasty employee, years before—who'd been in a car accident that had left him partially paralyzed. And then there were all Dad's donations to the Boy Scouts and the Special Olympics.

This was a little different, though. There were no newspaper articles or special plaques he'd be getting for helping Reggie Wiggins or Poor Chris.

"That's nice of you," I murmured. And it *was*. I wished my dad showed more of this side of himself to other people. The little hidden kindnesses that I knew so well.

"You want some peanuts, honey?"

"No thanks."

My father tipped backward in his chair and studied me. "You're so much like me, Ivy. I mean, I've always known that. But I can really see it right here, right now."

I looked down at my old jean shorts and pink T-shirt with the collar cut off. I couldn't remember if I had brushed my hair this morning. Feeling weird about both of these things, I stared at my sandals, hoping he'd look away.

"I'd have done the same thing, in your position," Dad continued. "You see a text like that, you start to wonder. You don't take bullshit from anyone."

234

I didn't look up but tried to smile.

"Well . . . why would I?" I murmured.

Dad laughed. "Exactly. Did I tell you about the time we had a spy come into one of our sprinkle parties at the Goffsbridge shop?"

"No," I replied, holding in a sigh.

"Oh. Well, it was quite a few years back. See, there was this young man at one of the kids' parties. And I saw him taking pictures on his phone. There was just something about him . . . didn't feel like he belonged there. I went up to the mom of the birthday girl, and I said, *Do you know this guy? Did you invite him?* And the mom says no. So I confront the guy, and he tells me that he's got a daughter who would love a party like this, so he came in to take a couple of pictures to show his wife. Now, the guy doesn't have a wedding ring on. So his wife? Come on. The guy was a squirt, he didn't seem old enough to have a kid. I chased him into the back parking lot and told him to get lost. I gave him a quick punch in the gut to show him I meant it. And he hobbled off to his car. I'm pretty sure he was from Snowy's Ice Cream Shop, because lo and behold, a month or two later, they were having 'build-a-sundae' parties that bore a suspicious resemblance to my sprinkle parties. Not as good, but the same idea."

"I don't know, Dad. He might not have been a *spy*. He could've been some kind of a . . ." I hesitated. "Kind of like a perv."

The word felt weird on my lips. Especially in front of Dad. We didn't talk about stuff like that generally.

"Well, sure," Dad offered. "But either way, the point is I can always sniff out when someone thinks they can put something over on me. And I think you can too. I think you get that from me."

"Well, I never heard that story before," I lied. He'd told it to me a few times over the years, but he sometimes got mad when you pointed out that he'd repeated himself.

"Now you know, honey. And you know what else I like about you? Not just that you don't take any bullshit from anyone. That's not the only thing."

I didn't reply. It would seem a little egotistical, a little leading, to say *What else?* like I did when I was a kid.

"You've got good survival instincts."

"You think so?" He'd never said that before.

"Don't think I've never noticed that you hardly ever go on the rides."

"Yeah, well . . ."

"Instincts." He pointed to his head. "Survival over thrills."

"I just don't find the rides thrilling. It has nothing to do with survival."

"Sure, honey. You might look at it that way. But I've known you since the day you were born, and you know how to take care of *yourself*."

He didn't wait for a reply. He tossed the empty peanut package in his desk drawer and got up. "I guess I'd better get back to that dough ball."

"You guys just frying the one?"

"For now. If it goes well, we'll fry a whole bunch more this afternoon and do a full practice-run doughnut after closing to-night."

"Sounds exciting," I said.

"It *is,* Ivy. I'm glad you said that. Look. If you've tended to the press contacts, you can probably go back to cotton candy."

"You sure you don't want help with the big doughnut?" I asked.

"I don't want you to get hurt. You can help us when the real one rolls around. Ha! Get it?"

"Naturally," I said.

"Good deal." Dad grinned, and then I turned toward the stairs.

TWENTY-TWO

The Rotor was in full spin when I walked by it. Ben was watching the riders from his little perch above it all. I stepped up there with him, keeping a few feet between us but watching alongside him for a couple of minutes. I wondered what it was like to see this all day, every day—people swirling around and around in a big tin can.

An older man was hooting wildly inside the cylinder.

A girl was yelling, "Hold on to your pancakes!" and giggling.

That's one thing I've always liked about the ride—people are more often laughing than screaming.

"I've got a wedgie!" some kid yelled.

Ben turned to me. "Almost every day, someone announces the status of their underwear."

Then he said into the microphone, "For those of you with your knees up, please lower them now. Lower them, so as I slow the ride, you can slide more easily to the floor. Thank you."

The ride came to a stop. As everyone was filing out, Ben said, "Did you want to talk about something, my friend?"

"Umm . . . yeah, I think so," I said.

It *felt* like I wanted to talk about something. I just wasn't sure what. I knew I didn't want to spin cotton candy, and I knew I didn't want to be alone anymore. I cast about in my head for something to say.

"Did you and Tim and my brother paint some rides last summer?" was what I came up with.

"Uh . . . yeah. We did." Ben shrugged. "Why? Your dad thinking of selling some more rides?"

"He didn't ever actually sell the ones from last year," I pointed out.

"Oh. Yeah. I guess you're right. Just trying to figure out why you were asking."

Ben glanced at the small group of kids—tweens, by the look of them—queuing up for the next spin. He was waiting for me to get to the point.

"U-umm . . . ," I stammered.

Ben tilted his head quizzically to one side for a moment, then reached for the microphone.

"Just a ten-minute wait before we load up the next ride, folks," he said into the mic. "Sorry for any inconvenience."

The kids who'd been waiting huddled, chatted for a moment, and then headed toward the Starship 360. I noticed one of the kids, with gelled hair and a Red Bull T-shirt, straggling behind. Poor kid. He didn't want to have to go upside down. I could tell.

"You didn't need to do that," I said.

"This way you won't be rushed. What's up? It seems like there's something else."

Yes, other things were up. But I couldn't very well say *Did you hear about me and Reggie? Do you think it was me that almost put him over the edge? Do you hate me?*

"Did anything weird happen while you were painting the rides?" I asked instead.

"Anything weird? Like did I paint myself red and pretend to be a lobster?"

"I don't know." I chuckled at the image, in spite of myself. "Just wondering if anything out of the ordinary happened when you guys were doing it."

While I waited for an answer, I watched the Red Bull kid part ways with his friends and go into the bathroom block. Good save, kid. *Don't wait for me,* I'll bet he said to them.

"Mmm . . . no." Ben's mouth contorted quizzically as he thought about this. "More generally, I thought it was weird that Chris and your dad were getting rid of the Yo-Yo. I mean, the Scream isn't that popular, so that kind of made sense. But the Yo-Yo still seemed to have a decent following. But then, executive decisions have always been beyond me."

"It might not have been exactly *executive*," I said slowly, thinking that my dad might have simply decided he didn't like the name or the look of the ride. That was just the way he was sometimes.

"Well . . . the kiddie rides that replaced them seem to be a hit, so *someone* knew what they were doing," Ben offered.

"Except that the sale of those rides never happened," I pointed out again. I wondered, for the first time, *why* this was the case.

"I'd be surprised if anyone wanted the Scream." Ben looked thoughtful for a moment. And in that moment, I noticed that his eyes were the color of hot cocoa. "That's a ride of a different era, I think."

"A traveling fair ride company would probably buy it," I said. "Just maybe not a newer amusement park."

I thought of what my dad had said on the recording, about Jason costing him a lot of money. Had he charged Jason with the grown-up task of selling the rides—as he was doing with me now with the press contacts—and Jason had dropped the ball? But why hadn't my dad sold them himself after Jason had gone, or had Chris do it?

"Makes sense," Ben offered. "But I don't know. This is all out of my wheelhouse."

"So the Yo-Yo used to be yellow and was painted purple. And the Scream used to be red but was painted . . ." I looked at him with a question on my face.

"Red. The same color. Just touched it up to be a little brighter."

"But why was the Yo-Yo painted a different color, then?"

Ben shrugged again. "Search me. Ask the executives."

He was right. My dad was available for asking. *If* he could remember where that impulse had come from. Sometimes he didn't have a great memory for details. Either way, I had a feeling it had to do with a fire sale on red and purple paint somewhere.

"I guess I will," I murmured.

Ben gazed at me for a moment, then at the Rotor controls.

"Was there . . . anything else you wanted to ask me, Ivy?"

"No. Sorry to hold things up."

"I think I need to get this next batch of Rotorists spinning."

"I get it," I said. "Of course."

I looked at the short line of people about to get on the ride.

"I think I'll join them," I said. "For old times' sake."

"Yeah?" Ben smiled. "You're gonna go for a spin?"

"Uh-huh," I said. I hopped off the metal platform and got in the back of the line.

Ben gave me a questioning sort of look when he let me on with the herd of kids and a couple of accompanying grown-ups. I just shrugged. I didn't understand the desire myself—the desire to be spun silly at this particular moment. I had a lot to think about. Maybe the Rotor could shake up the contents of my brain and bring something new to the top.

Ben went through the usual announcements: "Heads and backs flat against the wall, please. Feet apart. If you feel sick during the ride or for any other reason you need the ride to be stopped, please yell 'Stop.' Enjoy the ride, folks."

I pulled my shorts down as far as they would go on my hips, glad I hadn't worn a dress today. As the ride started spinning, I stared at my knees. When I felt ready, I lifted my gaze over the top of the ride, where people could stand and look down. You don't realize how fast you're going until you look up. I watched the heads of the spectators swirl. I was surprised to find the ride easier to stomach than I remembered.

Like Ben had pointed out a few days ago, spinning is easy. You just go around and around. You don't have to see anything upside down or sideways. You don't have to see the sky trade places with the earth. I felt silly as the ride slowed to a stop. Of course I wasn't going to learn or think anything new spinning around like that. But I hadn't wanted to go back to the cotton candy machine just yet. Where there'd be, admittedly, just more spinning. And staring into a slightly smaller tin can. It occurred to me that Ben and I spent our days in a similar way. I wondered if he was as sick of it as I was.

When I got off the ride, my feet felt a little funny on solid ground. But only for a moment. I turned to wave at Ben, but he didn't see me.

* * *

I sat behind the cotton candy machine and watched people stroll by. It was almost noon, when cotton candy appetites are usually at a lull. They tend to pick up at one-thirty or two.

I tried calling Jason back but didn't get an answer. A few minutes later, he texted me:

In class now. We can talk more tonight if you want.

I drummed my hands nervously on the side of the machine. I was going stir-crazy waiting for customers—waiting for distraction from all my issues and inadequacies. It felt like I should've known how badly Reggie had been struggling and that Chris's wife was sick. These things my father had told me made me feel incredibly naive and childish.

What's your problem? my brain kept saying. *Do you want to stay small?*

I grabbed a carton of floss sugar and studied it. Every word. *Super Floss Sugar! Makes 70–75 Cones.* Beneath the words was a picture of a clown with a bubble coming out of his big, happy red mouth, saying *Yummy yum!* There was a Shakespearean sort of ruff around his neck, a yellow daisy springing from his tiny hat. I wondered when the packaging was designed. In the '50s?

Clowns are often all about having something comically large or small. Giant feet. A teensy car. Big round nose. Tiny bike. I'd never understood why any of it was supposed to be funny. Was there something wrong with me? I suspected the answer was yes.

And I also suspected someone was standing behind me. I could feel it. I whirled around.

There was Lucas Andries, staring at me through his overgrown black swoop of bangs. The last of the riders who'd been with Ethan "that night." The one I hadn't talked to yet. Possibly intentionally, because my brother had implied he was shady.

"Hey," he said flatly. "I heard you wanted to talk to me."

I couldn't tell if there was a bit of a threat in that statement. I felt tiny seated in the shadow of his six-foot-plus frame. Even if his limbs were lanky, his joints knobby. When he smiled, Lucas kind of reminded me of Woody in the Toy Story movies.

But he wasn't smiling now.

"Who said that?" I asked.

"Anna," he replied. "Of course."

"Oh," I said noncommittally.

"*So?*" He sounded impatient.

"Well . . . I *did* want to ask you a couple of things, but . . ." I trailed off with a shrug.

Asking questions had gotten me into trouble. I didn't want to make things worse.

As seriously as I took my promise to Morgan, I was beginning to wonder if it was time to give it up. Someone else had broken down and gone to the hospital, and we were none the wiser about the sparkle scorpion. Maybe we both needed to face some sad realities: Morgan, that there was no knowable explanation for her finding Ethan's paperweight where she did, and me, that I was never really going to crack the secret of Ethan's fall. Or get my best friend back.

"She said you were surprised to hear that I saw Ethan go into the bathroom," Lucas pressed.

"Uh . . . no, I wasn't surprised. I just . . . She's the first one who ever mentioned that."

"Well, it's *true*. And you know what? If I had known he was gonna walk home, I'd have offered to drive him." Lucas pushed his hair out of his eyes and sighed. "*Really,* I would've."

"I know . . . ," I said carefully. "I'm sure all of us would have."

"You want to know one of the last things he said to me?" Lucas demanded, leaning in closer.

I hesitated. Judging from his pained expression, he *wanted* to tell me.

"Yes," I murmured. "I do."

"He said, *I'm pretty sure you farted. Because I know it wasn't me.*" Lucas made a sputtering noise, shaking his head.

I stood there speechless, because it seemed like Lucas was laughing.

"He and I sat next to each other on the ride." Lucas talked so fast and was so close a tiny drop of his spit hit me in the eyebrow. "And when it was over, when we were unbuckling our seat belts,

245

he was like, *Did you poop your pants 'cause you were so scared up there?* And I was like, *No, dude . . . did you?* He was all like, *Well, then you farted, at least, 'cause I could smell it up there.*"

Lucas's face was red. And I could see he was actually crying a little bit too. I glanced down at the clown carton because it was painful to watch. And because I didn't want Lucas to feel like he was being stared at.

"And that's what we were talking about when we got off the ride. Whether or not I farted. Which I hadn't, by the way."

"Okay," I said. I felt my hands pull themselves into fists, resisting the urge to reach up and wipe my eyebrow.

"And then he tried to get us all to go on again. And then he said, *I'm pretty sure you farted. Because I know it wasn't me.* And he went into the bathroom. And I guess Anna and Briony were too busy talking to see him. But *I* did.

"And my theory is that he was in there a while, till almost everyone was gone. And maybe that means he was kinda sick. Maybe he was throwing up, who knows? And then he tried his locker, and by then it was dark and he took off by himself. But that's what gets me. Maybe he *was* sick from the ride, or something. And that's maybe why he fell."

Lucas sighed, grabbed a napkin from my cart, and wiped his eyes.

"I'm so sorry," I said.

Lucas was silent, and I considered what else he might need me to say.

"I believe you," I offered.

"Thanks," he said.

"Do you want any cotton candy?" I asked. "It's on me."

"Sure." He sniffled. And I wondered if he had heard about Reggie. It seemed like maybe he hadn't.

As I twisted the cone for him, I told him what Ethan had said about me being a witch playing with cobwebs.

"That was very astute of him," Lucas said, taking the cone from me and staring at it.

I had a feeling he wasn't going to eat much of the candy. Which was fine. It was all air and empty calories anyway.

But he thanked me. And as he walked away, I decided not to read too much into the *astute* comment. I'm a lot of weird things to a lot of different people. And at least Lucas had been willing to come up and talk to me.

After he'd gone, I contemplated the *Yummy yum* clown for a few minutes more—and then slowly, uneasily took out my phone and Googled *déjà vu strong smell cold feeling*.

The first handful of hits came up:

Déjà vu weird smell—Epilepsy Foundation

Déjà vu—Epilepsy Foundation

Temporal lobe seizure—symptoms and causes—
    Mayo Clinic

People with epilepsy describe how they feel just
    before seizure

Symptoms of temporal lobe seizures—WebMD

Epilepsy? Now, that was an avenue I hadn't expected to open up. Ethan had worked for Doughnut Dynasty for years before he switched to Fabuland. My dad and his Dynasty manager would've known if Ethan was epileptic.

Still, maybe if I narrowed the search, something else would come up that applied to Ethan. Concussion, maybe, like I'd thought before?

I held my breath. *Maybe you need to stop asking questions.* Hadn't I just been telling myself that a half hour ago? *Maybe you stop here.*

But at the same time, I thought about how unusually protective Katy said Ethan's family had been lately. I curled my finger and started to click on the first site that had come up.

"Hey there!"

I gasped and dropped my phone, then looked up to see Ben standing beside me.

"Aw . . . ," Ben said, picking up my phone from the ground. The screen was cracked. "That was my fault."

"No it wasn't."

"I feel *terrible.*"

"Don't." I hurried to grab the phone from him. "Um, did you want cotton candy?"

"I was actually gonna ask you if you were having lunch soon?"

"Uh . . . what?"

"Can you break for lunch? You seemed like you wanted to talk more."

I wasn't sure if I should be touched by this offer or worried that he'd seen what I'd been searching for on my phone.

"Oh. Uh . . . sure. I guess."

"Well, I don't want to twist your arm."

"I've never liked that expression," I said absently. "But sure. Yeah. I'd like to."

We made our way to the Food Zone, and Ben ordered a pizza slice while I unpacked my yogurt and veggies from home.

"What do you do when it's not Fabuland season?" I asked him before any awkward silence had a chance to settle in.

He seemed to brighten at the question.

"I teach skiing in the winter. And work as a waiter at the same ski lodge where I teach. And I ski, of course. Sometimes I take classes at the community college."

This was a surprise. He'd never mentioned school before. Not to me, anyway.

"Are you trying to get a degree?"

"Not necessarily. We'll see. I only take one class at a time. They're expensive, and I have a short attention span. What do *you* do when it's not Fabuland season?" he asked.

I finished crunching on a red pepper stick, and hoped chewed-up bits of it weren't stuck on my tongue.

"I go to Danville High School."

"Well, I figured that. What else?"

I couldn't think of anything I did that could compete with hanging out in the mountains skiing for most of the year, in terms of casual coolness. I'd played the violin for a while but wasn't very good at it.

"I hang out with Morgan," I said. "At least, I used to."

"Not anymore?"

"She needs some time to herself, I guess." I tried not to mumble as I said this. And I chose not to mention the whole thing about her possibly switching schools—because saying it out loud might make it closer to reality.

Ben stretched, considering this.

"Everybody needs that sometimes," he offered.

"Yeah, sure. I don't know."

I didn't want him to ask again what I did outside of Fabuland. Homework and JV field hockey just didn't seem like good enough answers.

I hesitated. "Why don't you work up in the mountains in the summer, too?"

"I used to come here and work for Mr. Moyer and stay with my uncle, who knew him. Summers, starting when I was sixteen. It's a bad habit at this point." He paused. "I mean . . ."

"Never mind," I said. "I'm not offended.

"How old are you?" I blurted, since I'd been wondering for a long time.

Ben took a moment to finish his pizza crust before answering. "I'm twenty."

"Oh," I said.

Ben wiped his face with a napkin but missed a gob of cheese on his chin.

"You sound surprised to hear that," he said.

"You seem . . . older."

"I do?"

I tried not to look at the cheese. "Yeah."

But then I felt like I'd said the wrong thing. I wasn't sure if seeming older was a compliment. I wasn't sure if my question about his age might be interpreted as my assessing his viability as a romantic interest. Which was kind of mortifying. Especially since my question kind of *was*.

"Did you know Ethan Lavoie at all?" I asked, since at least that was a topic I was getting used to discussing these days.

"Not that much. I mean, he was a nice kid, of course."

I noticed the *of course*. It seemed like a weird thing to add, if you were giving a genuine answer.

"Someone told me recently they thought he was kind of philosophical," I said, deliberately avoiding using Reggie's name.

"Huh. I would never have used that word, but maybe I didn't know him well enough. What I remember about him was how much he seemed to know about music." Ben pointed an index finger upward. "You hear this stuff they pipe into the Food Zone? I'm sure you know it's on a loop—the same songs over and over again."

"It's a playlist Chris created. He worked on it for a couple of weeks to make sure only the cleanest and happiest possible songs get played." At that moment, an old '90s song called "Steal My Sunshine" was playing. Chris had been partial to songs with the word *sunshine* in them.

"Okay," Ben said. "Well, whatever it is, Ethan knew lots of the songs really well. He'd be like, 'Wait for it . . . wait for it . . . they're about to get to the crescendo.' He was into crescendos."

As Ben was saying this, I noticed that Zach Crenshaw was staring at us from behind the Pizza to the Rescue counter.

"That's funny." I tried to refocus my attention on Ben. "I don't remember that."

"Or maybe he thought *I* was into crescendos. Hard to know.

251

The first time he said it, I guess I was kind of encouraging him, like, *Yeah, yeah, that crescendo is really good.* And then after that we were, like, crescendo buddies. I hope I was interacting with him as sincerely as I could. Sometimes, thinking about it after the fact . . . I don't know."

Ben drummed his paper plate with the two burned remaining pieces of his pizza crust. "Did he ever ask you when your birthday was?"

"Yeah, that was interesting, his memory for that," I admitted. "Kind of amazing, actually."

Ben sighed. "It's rough. I really feel for the family. I don't know his mom. I've never met her. But it's a lot for Tim and Winnie to deal with, I'm sure."

I was quiet. The topic of Winnie seemed to paralyze me more and more each time her name came up.

"They were dealing with a lot before Ethan even died," Ben continued.

"Yeah?" I squeaked, unsure how eager I should be to hear more.

"They were both juggling a lot. Different jobs and stuff. Keeping an eye on Ethan was just an extra thing, but they were trying to make it work."

"Does Winnie have two jobs, too?" I asked. I hadn't heard that before.

"Well, no. I guess she lost her waitressing job a while back when that restaurant on Main Street closed, so she wound up back here for the summer. But Tim basically works two full-time jobs. And they juggle that one car. And I know sometimes Winnie would do some of Tim's jobs here for him, to help him make it to his deli shift."

"She'd do some of his jobs?" I perked up at this. "You mean *here*? At Fabuland?"

"Yeah. Like one day I saw her mopping the men's room floor in the restrooms by the waterslides. That's not, like, in her job description. That's Tim's. But she'd sometimes do that kind of thing if he got behind."

"Oh," I breathed. "So were they walking and driving Ethan home for a particular *reason,* you think? Do you think there was some special reason why they were doing that?"

"Well, why *wouldn't* they do that?"

"I was starting to wonder recently if Ethan had some kind of health problem that nobody knew about?"

"Like what kind of a health problem?" Ben asked.

"Hey!" someone barked behind me.

I craned my neck around. I'd been so focused on Ben that I hadn't seen Zach Crenshaw come up from behind. There was tomato sauce splattered across the front of his apron and an indignant expression on his face. He yanked his hairnet off.

"Can you give it a rest, hey?" he said. I wasn't sure who he was looking at—Ben or me. Bewildered, I smiled reflexively.

"What're you smiling at?" Zach demanded. "Don't you think you've done enough damage?"

"Hey . . . ," Ben said soothingly. "Is something wrong, Zach?"

"Yes. I heard Ethan's name again. And Winnie's."

"We were only saying nice things," Ben said slowly.

"It's not up to you to be judge and jury about what happened to Ethan, Ivy. I heard you were asking Tim about it, making him feel bad. And *everyone's* heard what you did to Reggie."

"Sorry," I whispered, staring at my sad carrot sticks, my little-girl lunch.

"And now you're . . . well, I don't care who your father is." I could feel Zach's stare boring into the top of my head, and I was too chicken to look at him. "He can fire me if he wants to for saying this, but you need to cut it out, what you're doing."

I was stunned silent for a second, then glanced up. Zach wasn't the only one staring at me. So were a few people dining near us.

"She's not doing anything," Ben said, standing up.

"He's not going to fire you," I murmured. It was the first thing I could think of to say. It was probably better than *It looks like you burned your last crust.* But not by much.

"Oh, but she *has* been doing something." Zach was angrily rubbing his palms against the sides of his apron. "I heard your question just now, and I know you've been making the rounds. First it was Tim and all kinds of funny questions with him. Real nice. And then on to Reggie. Do *you* know about how it turned out with Reggie, Ben?"

"It's not like she . . ." Ben trailed off.

He couldn't defend me. Nobody could.

"You'd better leave Winnie alone," Zach barked. "Do you understand? *Leave Winnie alone.* There's nothing you need to ask her. She has enough to deal with right now. She doesn't need to deal with you, too."

"Okay," I whispered.

"Good," Zach said. And then he stalked back to Pizza to the Rescue.

"What the fuck, Zach?" Ben yelled after him, but he didn't follow it up with any further comment.

He looked down at me as I pushed the remains of my lunch into my insulated bag.

"You want to get out of here?" Ben asked.

"Yes," I said, my voice a whisper now.

Ben waited for me to scooch out of the picnic table and then led me through the narrow aisle between rows of picnic tables, to the walkway that led to the rides area. I tried not to notice all the eyes on me. We were silent until we got close to the Rotor.

"When bad stuff happens," Ben said, "sometimes people don't know who to take it out on."

"I probably deserved that." I stopped at the Starship 360 and resisted the impulse to look up at the screaming riders. I was grateful to be here where all the other voices could muffle our conversation a little and make it feel more private.

Ben gave my shoulder a sympathetic pat. "No, you didn't."

"Did you know I went and saw Reggie last night?" I asked.

"Yeah," Ben said reluctantly, his hot-cocoa gaze shifting away from me. "I did hear that it was maybe you."

I didn't know why his reply felt like a kick in the stomach. What did I expect?

"Jesus. I *knew* it. Why didn't you ask me about it, then?"

I knew I wasn't angry at *him*, but I couldn't help myself.

"I figured you'd bring it up if you wanted to talk about it."

Ben shrugged and twisted his hands together. "It's not like I know Reggie that well. It's not really any of my business."

"Well, then you're smarter than me." I led him to the Rotor gate. "You know when to ask questions and when to shut up. I haven't been smart about that at all."

"It still doesn't mean you *deserve* it." Ben lifted the *Closed— come back in a few minutes!* sign and unlocked the gate to the ride. Apparently Winnie was too busy helping my dad to be substitute Rotor Lady during Ben's break.

"You're maybe too nice for this place," I said. "You don't want to be seen with me any more than you already have."

"Ivy," Ben said as I started to walk away.

I turned around, realizing it was the first time he'd used my name that I could remember. Instead of *my friend*. Up until now I wasn't certain he knew what it was.

"I have to go back to spinning my tin can," I said. "And so do you."

TWENTY-THREE

I didn't get a lot of customers that afternoon. Maybe the park-goers could tell from my face that I wasn't in a sugary-sweet kind of mood. Maybe lots of them had seen me being chewed out by Zach and felt awkward approaching me for their refreshment needs.

I didn't do any more Google searches on my cracked phone. It seemed like each time I asked a question, another person flipped out or started to hate me. I decided to table my research until I could be alone at home with my laptop.

Mostly I just sat with my chin in my hand, watching people go by. Thinking about some of the things I'd learned today.

It was obvious that Zach Crenshaw was still way into Winnie, for one. Or at least very protective of her. Beyond that, I was relatively certain it was Winnie who'd put the tape recorder in my dad's office. I hadn't had a chance to ask Ben if one of the du-ties that Tim sometimes handed off to Winnie was cleaning the main office. But probably I didn't need to ask. If she was cleaning a men's room for him, likely she was willing to do any of his duties for him. And she probably had regular access to Tim's keys.

And I thought about my dad always trusting Winnie with important jobs—closing, the carousel, the fried dough. At least, my dad *thought* fried dough was important. And then I considered whether he might be a little too trusting, in his overgrown-kid kind of way. Could he have any idea that Winnie was recording him? And *why* would she want to do that? To capture what a buffoon he could sometimes be? Didn't we all already know this without needing proof? Did she really dislike him *that* much as a boss?

And speaking of my dad being a little too trusting—wasn't it kind of weird, now that I reconsidered it, that he didn't seem to know what *kind* of cancer Chris's wife had? Was he just so distracted by his big doughnut that he didn't consider this a relevant detail?

I hated myself for being so cynical, but had Dad somehow confirmed Chris's wife's situation with Chris in an official way? Asked for a doctor's note? Probably it would be too cold to ask. And really, there were easier and less shady ways to weasel out of work, if Chris wanted to.

Was it possible that Winnie wasn't spying on my father, but on someone else? On Chris, perhaps? But again, why?

If Dad wasn't going to entrust me with his great doughnut experiment, I was going to quietly do some other things for him. Maybe some things he was a little too bighearted to do himself. Like check up on his right-hand man.

I signed out of work an hour early. I knew my dad was probably too busy today to notice.

* * *

At the hospital front desk was the same lady who'd helped me find Morgan's room last week.

"I'm trying to find a patient room," I said. "Her name is Trisha Nealy."

"Ah. Yes." The nice lady typed quickly on her computer. "She's on the second floor, room 215. Take the elevator up one floor and then take a right, then follow the numbers after the small lobby there."

"Oh."

I felt disappointed at the affirmation of Chris's wife's illness—though not for the right reasons. Some small part of me had expected a different outcome. As crazy as it seemed now, I'd really thought I might catch Chris in a horrible lie. And I felt guilty that this lady had been so helpful and polite, when my motives were so icky.

"Thank you so much," I managed to say.

I realized then that she expected to see me head in the direction of the elevators, so I walked hastily toward them, took one to the third floor, found a staircase, and came down a different way. Of course I had no intention of looking in on Chris's wife. I'd just wanted to see if she was really here.

I ended up back in the front lobby, and didn't turn around or look toward the receptionist as I held my breath and snuck out the front glass door. I was just about to step off the curb in front of the parking lot—and just about to breathe a sigh of relief—when I saw Tim and Winnie Malloy heading in my direction.

"Oh!" I said, panicking.

Winnie looked up from her phone and her mouth fell open. She was apparently as surprised to see me as I was her.

"Are you here visiting Reggie, too?" Tim asked.

"Reggie?" I shook my head. "No."

We were all silent as they both stepped up, joining me on the hospital sidewalk.

"Hey," Winnie said quietly. "I heard my blowhard ex was giving you trouble in the Food Zone. Sorry about him. I didn't tell him to do that."

I wasn't sure if I should hide my surprise. Or if I should be skeptical.

"Uh . . . it's okay," I mumbled.

"He thinks he's helping." Winnie rolled her eyes as if at a toddler trying to assist with a car repair or a cooking project.

I nodded, feeling an unexpected jolt of empathy for Zach. The very same words could be applied to me—to what I'd thought I'd been "doing for Morgan." To what I'd just done a few minutes ago, even. Telling myself I was doing it on my dad's behalf.

"We going in?" Winnie nudged her brother's arm. "I've got to get back to Fabuland after my dinner break. And you've got your shift at Drake's."

I studied her expression. She didn't seem angry at all. She seemed distracted. And Tim looked like he was thinking. He didn't look angry either. Just sad. As he had the other day I'd talked to him.

"I think I'm going to stay out here for a second," Tim said.

Winnie looked at her phone, shrugged, and then paused at the doors. "Meet me in there?"

"Yup," Tim said, and turned to me.

He waited for Winnie to clear the glass doors, sniffling and then clearing his throat. Once she'd disappeared from view, he said, "I hope you're *happy*."

"Happy . . . ?" I murmured.

"Because we *have* to tell people now. And we probably were gonna soon. Once Winnie felt ready."

"Umm . . . Should we go sit somewhere?"

"Nah. Here is fine." He stepped a few more feet away from the doors, and I followed. We stood next to a big concrete pot full of petunias. "It's something I've been wanting for us to be able to tell people. Besides, the only other person who knew was Zach, and who knows how long *he'd* be able to keep his self-important mouth shut. Especially after he heard *you* say something."

Tim was scraping his sneaker on the concrete of the hospital walkway, moving a piece of gravel around in a circle.

"*What?*" I tried not to sound as breathless as I felt. "What is it?"

"Ethan had a problem," Tim said. "About two years ago he started having grand mal seizures."

It took me a moment to take this in. "Uh . . . like . . . he had epilepsy?"

"I don't know." Tim shrugged as he looked up at me. "I don't know the difference. If there *is* a difference. I know he had what they call grand mal seizures. That's what my aunt, his mom, called them. She wasn't willing to say he had *epilepsy*. There was a chance something else was causing the seizures."

I stood there silent. I didn't know what to say. I glanced down at the pot full of petunias—they were so cheerfully purple and white. It seemed like a lie, to plant these things in front of a hospital, where people generally ended up when things went wrong.

"We think he probably had one on the bridge," Tim added. "That's the basic theory."

"Oh my God," I whispered.

We stood there in silence for a moment before Tim started to wipe his eyes with his palms.

"His mom had all kinds of rules for him about working at Fabuland. He could only go on certain rides. The mild ones. But she knew it would be really tempting for him. She was hoping he'd get Fabuland out of his system and find a different job at the end of the summer. She didn't have the heart to tell him no."

Tim wiped a tear from the outside corner of one eye. "It was a calculated risk. He'd only had, like, three or four of the seizures in two years. There was a risk of him having one at Fabuland, sure, and freaking everyone out. But we figured it would only be a few months and we'd deal with getting him a new job after that. I was talking to some of the produce guys at Drake's Grocery about letting him work there."

Tim paused, wiping both eyes with the shoulders of his T-shirt. "What we didn't consider was that Ethan might break the rules. What would happen then. Because it's possible that certain types of rides can trigger seizures."

So it was true that Ethan had gone on the Laser Coaster *because* Winnie and Tim weren't there to police him that night. It was a rare little window he had without them keeping tabs on him. And he took it.

I can't do it on another day.

"I'm sorry," I murmured.

And I really was. I had questions—like whether the police knew about Ethan's seizures—but decided to keep my mouth shut, for the moment.

Tim had stopped trying to wipe his tears away by now, and they were pouring down his cheeks. "We think that if he had a seizure, it must have happened on his way home. Either right on the bridge or maybe before. If it was before, he was probably disoriented afterward."

He was trying to catch his breath now. I wanted to reach out to him, but didn't think the touch of the boss's clueless daughter would be of much comfort to him.

"I'm so sorry," I whispered again.

A seizure. Not a concussion. Nothing on the ride that Reggie could've prevented.

"Zach knows about it, because he and Winnie were together when it started. And Zach told Winnie what you were asking Ben about today. And we wondered if you'd figured it out, or if you somehow had heard. Like maybe Ethan even told you. I know you would sometimes let him make his own cotton candy. Maybe he let something slip?"

I shook my head.

"No, I didn't know," I said.

I glanced at the brick building next to me—at the four stories of windows—and wondered which room Reggie was in. Wondered if there was some possibility he and Winnie were looking down on us.

"Déjà vu," I said. "It's something people feel right before a seizure."

"Yeah," Tim said. "I just wish he'd had some of the stronger warning signs. Like being dizzy."

"I shouldn't have been asking Reggie those questions," I breathed.

Poor Reggie. If he'd known about the seizures he wouldn't have let Ethan on the ride. *But he hadn't known.* Certainly hearing this would be even worse for Briony, Anna, and Lucas.

But it was the truth. And it *could* explain Morgan's sparkly scorpion mystery. If he'd had a seizure at some point before or after crossing the bridge, he would likely have been very disoriented and could easily have lost his way, taking the wrong path and then maybe backtracking. Dropping the paperweight somehow. The question remained *why* he would pull the sparkly scorpion out of his pocket in that moment. So that part was still a mystery. But if he was disoriented, maybe it didn't need to make complete sense. Still, my heart sank at the thought of it.

"I don't blame you . . . ," Tim said. "Winnie doesn't blame

you either. I mean, about Reggie. But I wish you'd let us all come around to talking about the seizures in our own time. There's already a lot of regret about that night, right? Winnie's still having a lot of trouble. You might not realize it, but it's been the roughest on her."

Because it was still unclear why she wasn't *at work that night,* I thought, but then pushed it down. Because it was cruel. Maybe almost as cruel as Zach Crenshaw seemed to think I was.

"I'm so sorry," I said again.

Tim sniffled and pulled up the bottom of his T-shirt to wipe his face.

"We're all sorry," he replied flatly. "I'm going up to see Reggie now. Thanks for talking."

He turned and walked through the hospital doors, leaving me alone with the lying petunias.

TWENTY-FOUR

I went to my dad's house, put on yoga pants, and crawled into bed even though it wasn't dark yet. And I wasn't sure I'd ever want to get out.

I briefly considered writing to Morgan, since her paperweight mystery had probably been solved. But I couldn't figure out how not to make such a text sound smugly satisfied. Of course, there was nothing to be smug or satisfied about. It was the saddest news ever, about Ethan's seizures. And I hadn't *solved* anything. Just forced some uncomfortable truths out of people who hadn't been quite ready to share them yet, and probably almost killed Reggie in the process.

I stayed under the covers and wondered what I'd say when Dad came home. I *could* tell him that I thought Winnie had been recording him in his office. But why would I do that? I still didn't know what to make of her. But given what Tim had just told me, I felt sorry for her and didn't want to be a tattletale. Even if

I wasn't sure whether I liked Winnie, I didn't want to be responsible for her suffering a fate like Carla's.

After about an hour in bed, I got a text from Jason.

Want to talk now?

I considered the question for a moment, then typed back:

No. And sorry I almost killed your friend.

After that text, the phone rang. I didn't answer.

I got up, pulled the tape recorder from my sock drawer, and crawled back into bed with it.

I started to listen to the recording again, paying special attention when Chris was on the phone.

I know, baby. I know. We're going to figure this out. Don't worry. I'm working on it. I know it's hard right now. Oh. No. No. Don't say that. Listen . . . No. Come on, now. Don't say that.

No, these probably weren't sweet nothings between Chris and Winnie. This was very likely Chris talking to his wife in the hospital. Trisha was having a hard time and he was trying to help her feel supported. And struggling to stay positive himself. This was Chris wishing he could be with her when my dad was making him work at the stupid Princess Parade.

I wasn't sure what was wrong with my brain that I'd wanted to make something else out of what he'd said. And I felt horrible for listening to the recording more than once.

I let the recorder slide down to the carpet.

My room was totally dark now. And my dad hadn't come home.

I pulled my phone under the covers.

I typed in *grand mal seizures,* with some difficulty because of the cracked screen. I found out that yes, a feeling of déjà vu was among many symptoms, called prodromal symptoms, that often appeared in the minutes, sometimes the hours, before the actual seizure. I hadn't been far off, then, when I'd speculated that Ethan might have had a concussion. It was a neurological symptom. I'd just had the wrong cause. For Ethan, it was likely a sign of an impending seizure rather than the aftereffect of a concussion. Grand mal seizures were usually caused by epilepsy, although there were other reasons a person might have them. There was also something called sudden unexpected death in epilepsy, which could cause a person to die from impaired breathing or heart failure during a seizure. But it was rare.

I typed in *grand mal seizures and Down syndrome.* Epilepsy was *slightly* more common in people with Down syndrome than in the general population, but not by much, according to the first couple of sites that came up. Next I tried *grand mal seizures and roller coasters,* and *grand mal seizures and amusement park rides.* There was some debate about whether certain types of rides could trigger seizures. One commonly cited trigger, though, was flashing lights. Something the Laser Coaster had in overwhelming abundance, especially at night.

I was beginning to feel sick from the weight of the information. I switched over to my texts from the past few days and considered calling Jason, but instead looked up *Shawn Colvin* and *Polaroids.* After digging an old set of earbuds from the drawer next to my bed, I listened to the song. And then again. I hadn't heard it since I was seven or so—the gentle thumping of a guitar at the beginning, the singer's lullaby voice, her humming at the close of the song.

An old feeling came crashing back—of hiding, of being in the dark, of letting myself be comforted even though I knew something indefinably unsettling was unfolding around me.

I repeated the song over and over, and then fell asleep.

TWENTY-FIVE

"Ivy . . . Ivy?"

My father's voice woke me up. It was still dark. He was standing in my doorway, backlit by the bathroom light.

"What time is it?" I mumbled.

"You want to see something awesome?"

I picked up my phone and looked at the time.

"A three-thirty a.m. kind of awesome?"

"When's the last time I woke you up in the middle of the night?" he asked.

I sat up. "Probably never. Are you okay?"

"More than okay. Come with me, honey. I want to show you something."

"Where?"

"Fabuland." Dad was grinning like I hadn't seen in a while. I couldn't help smiling in response.

"Am I going to look at a half-dozen dough balls?" I asked.

"Just come with me, Ivy. I'm gonna go down and make myself a quick cup of coffee while you get yourself dressed."

"Okay," I said.

* * *

We drove to Fabuland with the windows open. I don't normally drink coffee, but I sipped at the one my dad had made me, enjoying the sugar and cream and ignoring the bitterness beneath them. That and the breeze woke me up, and I started to feel better. I'd just let myself get too hot and stuffy under the covers, I told myself. I was fine now.

"I really wanted you to see this," Dad said as we pulled into the parking lot. "It'll be gone by morning, because we don't want anyone to see the practice one."

We walked to the east pavilion area of the park. And when we arrived, there it was: a golden-brown doughnut the width of a small house. Slathered with white frosting and glistening in the moonlight.

"It worked, honey," Dad whispered. "Look how well it worked."

It really was amazing. You could tell the doughnut was made of separate parts. But it didn't look like a shortcut. It looked deliberate because of the cute floral formation the parts made. I circled it, running my hand along the golden dough beneath the frosted top.

"How'd you get the balls all the same size?" I asked.

"Well, we mixed up each ball as a separate batch, with the

271

same amount of weighed ingredients. The balls didn't rise or fry to exactly the same height, but we trimmed some of the tops to make them uniform since they were all going to be frosted anyhow."

"Wow."

It really was like he, Winnie, Carl, and John had performed magic in the night. Way bigger magic than my little cotton candy machine could ever produce. I wished I'd been a part of it.

"Where is everyone else?" I asked.

"They had a long night. I told them to go home and sleep." He handed me a bucket of sprinkles. "Do the honors with me?"

"If you're just going to clean this all up by opening time, isn't it a waste of sprinkles?"

"I want to see what the finished product looks like."

I smiled. "Sprinkles never make things look anything but fabulous. You don't need to test that part."

"Of course not. But I *want* to. Come on. You first."

I took a handful of sprinkles and threw it at the doughnut.

He did the same. And then I threw another handful.

"All right!" Dad said. And after a moment, we were both laughing.

And I felt close to him—like I used to.

"Dad?" I said.

"Yeah?"

"So you heard about Reggie Wiggins . . ."

Dad stopped sprinkling and glanced at me. "Yeah?"

I gazed at the partially sprinkled doughnut, suddenly unable to make eye contact with my father.

"I was with him just a couple of hours before he did it."

"I know."

Dad half-heartedly threw a handful of sprinkles at the side of the doughnut. Most of the sprinkles fell into the grass.

"I feel bad," I said.

It wasn't very articulate, but it was straightforward. Which was the best way to communicate with my dad.

"You need to try not to," he said firmly.

I wasn't sure how I was supposed to do that. And that didn't seem like a question my father would be prepared to answer.

"Can I maybe do the doughnut media job from home for a little while?" I asked. "Probably I should stay away from Fabuland for a few days."

"You think that's gonna help you?" he asked.

I couldn't tell if his tone was concerned or skeptical.

"Maybe," I said, still sprinkling. "So, would that be okay with you?"

Dad nodded.

"People make mistakes," he offered after a moment's silence.

I didn't know if I'd ever heard him make that concession before. I wasn't sure if it was his way of telling me I was forgiven for whatever he might have heard about me and Reggie. For snooping through his texts. For being weak and hiding under the covers. For needing a few days away from Fabuland to figure out how to show my face. And maybe, too, it was his way of asking for forgiveness—for yelling at me earlier today, or for his generally demanding manner lately.

"Yeah," I said.

I took a giant handful of sprinkles and let them slip through my fingers, falling back in the bucket.

Fairy sand, I used to think when I would play with sprinkles as a kid.

I was around five or six when Dad filled a small kiddie pool with sprinkles and let my friends and me play in it. It was glorious. Like nothing else any other kid on the block had at her house, ever.

He did it just because I'd asked. *Imagine a beach of sprinkles,* I'd said. And he'd made it happen. Like so many things he'd made happen for me. Violin lessons. SAT prep courses. Birthday parties with bounce castles and wedding-style cakes. He made things happen. If you believed in him, he believed in you.

If I could forgive him, I had to think he'd forgive me too.

"Can I take a picture of this?" I said. "Not the whole thing, just a little glimpse of the frosting and sprinkles. Just as a teaser. I won't post it yet. Maybe the night before the event?"

"Sure," Dad said. "Good idea."

I took out my phone and started trying to capture a sliver of the doughnut from different angles.

"This is even cooler than I thought it would be," I told him, and meant it. "Cooler than I ever imagined."

TWENTY-SIX

The practice doughnut was dismantled before sunrise. Dad texted me pictures of the cleanup process and the aftermath. By opening time the next morning, you wouldn't have guessed the doughnut had been there. I knew, though, that hidden in the grass were a few hundred stray sprinkles.

Things were quiet for a few days. According to Dad, Tim and the rest of the maintenance staff did extra cleaning and spackling and painting to spruce up the place before the big event. I posted Facebook teasers and Fabuland ticket giveaways. I prepped the official press release while working from home in my pajamas.

FOR IMMEDIATE RELEASE

Danville, NH

Fabuland Theme Park will be hosting a special event on Saturday, July 21, featuring an approximately 30-foot doughnut that will be baked and constructed by Fabuland staff. Park guests will be invited to partake of the communal celebratory doughnut after an opening musical performance. Special food discounts, giveaways, and samples will be offered throughout the day.

Fabuland is the home of the famous Laser Coaster, which was designated one of New England's top ten roller coasters by Grayson's Travel Guides in 2016. The park also features an enhanced Little Adventurers area, which includes several new rides for the youngest parkgoers, ages 2 to 7. Since last summer, the park has been operated by new owner Edward Cork, well known in Danville for his ownership and growth of the beloved Cork's Doughnut Dynasty franchise.

DOUGHNUT DAZE SCHEDULE:

9:30	Seating area opens
10:00	Music by local band Hammer, Anvil, and Stirrup
10:30	Opening remarks
10:45	Communal sprinkling

11:00   Doughnut cutting and sample distribution

11:30   Performance and sing-along by guitarist Gary Ottemeier

Mr. Cork sums up his wish for the event: "This isn't just about a big doughnut. It's about our small community, and the big hearts within it. It's about coming together for something extraordinary."

Contact:

Ivy Cork, Assistant Press Manager

603-551-1992

IvyC@XBMail.com

With the release finally sent, I made lots of calls to the newspapers, regional magazines, and online events bulletins. I didn't text Morgan at all. I convinced myself I didn't have time. And it was looking like I'd have to figure out how to survive without her anyway.

To make sure my dad wouldn't regret this little break he'd given me, I was preparing an extra surprise for him. I'd made some headway with a young Channel 12 News reporter. Her name was Lexi Givens, and she seemed new to the job, from what I saw of her online. She was what my dad would call "a live one," and seemed really interested in our event. After I'd followed up on several phone calls and sent her some teaser photos of my dad's moonlit "practice doughnut," she promised she'd come and "check it out" with a cameraman. I'd added, in our final confirmation, that the event was going to have "a few extra surprises" for the community. I wasn't sure what I meant by that, but I figured it would end up being true. My dad always makes sure there are surprises.

Jason even made good on his promise to try to come, arriving late Thursday—two days before the big doughnut event. I was sitting on the back deck—watching Emoji stalking a sparrow—when I heard his old Toyota.

When I got to the front of the house, Jason was climbing out of the car, stretching and surveying the front yard. I wondered if it looked different to him. He hadn't been here since Christmas.

"Hey!" I called, and ran up.

I wasn't sure if we should hug. Sometimes we don't. This time he reached for a quick one. And then we sat on the steps together.

"The drive sucked." He sighed. "I should've remembered what 495 is like this time of day."

He looked even more tired than he sounded. His dark hair was growing over his ears, and his face was stubbly. He was wearing a plaid dress shirt with the sleeves rolled almost up to the shoulders. An odd style choice, but I could tell he was working on his ruggedly jaded writer look.

"Where's Dad?" he asked.

"Showering. He's going back to the park for another late night, probably."

"He's not making you go?"

"Umm . . . not tonight," I said softly. I hadn't told Jason that I'd been working from home. In fact, we'd barely communicated at all in the last few days.

"Hmm," Jason said. "Maybe he'll want me to go in."

"You heard anything about Reggie?" I asked.

I'd been worried about Reggie. But since I hadn't been at Fabuland, I hadn't had an opportunity to hear any updates.

"Heard he went home from the hospital—yesterday, I think."

"Good," I said, relieved. "So, how close are you two? Or . . . how close *were* you?"

"We smoked the occasional joint together in the parking lot after work last year, if you want to know the truth."

Jason looked at me sheepishly, as if I was supposed to be scandalized. On the contrary, I wondered how he was so lucky to have a casual friend who trusted him like that—smoking pot a few steps from Fabuland, just out of view of our father.

We sat in silence for a few minutes. I followed his gaze to the right of the steps, where the ghost of our mother's old flower garden grew. It used to be a medley of tulips, lilies, irises, and a rotating variety of annuals. Now only the hardiest of perennials lived there—crowded irises and a couple of yellow Asiatic lilies that grew each year just to be immediately munched petal-less by the little orange beetles that lived in the garden. The bare, pointy green stems were always a weird reminder of my mom's bygone presence at this house.

The screen door creaked behind us. I turned to see Dad, hair still wet from the shower but already combed away from his face.

"Kids," he said. "I'm going to let you catch up. But tomorrow I want both of you at Fabuland. It's the last day before the big day. I'm going to need you both around. Especially you, Ivy."

I stood up, but Jason stayed seated.

"Hi, Dad," he said, nodding a little.

Dad patted him on the shoulder. "Glad you made it. Good to have you both here at the same time. We're a one-of-a-kind team, you know?"

I couldn't read the expression on Jason's face.

"Yeah," I said.

Dad patted his pockets until he found his keys. "It's nice to be back, isn't it, Jason?"

"Yup," Jason breathed, glancing toward the garden again.

"Yup," Dad repeated before heading to his truck. He revved the engine and waved to us as he roared away from the house.

"Where's Emoji?" Jason asked, watching the truck speed down the street.

"I don't know," I said. "I saw her in the back before you got here. Hiding in the wilderness now, I'm guessing."

"I hope she knows to stay out of the way when Dad's amped up and driving like that."

"If she didn't, she'd be dead by now."

"Wouldn't we all," Jason said.

I slapped a mosquito that had settled itself near my elbow. "I wouldn't go that far," I said.

"No," Jason said. "I guess you wouldn't."

The mosquito already had blood in it. Gross.

"You think you'll go see Reggie while you're home?" I asked, deliberately changing the subject.

Jason shrugged. "Maybe. If he wants visitors."

I nodded and said nothing. Jason was quiet, too. A bird started squawking in one of the two maple trees that separated our house from our neighbor's. Probably Emoji was nearby.

After a while, Jason's road-weary gaze met mine.

"I decided I'm ready to tell my Yo-Yo story now." He hesitated. "If you're ready to hear it."

He seemed to be waiting for my response. I heard my stomach growl. I couldn't think of the last time I'd eaten.

"I thought I'd already heard it?" I asked.

"No. I was going to tell you the rest the other night, but you wouldn't answer your phone."

"Sorry about that. I wasn't much in the mood for talking to anyone."

That was an understatement. I didn't know how to say to my brother, *I was so depressed I'm not sure how I ever got out of bed*. But since I *had* gotten out of bed, maybe it didn't matter now.

"Dad asked me to paint that ride because he wanted to sell it," Jason explained. "Originally, I was going to repaint it yellow. But while I was up there doing it, I noticed this spot where the ride was rusted so bad that the metal was as thin as paper. I went to Dad and told him about it, but he didn't seem all that surprised. I almost thought maybe Mr. Moyer had known about it and told him. Warned him. And that's why Dad was getting rid of the ride."

Jason was talking fast, almost breathlessly. As if he was afraid I might stop him. "Which, on the one hand, was a relief—that the ride wasn't being used. But then I was like, maybe we shouldn't paint it. If you're going to sell it, you should leave it unpainted and make a full disclosure about the rust to whoever buys it so they'll know it needs a major repair and the price can be negotiated."

"And what'd Dad say to that?" I asked.

"He said I was being naive. That of course any buyer would have the ride inspected before they'd put it into service at a park or carnival. That in the meantime, rides are hugely expensive and we needed to get the best price possible."

Jason looked out across the overgrown front lawn. "And then he had me switch to purple paint. To hide the rust better. Because it was apparently worse than he'd realized."

"Maybe he just—"

"And I *did* it," Jason interrupted me. "I just went ahead and painted that ride even though I knew full well that that whole car beneath the rust could easily come flying off and kill whoever was riding it."

Jason shook his head. I felt a tightening sensation in my shoulders and a general feeling of dread similar to what I'd felt under the covers the other night.

"I dragged my feet on posting the sale to the end of the summer. I kept coming up with reasons I couldn't sell the Yo-Yo. That the secondhand-ride site was down. I didn't have all the paperwork. Eventually, it was too late for me to sell it. Thank God."

"And then my first week back at Syracuse I couldn't stop thinking about it," he said. "So I texted Chris and told him about it. I said, *Don't let my dad sell that ride.* I made it sound like it was my fault, my doing. Like Dad didn't know about the rust. And I guess maybe Dad just didn't understand the seriousness of it, since he didn't see it for himself."

"Was that the main reason you didn't come back this summer?" I asked.

"I don't know. Maybe." Jason rubbed his eyes. "I just couldn't believe I'd actually *done* that. That I'd almost let Dad sell it. That I could've killed someone because I couldn't say *no*. And there was also this feeling like, *I've got to get out of here before something goes* really *wrong with this whole Fabuland thing.* Because the way Dad cuts corners and 'forgets' the rules sometimes, Ivy, I just can't help but feel like there's gonna be a disaster someday. Maybe not now, but someday."

Emoji came up and twined around my legs. Jason reached out to pet her. I was grateful for her presence because it filled the silence a little, buying me a minute to decide what to think. Or at least what to say.

"And I got tired of hearing that it was all because I didn't think like a businessperson. That I didn't see the bigger picture. When *he* was the one who didn't seem to understand how bad the rust was."

"Maybe you should've taken a picture of it and shown it to him," I offered. Our dad was a "seeing is believing" kind of guy. And remembering that seemed to loosen the tension that had been building in my shoulders.

"Yeah, maybe," Jason muttered. "I don't know why I didn't think of that. I just ended up feeling like the inadequate one in the whole situation. Not being able to talk to Dad about it effectively myself. Painting the ride anyway. Making *Chris* have the hard conversation with Dad."

I thought about his words for a moment. For some reason the word *inadequate* popped out at me.

"Do you remember Dad ever saying something like, 'I've always known you wanted to stay small'? Do those words ring a bell?"

Jason scratched Emoji vigorously behind the ears. She made some weird satisfied noises with her tongue.

"Did you hear the question?" I asked.

"Yeah. Umm . . . Dad used to say it to Mom."

"Not to you or to me?" I didn't have time to hide the surprise in my voice.

"No." Jason scowled. "Why would he say it to us?"

"Like, 'Don't ever grow up.' Or, like, 'You don't seem like you ever want to grow up.' "

"No," said Jason. "He used to say that to Mom when she started going to night school, to get her teaching certification."

"So he never said it to me or you?"

I felt I had to ask it again to make sure. The words had felt so ingrained in my memory as something that was meant for *me*.

"Well . . . not that I remember. Has he started saying it to *you*?"

"Uh . . . no." I paused. "I was just trying to remember it better."

"Right. Along with the couch cushion fort. Probably because they happened around the same time. That's what Mom and Dad always fought about. Her staying out late for her classes and being at the library. He didn't ever want her to do that program. That was the beginning of the end for them, you know?"

"So what did that mean . . . her wanting to stay small?" I asked. "Like she wanted to go back to kindergarten?"

"Oh, you know . . . that was when Dad was really growing the business, opening several different branches at once. He wanted her to be his business partner, to really go for it with him. And what she wanted to do was be a kindergarten teacher. Like he was going 'big-time,' and she was doing the reverse, going 'small-time.' In Dad's view, anyway. They fought about it all the time."

I closed my eyes. Yes, that sounded right.

I've always known you wanted to stay small, honey. I've always known that about you.

It was a mean thing to say. I couldn't really remember what our mom used to say in response. Maybe because she spoke so much softer than him. Maybe because she didn't argue so much as deflect.

"This was all while you were in elementary school," Jason said. "Dad thought Mom's going back to school meant she didn't really believe in Cork's Doughnut Dynasty anymore, or believe in the goals they'd talked about, to make it a much bigger enterprise."

"Right," I said softly.

I remembered them always fighting when I was in the first or second grade. I didn't remember the content. I probably had never really digested the content, actually.

"I guess it can be hard to think someone has stopped believing in you," I said.

"I guess," Jason admitted. "That's one way of looking at it. Look, I'm kind of hungry. I'm going inside."

I followed him into the house.

◆ ◆ ◆

We didn't talk much more that night. Jason got a text from Dad asking him to mow the lawn, so he was outside doing that as the sun set.

I watched TV and tried to go to bed early but couldn't sleep. Eventually, I turned the air conditioner off and opened the window by my bed. Sometimes I preferred to listen to crickets on a summer night. Even when I was six years old I felt that way—that it was better to be hot with the crickets than to be at the perfect temperature with the guttural noise of a machine in your ears.

I closed my eyes. The crickets persisted for what seemed like hours. When they finally faded in my ears, a zooming sound replaced them. Like a car was whizzing by both my ears. I opened my eyes to see there were no cars. I was strapped into a seat. Morgan was beside me. She was screaming—but in a genuinely scared way, not in a fun way like last summer. Before I could figure out where we were, the ground had smacked into us. We lay broken on the concrete.

I sat up with a gasp. It took me a minute to catch my breath. The crickets started again, helping slow my heartbeat but not staving off the realization of where Morgan and I had been in the dream. We were in the Yo-Yo together. And it had come apart, flinging us both to the ground.

When my legs felt firm enough, I got out of bed and stumbled to my father's bedroom door.

"Dad?" I whispered, tapping the door and then opening it slightly.

I saw with relief that he was in bed. He hadn't spent another night on his office couch, obsessing about doughnut measurements or the exact right color of frosting or bleacher rentals.

I could hear him breathing in his sleep. He was probably exhausted from these last few days. This whole summer, even. It wouldn't be fair to wake him up now to ask about what Jason had said about the Yo-Yo. Nor would it be smart. Jason might wake up and hear me, and he and Dad might argue. And I kind of knew what our dad would say anyway.

I thought the ride was fine. I didn't know there was any rust. I took it out of service as soon as Jason told me. Why do you think it's sitting unused behind the parking lot?

And that would sound reasonable to me, wouldn't it? Because, as Katy had pointed out, sometimes Jason wanted to see things from his side. I understood that. We were all like that sometimes. And now wasn't the right time to make an issue of this either way. The Yo-Yo was last summer's concern. We all had other things to worry about right now.

I went back to my room and let the crickets sing me back to sleep.

TWENTY-SEVEN

Dad was already gone when I woke up. But my phone was full of text requests from him.

Hey Ivy. Some final social media ideas for today. $1 hot dogs tomorrow between one and two o'clock and free burgers for early birds (arrive between 9 and 9:30, get a voucher).

Delicious pics to go with those reminders, too! Be creative.

Then tonight, pics of the bleachers being set up?

Remember: Final calls to any contacts who haven't already committed to sending someone.

Jason was still asleep. I wondered if he had received a similar list, but didn't awaken him to ask. I drove to Fabuland alone and parked in the customer lot so I wouldn't have to look at the two retired rides.

Since my dad hadn't said anything about cotton candy duty, I didn't go to my station. Instead, I strolled around the park taking pictures.

It was actually nice—if a little surreal—to be back at Fabu-land after a few days away. I wasn't sure if it was the bright morning sunshine or the new coats of paint in unexpected places—like the entrance to the bumper cars, or the front door of the administration building—that made the place seem to pop and sparkle.

Nobody was at the carousel yet. I took a picture of a particularly eager, openmouthed horse, making a mental note to find a doughnut later in the afternoon and snap a picture of the same horse with a doughnut in its mouth.

Inspired, I started staging more photos to post on today's feeds.

I started with a pile of economy-size boxes of confectioners' sugar in the back room of the pavilion, with a giant see-through tub of sprinkles on top of the pile and a set of metal mixing tubs beside it.

We can't wait to mix up a few pounds of perfect pink frosting tonight! I typed as a draft caption for the photo. I wasn't certain my dad had settled on pink. And surely it was being mixed up in the morning, not the night before, but that didn't sound as exciting as an all-nighter kind of process.

After a couple more photos, the park was open, and I realized I was kind of starving from going a couple of days without eating much. As I neared the main fried dough stand, I could smell it. And for the first time since the beginning of the summer, it actually smelled good to me. Irresistible, even.

I was surprised to see Winnie tending the stand. I'd have thought my dad would have her at one of her more important posts, or helping with preparations for tomorrow. But then, the practice doughnut was finished, and the most frenetic of preparations probably wouldn't start until after closing tonight.

Winnie already had two customers as I approached slowly, weighing my hunger against the awkwardness of encountering her again. A girl who looked to be about seven was standing at the counter with her mom, shaking a pile of powdered sugar onto her dough. It was taking her forever. Those sugar shakers have tiny holes so people will give up before they end up taking all the sugar.

Winnie was handing change to the mom.

"It's *sooo* good with a coffee in the morning," she was saying. "Enjoy it."

"Just once. Just once a summer," the mom was saying.

"I'm not telling anyone, don't worry." Winnie laughed and winked at the mom.

Why couldn't I be like that with customers? So flirty and so natural? No wonder my dad put Winnie on so many of his "important" jobs.

I watched the mom and daughter walk away from the stand. Winnie tidied the counter, wiping it and then lining up the cinnamon and sugar shakers. Then she stretched her back and cracked her neck.

Winnie looked up and out and caught me looking at her. She stared at me for a moment. Then she folded her arms.

"Did you need something, Ivy?" she called.

"Umm." I turned my head this way and that, as if there might be another Ivy standing on either side of me.

She gazed at me with her gray-lidded, heavily lashed eyes.

"You okay?" she said.

"Yeah," I said. "I'm gonna have one piece of fried dough, please. No special topping."

Winnie nodded and put a flap of dough into the fryer behind the counter.

"Since we've got a second," I said, "I just wanted to apologize. I didn't get a chance to at the hospital. I'm sorry about the Ethan stuff. The seizures. I didn't know. I didn't mean to force the subject."

"You don't really need to apologize. If you're still worried about whatever Zach said, you can just forget it. He sometimes doesn't think before he opens his mouth."

"I guess I was trying to help Morgan. It probably sounds dumb now, but . . . she had questions and I thought I was being a good friend by asking them. I wasn't thinking enough about how it might be . . . hurtful."

Winnie didn't reply. Instead, she turned around and fished my dough out of the fryer with metal tongs. She slapped it expertly onto a paper plate, then turned to shove the plate in my direction. Something about her movements reminded me of the day of the Princess Parade. The stray pendant necklace that had hit Chris in the head.

"Do you want butter on that?" she asked.

I hadn't thought a great deal about that day for about a week now. The surprise on Chris's face. My dad bent over right after it happened.

Winnie picked up a greasy brush from the counter and poised it over the metal vat of butter. I tried to process her simple question. But my mind was tied up in a distracting thought.

Maybe my dad had *ducked*.

And that thought—along with my vague annoyance at Winnie for not acknowledging the heartfelt things I was trying to say—pushed my next question out of my mouth.

"I have your recorder, by the way. Would you like it back?"

Winnie's gaze shot up and she gave me a look I didn't understand. Like at the hospital, I was surprised that it wasn't exactly angry.

"I . . . um" was all she said.

"Is that a yes?" I said. "I don't have it with me right now. But I can get it back to you if it's yours."

Winnie tapped the brush against the counter, her mouth slack and noncommittal.

"You didn't say if you wanted butter or not," she said, making pointed eye contact, not blinking.

"Sure." I stared back at her. "Go for it."

Winnie brushed the dough quickly. As she did it, my phone vibrated. I glanced at it. My dad had texted: *WHY IS NO ONE AT THE COTTON CANDY STAND?* I sighed and put the phone back in my pocket. Winnie pushed the dough over to me, little yellow rivers separating its big puffy bubbles.

"You really *do* care about Morgan, don't you?" Winnie asked, still studying me.

"Yeah," I said, resignedly shaking cinnamon sugar onto my outrageously unhealthy breakfast. "I do."

"Does she talk to you anymore? Have you spoken in the last couple of weeks?"

I put down the cinnamon sugar shaker. I wondered if these questions were designed to distract me from the one I had asked her. Which she hadn't answered.

"Why were you recording my dad's office?" I asked.

I wondered how long we could go on like this, actively ignoring each other's words.

"I think I know why," Winnie said slowly. "And it doesn't have all that much to do with Ethan."

"Wait. Then . . . *why?*"

I'd broken first. Because Morgan was, of course, my soft spot.

"If you really want to know, I have something to show you," Winnie said, lowering her voice.

As she said it, two guys came up behind me. They were about my age, and engaged in very profound conversation:

"Dude, I don't want Bavarian cream topping. That's too *much*."

"Well, then we can't split one. It's my favorite way to do it and I only get to have this, like, once a year."

"It's on my laptop," Winnie hurried to say. "Do you know where my house is?"

I shook my head.

"It's Fifty-Six Hauser Street. Not far from Morgan's. Can you come after six?"

"Yeah," I said, and then Winnie turned her attention to the customers.

I went back to my cotton candy. And I stayed there most of the day, watching the clock and conducting the last few bits of doughnut media business on my cracked phone. I posted a couple of Dad's promotions, one photo, and answered a last confirmation email from Channel 12 News. My dad was being a little too annoying to deserve this extra media surprise, in my opinion. But he was going to get it anyway.

* * *

The Malloys' house was a small one-story ranch the color of pistachio ice cream, its yard surrounded by a cyclone fence and covered with clover. As I looked at it from my car, I had a passing thought that it resembled a house leprechauns would live in. The word *lucky* passed through my head, but I shook it away. I didn't think of myself as being lucky, but I didn't think it of Winnie Malloy either.

Winnie opened the front door before I got to it. She must have seen me parking.

"Is your brother here too?" I asked.

Winnie shook her head. "No. He's working his deli counter shift. And my mom's out with her boyfriend. So nobody else will hear."

Hear what? I thought as she led me into the kitchen, which smelled like someone had recently been frying bacon. It was a pleasant room, though, with a long windowsill decorated with colorful little teapots.

"I'm glad you came right at six," Winnie said. "I'm supposed to go see Reggie in a little bit, and I was afraid you'd come late and I'd have to miss out."

She had a laptop set up on the kitchen table, and I tried not to act too self-conscious at the mention of Reggie's name.

"You want any water or anything?" she asked, settling herself in front of the computer.

"No. Why, is this going to take a long time?"

"Uh . . . no. You should sit down, though."

I did. I pulled her voice recorder out of my bag and plunked it down on the table. "Here. Take it. There's nothing on here that anyone cares about, I don't think."

Winnie nodded, unsurprised, gazing at the computer screen.

"Before it disappeared, I was downloading stuff from it onto my computer," she said.

Two of her fingers hovered over the mouse. The screen showed a list of items, about twenty, with little audio play buttons next to them. I had to remind myself to breathe.

"I'm going to play you something," she said.

I felt my chest start to seize. "Okay," I managed to say.

"And I'm playing you this because you care about Morgan." She took a deep breath. "I can tell you do."

"*Okay,*" I said, growing impatient.

She bit her lip and studied me for a second.

"It's not fair of me to ask you if you *really* want to hear it, I'm realizing now. Because you don't know what you're gonna hear." She hesitated. "*Do you?*"

My chest was so tight I could barely get the words out of my throat.

"Umm . . . maybe you should just play it?" My voice came out squeaky.

Winnie's gaze shifted from me to the laptop's keyboard, which I noticed was full of crumbs and cat hairs.

"I want you to know I'm not a mean person," Winnie said. "Morgan asked me to delete it. But in a way, I kept it *for* her . . . because I wasn't sure anyone would believe it if they didn't hear it for themselves."

I watched her hand on the mouse, and I watched the little arrow on the screen hovering between the Play buttons numbered eleven and twelve.

"Which one is it?" I asked. "Eleven or twelve?"

"Twelve," she said, her voice barely above a whisper.

I gently pushed her hand away and clicked number twelve.

The recording started with the squeaking of a door. My father's voice followed.

"Come on in, honey. You looking for Ivy? She's out of town, you know."

"Yeah. I know. I'm not looking for her." My stomach dropped. This second voice sounded like Morgan's. "I need to take next Sunday off to watch my brother, and I couldn't find Chris to ask him."

"What's happening next Sunday?" Dad asked.

"My mom has to work extra and his day camp doesn't run on Sundays."

Yes. Definitely Morgan.

Dad's chair creaked. "You know Sunday's a busy day for us."

"Yeah. It would just be this once," Morgan said quickly.

"Okay, honey. I know you're good for it."

"Thanks, Mr. Cork," she chirped.

"Please, honey, you know you can call me Ed. We know each other well enough for that, right?"

A soft laugh. "Um. Right. Okay."

The tone of her reply made me suck in a breath. Winnie glanced at me. I focused my eyes on the saltshaker in the middle of the kitchen table.

"Hey . . . was it you I saw out by the wave pool yesterday in that red bathing suit?"

"Uh . . . yeah, I guess. I was there during my lunch break. Emma and I were just cooling off because it was so hot. I don't usually do that, but it was ninety-five degrees."

"You can do whatever you want on your break. I wasn't complaining."

A pause. Winnie bit down on her lip and stared at the laptop, clearly afraid to look at me. I returned my gaze to the saltshaker, my heart starting to pound hard.

"I just liked how you looked in that bathing suit."

I lost focus on the saltshaker and felt the kitchen start to slip sideways. Winnie, the kitchen table, and I were all sitting on a slant. Soon we'd be on the ceiling.

"Oh," Morgan said.

"You look nice in that. You look like a lifeguard."

Morgan laughed a little. "Uh . . . oh!"

"I bet you'd look even nicer in a lifeguard chair. How'd you like to sit up in that lifeguard chair?"

I gripped the sides of the kitchen table and closed my eyes. I didn't care if Winnie was watching me.

"Where?"

There was a shifting, a creaking, and then their voices moved away but were still audible.

"See?" my father said. "See that chair? I'd love to be able to look out that window and see you sitting up there. That'd be a nice view."

After a pause, he said, "Lifeguards get paid quite a bit more than what you're making in the Food Zone."

"I'm not a lifeguard, for sure."

I put my hand to my mouth—because I could feel it hanging open, and I didn't have the mental capacity to close it. My brain was too busy trying to form an impossible denial. *Maybe this isn't Morgan's voice. Maybe it isn't my dad's. Maybe the girl is actually Winnie. And maybe the man is Chris.*

"Maybe you'd like to sit up there and try it out. Maybe you could see how it feels. Just for a couple of days. We're short one lifeguard right now. And Chris is too busy to fill the position really quick. So just for a couple of days, right?"

Morgan let out a little *huh* kind of laugh—the kind she used on drunk boys who tried to talk to her at parties. The kind she used on teachers who told dumb jokes. I didn't have a laugh like that because I didn't know how to pretend at the same things she did. But she had one. I knew it well because it had saved us more times than I could count. There was no denying it was her.

"How would that be?" my dad pressed.

"Oh, I don't know. I don't think you realize—"

"Realize! I realize a lot of things. I'm a realizer, actually. I'm a pretty darned good *realizer*. And I realize that you could use the extra money, and I could use the view."

Silence.

"Think about it, honey. I'll set it up with Carla. Just while we're short that one lifeguard. I'll tell her I know you and you can just slip in for a few days."

"Umm . . . umm . . . I'll think about it?"

Winnie tapped the mouse. The voices stopped.

"Is there more?" I whimpered.

"If they talked about it again, it wasn't in the office."

Winnie watched me as I tried to recover my voice.

"Do you want some water or anything?" she asked.

I shook my head and tried to take a deep breath, which I choked on.

"You sure?" said Winnie.

"Yeah," I said quickly. "So Morgan knows you have this?"

"Yes. I told her about it. And I warned her . . . I warned her that he might . . ." She trailed off, clearly remembering who she was talking to.

I picked up the recorder from the table and put it in her hands. When our fingers met, it seemed she was shaking worse than me.

"Take this," I mumbled.

"I'm sorry," she said softly.

"What're *you* sorry for?" I whispered.

I didn't wait for an answer.

I knew the answer. She felt sorry for *me*. That I had to be the daughter of the person speaking to Morgan on the recording.

Morgan.

Oh my God. *Morgan.*

A picture of her flashed into my head. Standing in my father's office. Trying to smile politely, trying to hide her reversed canine tooth, as my dad said, *I'm a pretty good realizer.* The kind of statement we used to laugh at together.

I got up. I ran out of the house, the word *lucky* echoing in my head as I stumbled across the long swath of clover, over the sidewalk, and into my car.

TWENTY-EIGHT

Morgan's house was about two minutes from Winnie's. I drove over there in a blind panic, praying that no dogs or small children got in the way, because I wasn't sure if my reflexes would work. I was gasping and crying as I pounded on Morgan's door. When no one answered in the first few seconds, I just pushed the door in, barging in, screaming, "Morgan! Morgan!"

As always, the house smelled like lavender and Stinkangel. I could hear the television on in the next room. It sounded like something with zombies was playing. I could hear them gurgling and gagging.

"I need to talk to you!" I screamed.

Morgan appeared in the living room doorway. She was wearing black leggings and a long tank top. Stinkangel came up behind her, nails scratching fervently on the hardwood floor. When she saw me, she gave a single bark.

"Are you okay?" Morgan said softly.

"*No!*" I wailed.

She led me into the living room and put the TV on mute. I was right about the zombies. They continued to stagger and flail across the screen in silence.

I flopped down on the couch in a manner not unlike the zombies. I was feeling a little undead myself on the cramped old love seat, where Morgan and I used to squeeze in together and watch movies when I'd sleep over. Where Morgan used to pull her red fleece blanket over us, and our knees would touch.

She sat with me now but hugged the opposite arm of the couch, still keeping her distance. Now I sort of understood why.

"Winnie played me something she recorded," I said hoarsely. "You and my dad talking."

Morgan's eyes went wide and the color drained from her face. I felt like I'd just slapped her.

"I want to ask you if it's true, but I know it is." My voice was trembling. "There's no way that was someone else."

Morgan covered her face with her hands and I looked away. A guy on the screen shot a zombie in the head, and blackish ooze poured out. I stared, feeling like I might have a similar substance in my head and heart right now.

"Please say something," I murmured.

"Winnie shouldn't have done that," Morgan mumbled. She yanked the old red fleece from the back of the love seat and wrapped herself in it, covering her shoulders and pulling up her knees.

"But she *did*," I said softly.

"I don't think I can talk about this," Morgan said, gripping the fleece with both hands and pressing her fists over her mouth. "Not with you."

"Please," I said. It was all I could think of to say.

"You would have trouble understanding," Morgan added.

I stared into my lap. "I'll always have trouble if you don't say anything."

"I just mean . . . you don't know how it is for me. To need a job at Fabuland so badly, to help my mom. She can never get enough hours."

"Okay," I said. "I hear you. Tell me more."

"You have no idea what you're asking for, Ivy."

I could feel tears coming to my eyes again. "Then tell me before I can change my mind."

Morgan was quiet again. Then she closed her eyes, sank backward into the love seat cushions, and whispered, "Okay."

She kept her eyes pressed tight, but started talking. "This will be like the story swap in Mr. Tomlinson's class."

"How's that?" I asked.

Mr. Tomlinson was our ninth-grade English teacher. Morgan had loved that class. She always wrote horror stories, usually about cloning or botched medical experiments, and always got As. Sometimes I wondered if it was her taste for weird things that allowed her to be friends with me the way other kids couldn't.

"Remember when he always paired up kids to critique each other's stories?"

"Yeah," I said, casting my mind back, trying to recall what exactly the rules were.

We had to say what we liked and didn't like about each other's writing. The critic got five minutes to talk. The writer was not allowed to interrupt. *You can quietly think what your reader is saying is crap,* Mr. Tomlinson said. *But you can't interrupt. You don't try to defend your work to them. You just take it in.*

"So you can tell me when it's been five minutes," Morgan said. "And if I'm not done by then, you can decide if you want me to say anything more."

"Okay," I agreed, and decided to close my eyes too.

I wanted to reach out and grip her hand—like we'd done right before we'd rode the Yo-Yo together that one time. But I knew she probably didn't want me to touch her. And anyway, it was probably already too late. We were already speeding toward the concrete.

"Winnie played it for me," Morgan said. "She played it for me right after she heard it. She had to admit she was recording in your dad's office, first of all. So there was that. But anyway, she played it and told me she was worried about me. That I should avoid getting into that kind of situation with Mr. Cork at all costs. Because Winnie had gotten into something like that last summer, and she regretted it later. Regretted it really bad."

"Something like . . . what?" I mumbled into the darkness behind my eyes.

"Shh," Morgan said. "If I keep having to remember you're there, I won't be able to say everything."

I nodded before remembering that she couldn't see me.

"Winnie had started recording because she was so angry about what happened to her," Morgan went on. "She thought she'd catch him referencing it sometime, or doing something like that to someone else. And she was right. She caught it. But she didn't have the heart to spread it around, like was probably her original intention. She just played it for me and told me I really needed to be careful. It had started like that with Mr. Cork and her. But then it got out of hand and she didn't know what to do. Last summer, Mr. Cork started making more serious moves and then they were kind of together, for a little while. Just a couple of weeks, really. Winnie felt bad about it after and didn't want to go back to Fabuland after that, but this year she needed the job again. So she came back but tried to never be alone with him. Like at night. Like at closing. It wasn't hard, I guess, at first. Until Chris started flaking out on his nights."

My breathing started to feel funny—like my lungs couldn't keep up with the number of breaths my mouth was trying to take.

"She was surprised she got to keep her job, but by the start of this summer he acted like he'd forgotten the whole thing. But *she* hadn't."

I tried to take a deep breath. I knew it was audible—slightly gasping. Morgan ignored it. Maybe she thought it was Stink-angel.

"I wasn't sure what to believe from Winnie in the beginning. And when at first I said that that lifeguard stuff was just him joking around, just him trying to do me a favor, she told me I needed to wake up. I was like, yeah, whatever, Winnie, I think I can handle it. I've known this guy since I was a kid, you know? But it didn't take long after that for me to really understand."

My eyes flew open. "Morgan?" I said, my voice cracking. But she went on, the words tumbling out now.

"After everything that happened with Ethan, I went to Mr.

Cork and I told him that with everything else I was going through, I was feeling like I couldn't do that job anymore . . . I shouldn't be in the lifeguard chair, that it was a bad idea. He said he understood. He didn't want me to feel bad. And then he, like, hugged me, which was weird because I know he's not very huggy. *You've* told me that, even. But then it wasn't really a hug at all, exactly. Because he was kissing me and . . . but he *couldn't*. Because I pulled away. And I ran."

I grabbed Morgan's arm and squeezed so hard she yelped.

"Sorry. It's been five minutes," I managed to say. "You can stop talking."

Morgan wriggled away from my grasp, keeping her eyes shut. "And then, for the next couple of days, I couldn't really believe it had happened. Thank *fuck* you weren't around. What would I have said to you? I felt like I was going crazy. I stopped sleeping. I stopped eating. You were coming home. How could I even look at you? It didn't matter *what* I did to get away from it. And then there was the thing with Ethan, too—something wasn't right there either. I just had to do *something*. It was pure adrenaline that made me climb up the Ferris wheel. And then it was such a relief to be up there, away from it all. I just needed to do something that would get me out of all this, at least until I had time to think. And it worked, kind of. But not really. Because what do I do now?"

"Stop *talking*!" I shrieked. Because the whole room felt scattered. The love seat was sideways and I was sliding off.

Morgan finally opened her eyes and stood up, staring at me, her eyes flashing as she watched me struggle to get up off the floor.

"I mean, really, Ivy. What the fuck do I do now?"

"How would *I* know?" I stood up too, barely managing to keep my balance.

"Exactly!" Morgan screamed.

Stinkangel yipped. I turned and gazed into her crusty little brown eyes.

"Your dog is gross," I hissed.

"But *I* love her!" Morgan was still screaming.

I looked at the floor and then the television screen. The zombies were still going at it, climbing clumsily through a car window and feasting on a screaming driver. Morgan also watched for a moment. It was easier than looking at each other.

"Then maybe we understand each other better than you thought," I mumbled.

Morgan didn't reply. She just stared at me.

"On the Ferris wheel," I said. "Why did you say *Ask Ethan* instead of telling me any of this?"

Morgan looked away from me, into the television. And then she burst into tears.

"I *do* care about Ethan. About what happened to him. And I know it was really messed up to say *just* that. But looking at it all now, wasn't Ethan's dying still worse than everything else? And how was I supposed to say *both* things? How was I supposed to say the *other* thing out loud?"

I stood there shaking my head for what felt like forever. Morgan wiped her tears away and waited for me to say something.

"I don't know," I admitted finally.

I turned to go, and she didn't stop me.

TWENTY-NINE

The sun was starting to go down as I parked at Fabuland.

It was almost dark by the time I reached the Starship 360. It was in full swing, and there was only a handful of people waiting to go on next. I didn't watch the ride as I waited for my turn. I didn't want to change my mind. On the drive over, I'd convinced myself that this was what I needed to do in this moment.

My heart and my stomach felt numb as those of us waiting were herded onto the ride. Whatever happened in the air, I decided, could not be worse than what I'd felt at Morgan's house. So what if I fell right out of the sky, really? The worst had already happened.

I got onto one of the black seats and buckled the seat belt. I was in a row all by myself. The ride operator—whose name I think was Dave—did only a cursory check of everyone's belts. Then the familiar hum of the ride's motor and the initial creaking of its metal started. I thought about how many times I'd passed this ride, heard these sounds, and dreaded the day I might find myself here. Among these people who loved to see things upside down. I'd never seen the park that way. Any time I'd been forced into going on a ride like this, I'd kept my eyes shut tight and made myself breathe after every count of five.

How come so many people handled this better than I did? Seeing the horizon rise, and the ground disappear? Seeing all blue sky for a moment? Realizing that your feet don't really have the permanent place on the ground you thought they did? Realizing how easily you can be lifted and thrown?

I forced my eyes to stay open as the ride started. I watched the ground become sky. And found I was too heartbroken to feel much fear.

Around me, people were screaming and hooting, but there was a dark place in my brain that had become completely silent.

I loved my dad. I loved his passion for spectacles and his belief that he could make them happen better than anyone. I loved that he made me a part of it. I always had—whenever he had been willing. For as long as I could remember. Probably longer. And I loved that he had made me a sprinkle sandbox.

But I believed Morgan.

I didn't know if I was allowed to do both. It didn't seem like I could. Or like I should. But I *did*.

For the last two summers I'd rushed in and out of this park, running from the cotton candy stand to the waterslide to the administrative office. Surrounded by people seeing it from every which way all the time—people willing to go upside down and sideways. And yet I'd kept my eyes shut, and looked at it only one way.

Even just a few days ago, I'd convinced myself that Winnie had backed out of her shift whenever Chris had done the same because she wanted to be with *him*. But the *real* explanation was obvious, if you could just turn it upside down for a second. It wasn't about who she wanted to be with. It was about who she *didn't* want to be with. Who she was avoiding. Alone at night, particularly.

And now I thought too about *Shiny Penny*—the young woman at Doughnut Dynasty who used to laugh at Dad's jokes. About how she'd left the job suddenly, and Dad didn't seem to know why or where she'd gone. At the time, I couldn't articulate why that had bothered me. But I'd only been thirteen then. I was older now.

It had been here from this perspective the whole time— creaking away in the background, behind all the good-natured screaming. I'd always heard it, humming along in the distance, day in and day out. I was just afraid to open my eyes and look.

THIRTY

It was officially my night with my mom, so I didn't need to make excuses with my dad. After I'd gotten off the Starship 360, I drove to her place. I had no idea where Jason was. He was over eighteen, so he didn't have to honor old custody arrangements anyway.

My silence was making my mom nervous. I felt bad for that, but I couldn't bring myself to say much. She flitted around me in the kitchen, preparing me a sandwich I didn't ask for, followed by a bowl of blueberries.

"I bought them to make a pie," she said, pulling up a stool to sit with me at the kitchen counter. "But I got some extra for eating."

I nodded. Blueberry pie was Jason's favorite dessert. Maybe she had designs on making him stay longer. It was kind of sad, actually. She could bake all she wanted—the length of Jason's stay would only ever come down to how long he could endure Dad. And Dad was something she couldn't control. She'd figured that out a long time ago.

"Tired?" she coaxed.

"Yeah," I admitted.

"Maybe you should try to go to bed early."

I took a handful of blueberries out of the bowl and put them on the counter in front of me. I started to arrange them into a little design. At first the blueberries formed a flower. But I had leftover blueberries, so I started over.

"I have a question," I murmured.

The berries formed themselves into a spiral, my fingers working furiously. I was thinking about my father—about how he had always seemed to steer Mom around by the elbow or the shoulder. Sometimes his grip was gentle. Sometimes it wasn't. It all seemed to depend on how much effort she was putting into making him feel good. Or making him look good.

"Yeah?"

"You didn't fall on the ice when I was seven, did you?"

Mom didn't look angry. Just a little sad. Her eyes flickered to the countertop and she ate a single blueberry.

"What?" she said, even though it was clear she'd heard me.

"When I was seven. You hurt your arm. You said you fell on the ice."

I was still adding blueberries to my spiral, but it was getting too big and sloppy. A blueberry rolled off the counter.

"I don't want to upset you," I said. "I just want to know. I think Jason knows, but he'd never tell me."

My mother put her hands over mine, stopping their frenetic movement but sending more blueberries rolling off the counter.

"No," she said after a moment. "I didn't fall on the ice."

"I'm sorry," I breathed.

I didn't say anything else. I couldn't tell if she wanted me to. The look in her eyes reminded me of Morgan's earlier that day. And even Morgan's on the Ferris wheel.

Like I had betrayed her somehow, just by not knowing—not seeing—for so long.

THIRTY-ONE

I waited until my mother was asleep to leave. It was after eleven by then—long past Fabuland's closing time, so it was unlikely I'd run into any last few workers shortcutting through Brewer's Creek Park.

I parked my car on Brewer Road and walked through the woods, shining my phone's flashlight ahead of me. I was still too numb to be very scared. When I got to the trestle, I sat down on the edge and looked down. Nothing but blackness this time. It was too dark. The stream wasn't visible, so I couldn't see myself at all.

I thought about my father and my mother. My father and Winnie. My father and Morgan. Somewhere deep in my heart, I'd known about it all along. "It" wasn't the fact of any of these relationships in particular, but the reality of who my dad was. What he was capable of. If I was going to be honest with myself, I'd sensed it for years, without being able to put it into words.

I was his exception. But that didn't mean I couldn't see it. As much as I'd tried not to.

I stared into the blackness below the trestle. Last time I was here, I'd considered the possibility of Ethan jumping. And yet I'd never really believed he had jumped.

The one I'd wondered about all along was *me*.

Because how could I live with being his daughter? In this moment, I couldn't think of anything more lonely, even if Jason could almost understand. I was my father's exception. Just for now, as Jason had once been? Or forever? Was I *lucky*, then? Or terribly unlucky? Or was I worse than my father, to know what I knew and still accept him and all the nice pretty things he offered only me?

It wasn't just those things that had made me so sure I loved him in the past, was it? Because if it was *only* those pretty privileged things, I wouldn't be a very good or genuine daughter, would I? If my love could drain away as fast as it had today, was I ever a loving daughter, really?

Was it ever real? Was any part of it *still* real?

And how could I *not* hate my father but somehow, simultaneously, manage not to hate myself?

I started to cry.

And kept on crying for a while. The crickets seemed to kick up their song just for me. I sniffled myself into silence and reminded myself I didn't *really* want to be here. Sitting at the edge of the trestle, staring into the blackness below.

I thought of texting Jason, but I knew he wouldn't have an answer. He'd barely started to figure out how to live with himself. I could tell. And as I'd pointed out to him a few days ago, it was different for me. There was a part of this he could never understand. I had to figure that part out myself.

I turned off my phone.

More tears rolled down my face, and I tried to make a plan.

At the very least, my father had to know that I *knew* and I *saw*. That now I *knew* the things I'd pretended not to see. And that I wasn't willing to pretend anymore. He would need to change to get back in my favor—however long it would take, and for whatever it was worth. The specifics of how he would change weren't up to me. I knew he didn't take kindly to being told what to do. And there were some things it wasn't up to a daughter to tell a father to do. Just as the reverse was true. But if he understood and cared how much he had hurt me, maybe he would start to see how much he'd hurt *everyone*.

Tomorrow I would go in to work and do everything he wanted. To show him I still had a reserve of love for him and believed in his big ideas. And that I still wanted to be a part of them, to a point. But after that would be the hard part. I would tell him I knew about Winnie and Morgan. And that I needed for him to be better.

Tomorrow. I mopped up my tears with the hem of my dress.

Tomorrow. After the giant doughnut. After the photos were taken and the crowds went home. After he got to see all his hard work pay off. After all that, my real work would start.

I drove back to my mom's apartment and fell into bed with my clothes on, exhausted by all the things I knew, and all that my lucky life now demanded of me.

THIRTY-TWO

There were already a dozen workers buzzing around the grounds when I got to Fabuland.

Jason was waiting for me near the main entrance.

"Are you okay?" he said. "You look tired."

"Just sleep deprived. And excited," I lied. I'd decided last night I needed to get through the day before saying anything else to him. "What's happening? Has Dad given you an official job yet?"

He handed me a shovel with its long, sturdy wooden handle painted with lavender and white stripes.

"Who painted the shovels?" I said, surprised our dad hadn't asked me to help.

Jason shrugged. "One of the girls who does the game booths, I think. He wanted me to make sure and save you this one. He thought it was the prettiest."

"Oh." I took the shovel reluctantly.

"Wait'll you see the doughnut. Jesus. It *is* something."

Jason led me to the open area in front of the Laser Coaster. And there it was. Ten beautiful golden puffs, nearly my height, arranged in a circle. They looked bigger here than they had on the lawn behind the pavilion—probably because the space was more crowded.

I stepped up close to one of the puffs and ran my hand along its side. It was firm and crisp on the outside, but soft when you pressed. It was perfect.

Jason led me up into the Starship 360 ride, from which the view of the whole doughnut was better. There was white frosting across the tops of each puff.

"What are the shovels for if it's already frosted?" I asked.

"They needed to frost some of the tops early since they were trimmed to make them all the same height," Jason said. "But the frosting will be finished as part of the festivities at nine-thirty. Dad liked the idea of making a little show of that part."

"Right," I said, noticing that Jason didn't have a shovel. "Are you going to be frosting too?"

"Not if I can help it. He's got me on sound equipment with Chris. I'm 'assistant sound administrator,' apparently."

"Chris is here?"

"Yeah. Just for the day, I guess. By the way, in addition to whatever else Dad's got you doing, I'm pretty sure you're in charge of sprinkles. Like, putting them in the cute little buckets he got and making sure they get distributed in an . . . organized way."

"Sprinkle administrator," I mumbled as he steered me toward the Food Zone.

* * *

I put sprinkles into little buckets and sandwich bags until nine o'clock, when people started coming into the park and the first musical act started setting up near the bleachers. I was glad for the excuse not to have to go to the office and see my dad face to face. I still had no idea how it would feel to talk to him, so I welcomed the numbing distraction. Even if it did keep reminding me of my sprinkle sandbox.

By now there was thick plastic purple tape—like crime scene tape, but festive—around the immediate vicinity of the doughnut so no one would touch it before they were given permission.

I was lining up the last of about fifty buckets of sprinkles along the first row of the bleachers when my father thumped me on the shoulder.

"Ivy."

I felt myself recoil but sucked in a breath to hide it. When I turned around, I saw he was standing with a tall, blond young woman with prominent teeth and severe-looking glasses.

"I want to introduce you to someone," Dad said. "This is Lexi Givens. She's from Channel 12 News."

"Oh!" I exclaimed, rearranging my face and forcing a smile as I extended my hand. I'd forgotten all about her. Another welcome distraction.

"Nice to meet you after our chats on the phone." She shook my hand. "My camera guy and our assistant are looking for a good place to set up. Can you tell me where would be okay? We want a good view of the doughnut and the opening speech, but don't want to be in the way."

"Ivy here'll be happy to help you." Dad beamed. "I'll be fairly busy and don't want anyone to feel neglected. Ivy will show you around and—"

"Actually, Mr. Cork," Lexi said, "I'm sorry to interrupt, but before the festivities get started, I was curious if this event is in some way commemorative of or going to recognize the young man who died a few weeks ago?"

Dad looked taken aback.

"Um, Ivy here can answer your questions, and I'll see if I have more time after the doughnut festivities are over."

Lexi pushed her glasses more firmly up the bridge of her nose. "Okay. I hope you'll have time for a few comments after the main presentation then."

"Let's hope, yeah. In the meantime, Ivy's going to give you an exclusive look behind the purple tape, let you get up close to the doughnut, even touch it if you want—but no tasting for now! And she'll give you a blow-by-blow of how we constructed the doughnut. But I've got to run. We've been having problems with the microphone, and I've got a few more things to square away."

With that, my father was off, winking his appreciation at me for this media win, then jogging toward the administration building, where he was probably going to reconsider his "re-marks" and whether they should mention Ethan. I breathed a deep sigh of relief that he was gone, turning away from Lexi so she wouldn't see it.

"Feel free to film from anywhere," I told Lexi, turning back to her with a smile. "Even from behind the purple ribbon, if that helps you get good footage. We just didn't want anyone rushing the doughnut before the official time."

Lexi nodded, and waved to two guys who had just appeared from the other side of the bleachers, one with an enormous camera on his shoulder, the other carrying a duffel bag and a tripod.

"This is sur*real*," the tripod guy said when he came over to us. "What next? Did this guy fill one of the swimming pools with some steaming-hot coffee?"

Lexi ignored him, blushing a little as she turned to me. "I meant to ask about your name, after our emails. Ivy Cork. You're a Cork. Are you the owner's daughter, then? He didn't say."

"I am," I said softly. And then I had a sudden fear she was going to ask me to make some on-camera comments.

"Listen, you guys make yourselves at home and film from wherever," I said. "We're just so glad you're here. I've got a few things to do before the official start."

I tried to look busy and important as I walked away. But then I went back to my sprinkles.

＊ ＊ ＊

By 10:29, the bleachers and Starship 360 were filled with people, and the local band was just finishing its plodding version of "What a Wonderful World." As the song ended, Dad stepped up to the microphone.

He tugged at the lapels of his dark-blue suit coat, stiffening its shoulders, before he spoke.

"Over the past couple of weeks, people have been asking me why," he said, and then paused for a moment and looked out at the crowd. "Why do *all* this?"

He stretched one arm out, floating it slowly over his view of the doughnut.

"And I have two answers," Dad continued, glancing at the news camera that was hoisted up on the tripod to the side of the platform. "One, because it's fun, and so, why not? And the other is that it's a gift to *you*. You, our community. Thank you for coming to Fabuland and making it the great and spirited place that it is."

Dad puckered his lips for a moment, thinking. "And the other reason is that I'm in the business of making beautiful memories. And I'll bet there's not a single kid here today who's going to forget the day they saw a huge doughnut and got to take a big bite out of it. Well, I guess that's three reasons. But anyway, I hope you all have a great time helping us decorate the doughnut. We've got folks going around handing out buckets and bags of sprinkles."

Dad glanced at me and I held up a bucket and a bag, then nodded at Emma Radlinger and the other Fabuland employees I'd managed to corral to do the same.

"So we'll sprinkle it up, boogie to some music, have a good time. And then at eleven o'clock, after everyone's had a chance to look at the doughnut, take some pictures and whatnot, we'll remove the purple tape and everyone can come and grab themselves a bite. Sound good?"

A tentative cheer rose up from the crowd in the bleachers,

followed by a smattering of applause from the crowds on the ground and in the Starship 360.

"Now, before we start the sprinkling, I also wanted to say—"

"Excuse me!" A loud, almost robotic-sounding voice came from the Starship 360. When I looked over, I saw that the voice was coming from Winnie. She was standing on one of the ride's seats, holding a megaphone.

I glanced from Winnie to my dad, my pulse quickening.

My dad looked stunned, and Winnie pressed on.

"I'm sure Mr. Cork won't mind if I say something on behalf of my cousin, Ethan Lavoie, who worked here at the beginning of the summer until he died on June twenty-ninth. We all miss him, and he is here in spirit."

I looked back at my dad. He nodded, trying to look solemn but clearly, to me, brimming with nervous energy. His mouth was twitching, but his eyes were wide and unblinking. These were clearly unplanned remarks, but he didn't want to step on them, given the sensitive subject matter. And given that this might make a longer and more nuanced story for Channel 12 News. I started to breathe a sigh of relief.

"Ethan loved Fabuland," Winnie continued. "And he would've absolutely loved what's happening here today, more than anyone I know. Which makes it even more difficult to share what we have to today."

She reached down and yanked at the shirt of the person next to her. It took me a moment to realize that it was Reggie. He was pale and way thinner than the day I'd seen him. His face looked wrecked. I wondered how he could've been released from the hospital looking like he did. But still he stood up and Winnie handed him the megaphone.

"Hello," he said absently into the megaphone, and then, as if startled to hear his voice so loud and distorted, muttered, "Oh shit."

The crowd remained silent except for the sound of a small girl in the bleachers laughing—probably at the unexpected use of profanity.

Winnie took the megaphone back from him. "Reggie has something to say about the night my cousin died. He told me yesterday, and while we thought about going to the police this morning, we decided we didn't want to miss this event. We didn't want to miss the opportunity to first tell the story in the presence of all of you. Reggie?"

I was holding my breath as she handed him the megaphone again. Dad dropped his microphone and started to move to the edge of the platform. The Channel 12 News cameraman picked up his camera, hoisting it to one shoulder and turning it toward the Starship 360 instead of the stage.

"Ethan Lavoie didn't die falling off the trestle in Brewer's Creek Park," Reggie cried into the megaphone. "He died at Fabuland. He died on the Laser Coaster."

He collapsed back into his seat, but Winnie pulled him up again.

"Can you tell us how, Reggie?" Winnie pressed. She was shouting, so as not to interrupt Reggie's use of the megaphone.

My father had jumped off the platform now and started running for the smaller, higher perch that held the Starship 360 controls.

"He wanted to go for one last ride," Reggie said, somewhat robotically. "After his friends left and he came out of the bathroom, he was begging me for one more ride. It was just him and me, and he was so excited, I just gave in. Like, why not? But after about a minute on it by himself, he stopped screaming. I didn't know what had happened. But when I brought him down to the exit area of the ride, he wasn't conscious. He wasn't moving."

Dad appeared to be pressing a couple of buttons at the Starship 360 controls. Everyone was so focused on Winnie and Reggie that not many other people seemed to notice. Reggie was weeping into the megaphone now. The crowd was completely silent. But I was watching my father, thinking of him screaming, *I always knew you wanted to stay small. Just a small person, I guess.* And dragging my mother to another room by her elbow. The image darkened, eclipsed by a blanket provided by Jason, muted by folk music playing through earbuds.

The Starship 360 started moving. A couple of people gasped in surprise. A few people on the Starship 360 squeezed themselves into the already crowded seats. Others tried to hold on to its metal sides to steady themselves. Winnie stepped down from the seat she'd been standing on, staggered into Reggie, and then steadied herself.

"I tried to wake him up," Reggie sobbed, still standing and gripping the railing in front of him with one hand. "Nothing. There was nothing. I know now that he'd probably had a massive seizure up there, but I didn't know then. I was in shock, seeing him like that. I ran to get some help. The only person left was Mr. Cork. By the time we got back to the ride, it was obvious Ethan was dead. No heartbeat. We both tried to take his pulse."

The ride was picking up speed.

"Shut it *off*!" someone yelled. It was Ben, who was pushing his way down the bleachers.

"I'm so sorry," Reggie was saying, struggling to keep his footing but continuing to hold the megaphone close to his mouth. "But at least whatever happened . . . it was fast. Ethan didn't die confused in the woods. He died on the roller coaster."

I rushed to the ride operators' platform.

"Dad!" I screamed. *"Dad!"*

Dad didn't hear me, or didn't want to. He elbowed Ben away from him.

"Let's clarify this for everyone here!" Winnie shouted. "Including this news camera, and that police officer over there. Ethan didn't fall off the bridge, did he?"

Adrenaline shot through me as I rushed up the steps of the Starship 360 control platform, toward my father. He stood his ground, seeing me but staring through me. For a moment, I glanced around for Jason, but didn't see him anywhere in the crowd.

"No." Reggie was wailing. "He never left the park. He died on the ride."

The Starship 360 was quickly picking up speed. Within a minute or two, all these people would be upside down. A few people seemed to understand this. I heard seat belts buckling.

But some still looked bemused, as if this might all be part of the program.

"Why . . . why did you . . . ," Winnie was saying. She was faltering, trying to steady herself by holding on to Reggie's shirt.

"Mr. Cork decided not to call the police. Ethan was already dead. We needed to deal with this privately, he said. For the good of everyone. Someone dying on a ride, a kid with Down syndrome, so early in the summer, under fairly new ownership. He said we'd probably be shut down. Maybe for weeks, maybe longer. Lost jobs. He said I'd probably be investigated, especially since it was after hours and what was I doing, torturing a poor scared kid?"

The ride was doing a one-eighty by now. People were screaming and trying to steady themselves. I ran across the platform. The screams were intensifying, growing louder and more terrified. Reggie was trying to stay on his feet, hanging on to Winnie, still speaking into the megaphone.

I realized then that I was still holding the lavender-striped shovel.

"Mr. Cork convinced me. Just for that night, really. But after that it was too late. I'd already helped. He put Ethan in his truck and then after midnight we drove around to the other side of Brewer's Creek Park."

"Move!" I yelled at Ben.

He did. He ducked. I pulled the shovel back like a baseball bat. I avoided Dad's head and I swung. Hard. The shovel blade landed in the middle of his chest and there was a *PUMF!* sound.

"Who threw him over the bridge?" Winnie was screaming.

"We both did," Reggie sobbed. "Mr. Cork asked me to. We parked up on Braeburn and carried him down the path."

Dad went flying off the ride operator's platform, arms flailing. There was a loud *crack* as he hit the concrete. I winced, because it sounded like the crack was his head.

It was hard to hear Reggie because so many people were screaming now.

I rushed to the red emergency stop button and slammed it. The Starship 360 started to slow down. The screaming started to die down too.

There was a long pause. People on the bleachers and the ride looked around, clearly wondering if it was over.

Winnie and Reggie were still talking into the megaphone, taking turns again. But I didn't catch all the words as I rushed down to where my father lay. "Business decision" was repeated, along with "very sick man."

My father was unconscious, but one hand was moving and an indistinct mumble came out of his mouth. I noticed a trickle of blood on the pavement beneath his ear.

"Dad?" I said, feeling tears come to my eyes. "Dad, I'm sorry. I had to."

In my dream it had been me lying broken on the concrete, unconscious to myself and everything I was—everything we had been as a family. In my dream, it only hurt for a second and then it was over. But I knew this particular pain might be with me forever. It was a part of me—a part of who we were together.

"Is he okay?" Jason asked, kneeling next to me. Ben was behind him.

As he asked the question, an image flashed in my brain. Of my father and Reggie clumsily carrying Ethan's lifeless body down the path from Braeburn Road—the quieter, less traveled road into the park, where they wouldn't be seen. In the dark, in their panic, they don't see Ethan's prized blue sparkle scorpion fall out of his pocket, onto the path.

"I don't know," I said, pulling myself up to my feet, taking a step away from my father. "Call an ambulance."

THIRTY-THREE

I rode in the ambulance with my father. He woke up enough to ask what had happened. But thankfully the EMT took over, asking him questions before I had a chance to say anything.

Do you know what day it is, Mr. Cork? How many fingers am I holding up? Who is the president of the United States?

I was still speechless, anyway. I was having trouble believing what had just happened.

Jason met us at the hospital and took over from there. He went with Dad to the examination room, for the stitches on his head, for the CT scan. When Dad was resting and waiting for the results, Jason visited me in the waiting room.

"Well, *that* didn't go as planned," he said in lieu of a greeting.

I wasn't sure if he was expecting me to laugh. Or cry. Or both.

"How is he?" I asked instead.

"They'll probably keep him overnight, since he lost consciousness." He hesitated, then grinned. "But then, we both know how easily Dad bounces back from a concussion."

I cringed and Jason sat next to me.

"There are police officers waiting to talk to him," he said softly, "but I guess the doctors aren't letting them yet. I guess you don't question someone when they might not be right in the head."

"If they're waiting for him to be right in the head, we might all be here a very long time," I murmured.

"I meant they're waiting to make sure there's no brain trauma before he talks to the police," Jason said. "How are you holding up?"

"I wonder if Dad remembers what happened to him," I said, ignoring Jason's question.

Jason went over to the vending machine and stared at its contents for a moment. I think he was actually staring at his reflection in the clear plastic.

"The funny thing about Dad," he said. "Well, not *funny*, but you know what I mean. . . . The interesting thing about him is that he selects what he wants to remember. Your part will fall into the story however he wants to tell it. Maybe you missed Ben and hit him instead. Someone else had the shovel and you were wrestling it away from them. Or maybe the Starship start button got bumped by accident, and *he* was the one trying to turn it off. And anyway, how much do you really still care what he thinks, at this point?"

I stared at my hands. One of my palms still had a slight lavender mark from the freshly painted shovel. I was glad it was there.

"I'll probably always care. You know?"

Jason nodded. "I'll stay here tonight. You don't need to. You've been on right-hand duty a little too long, I think."

"Jason," I said slowly. "Did you know about Dad and Winnie?"

Jason looked stunned. "When did you find out?"

"Yesterday," I admitted. It felt like the answer should have been *A long time ago*.

"I thought maybe that's why you'd been asking about her. But I didn't say anything because I wasn't sure."

"Probably a smart choice," I admitted. "I had some fuzzy suspicion about it in the back of my head, I think. But I wasn't ready to . . . *look* at it."

"I walked in on them," Jason said. "In his office. Last summer. He had his arm around her. They heard me at the last second but I caught them pulling out of a kiss. I mean, she was nineteen, I think, but . . ."

"Uh, let's not . . . ," I mumbled. If he kept talking I'd probably have to go puke somewhere.

He snapped his mouth closed, clearly understanding.

I considered the lavender marks on my hands once more. Maybe I could somehow keep them there forever. Have them tattooed on. I had a feeling that I would want to remember for months to come—probably years—how it felt to swing that shovel.

"So that's the *real* reason you didn't want to come home?" I asked.

"Six of one, half dozen the other," Jason said. "I just couldn't

332

handle him anymore. I'm sorry I left you to deal with it. Maybe I convinced myself your innocence was bliss."

I nodded. "I think I'm going to take you up on your offer. I think I'm going to go home to Mom for a while."

Jason stepped away from the vending machine and turned to give me one of his quick, awkward hugs. Apparently he didn't need me to say it outright—that I wouldn't be able to stomach being summoned to my father's side.

"We'll be okay eventually," he said.

He didn't sound very confident. But we'd have to go with it. For now, it was what we had.

THIRTY-FOUR

My mother seemed delighted at the opportunity to distract me all night long. We binge-watched two-thirds of a trashy Netflix mystery series and ate practically the whole blueberry pie, saving Jason one slice. My phone buzzed nonstop as Lexi Givens tried to call, and a few other news contacts—some I'd never heard of. Eventually I shut the phone off.

When I turned it back on in the morning, I ignored all the messages and texts except the one from Jason at 8:20 a.m.

A couple of police officers in Dad's hospital room, he reported.

You want me to come? I offered.

No. I think they'll be in there awhile. Will let you know. By the way, Chris swung by the waiting room last night to let me know he's no longer working for Dad.

Lucky duck, I wrote back.

I grabbed my keys and drove to Fabuland.

Nobody had locked the gates the afternoon or evening before, apparently. I tried to picture what happened after Dad and I left in the ambulance, and Jason followed in his car. Chris hadn't bothered to close up. He was probably in shock. Probably went straight back to his wife's side, and good for him for that. Nobody else considered themselves part of management. Nobody else really cared. Winnie and her friends probably took off. Spooked parkgoers probably dissipated quickly, not knowing whom to ask for their money back. I wondered if the second musical act my dad had hired had attempted to play a few songs, in spite of everything.

When I reached the center of the park, the giant doughnut was about mostly intact. Armfuls and mouthfuls had been taken off the sides, and some off the top. There were gobs of sprinkled frosting on a couple of bleacher seats. An overturned bucket lay beneath the Starship 360.

As I approached the doughnut, I saw a squirrel run away, escaping over the fence behind the bleachers. I was glad someone was enjoying it, for all my father's efforts. I hoped the trees behind the fence were full of fat squirrels on sugar highs.

I'll bet there's not a single kid here today who's going to forget the day they saw a huge doughnut. . . .

If nothing else, my father was probably right about that one.

I pulled off a chunk of the doughnut and took a bite. It was stale, of course, but I was hungry. Then I went to my dad's office and found some paper and a Sharpie to make a sign for each entrance:

CLOSED DUE TO FAMILY EMERGENCY

Before I drove out of the park, I put the same thing up on Dad's LED sign.

I wondered how long the signs would stay that way. I had a feeling someone else besides me would end up taking them down. Maybe someone I didn't know and never would. That wasn't such a tragic thought. Now that I'd seen Fabuland upside down and sideways, there might not be much else for me to see here.

In the meantime, there was a place I would much rather be.

THIRTY-FIVE

Morgan opened her front door.

"Hi," I said. "I wanted to talk to you."

Morgan appraised me with sad but knowing eyes.

"I saw what happened at the doughnut thing," she said.

"Yeah?" I tried to ignore the jump in my pulse. I was going to have to get used to this version of myself—the one that had smacked my father unconscious with a shovel. "You been watching the news?"

"I don't need to," Morgan admitted. "The clip is everywhere. Facebook, Twitter."

"I'm famous," I said dryly. "My dad should be proud."

"Is your dad okay?" Morgan asked.

"No." I shifted my weight from one foot to the other. "He never really has been, though."

Morgan hesitated. "That's not how I meant the question."

"I know," I murmured. "But it's how I meant the answer."

"Are *you* okay?"

"I don't know. It turns out I'm kind of crazy. I mean, did you see what I did?"

"Well, you *had* to."

"Probably I wanted to. So there's that, too."

Morgan considered this for a moment, then bobbed her head, conceding.

"Well, if it *was* crazy, it wasn't any more so than climbing a Ferris wheel in the middle of the night."

"I don't know, Morgan."

Morgan pulled the front door open wide. As I stepped inside, Stinkangel came over and sniffed my left foot.

"I'm sorry I said she was gross," I mumbled. "I didn't mean it."

"I think you actually did," Morgan said. "But that's okay. Come on, come in."

The TV in the living room was playing some kind of alien apocalypse movie, but Morgan immediately shut it off and wedged herself in one corner of the love seat. Stinkangel jumped up between us just as I was settling into the other corner.

Morgan asked me to tell her everything, from the moment I left her house yesterday until now. Down to every last sprinkle. As we talked, Stinkangel rolled and writhed between us, scratching her forever itches, yipping at her invisible fleas, making the olive-green upholstery fabric even hairier than it already was. We talked above her noise, ignoring her strange soggy odor, almost forgetting she was even there.

When I finished, Morgan asked me if I'd had breakfast.

I thought about the few bites of stale doughnut I'd had.

"No," I admitted.

"I think we have some eggs," Morgan said. "You need to eat breakfast."

She led me to the kitchen and thumped around in the cabinets and fridge, pulling out a container of yogurt, half a loaf of bread, and the egg carton. She cracked the last two eggs into a bowl.

She whisked them for a few seconds before looking at me and saying, "The Pimple Popper?"

"What?"

"For a ride name."

"Oh," I said, looking down. I opened the bread and stuck two pieces in the toaster. I wasn't sure I was up for this game, but after a minute I thought of a new one.

"The Mindfuck," I said.

Morgan swirled a bit of melting butter in a pan on the stove.

"The Old Switcheroo," she replied.

"The Delusion," I countered.

Morgan smiled and poured the eggs into the hot pan.

"That one wins for today, I think," she said softly.

I watched her jostle the eggs with a spatula until the toast popped up.

She was letting me win this time. But I'd take it.

ACKNOWLEDGMENTS

Many thanks to:

Lisa Walker and Sarah Hawker, my kind and generous early readers.

My wonderful agent Laura Langlie.

My patient and insightful editor, Monica Jean, for taking a chance on Ivy and giving her story so much thought and attention. Jen Heuer and Alison Impey for the stunning cover. Also Colleen Fellingham, Heather Lockwood Hughes, Alison Kolani, Cathy Bobak, and the rest of the Delacorte Press team.

My brother Dan, always willing to reply to my political apocalypse texts with a motivational KEEP WRITING.

Sarah Guzzetti, for the gift of a priceless story about a certain Western Massachusetts restaurant that shall remain nameless. *It is what it is.*

Ross and Eliza. You two are the best.

ABOUT THE AUTHOR

Emily Arsenault is the author of several literary mysteries, including *The Broken Teaglass*, a *New York Times* Notable Crime Book; *In Search of the Rose Notes*, a *Wall Street Journal* Best Book of the Year; *The Last Thing I Told You*; and her young adult novels, *The Leaf Reader* and *All the Pretty Things*. She lives in Shelburne Falls, Massachusetts, with her husband and daughter.

emilyarsenault.com